Hot Air

A NOVEL

Bob Katz

A BIRCH LANE PRESS BOOK
Published by Carol Publishing Group

A Birch Lane Press Book
Published by Carol Publishing Group

Editorial Offices
600 Madison Avenue
New York, NY 10022

Sales & Distribution Offices
120 Enterprise Avenue
Secaucus, NJ 07094

In Canada: Musson Book Company
A division of General Publishing Co. Limited
Don Mills, Ontario

Manufactured in the United States of America

Library of Congress Cataloging-in Publication Data

Katz, Bob.
Hot air : a novel / Bob Katz.
p. cm.
"A Birch Lane Press book."
ISBN 1-55972-021-2 : $ 17.95
I. Title.
PS3561.A7516H68 1990
813'.54—dc20

Hot Air

A NOVEL

CHAPTER 1

Alchemy is what's really needed, yet we who eke a livelihood from these flimsy, modern conceptual endeavors usually persist in a feverish panning for gold. Screaming tabloids, ranting TV talk shows, rural roadside billboards, emergency news bulletins—the whole sprawling detritus of popular culture forms a cascade of glistening notions which wash over us. Our overburdened minds function, appropriately, as sieves. Occasionally something that glitters gets noticed, and saved.

Recently the lecture agency I run, Frankly Speakers, was sorely outmaneuvered by our most cut-throat, amoral, undeserving, and sophisticated competitor, those unabashed mid-town Manhattan hucksters from Smooth Line Presentations. As insatiably aggressive as pit bulls in heat, and equally constrained by ethical qualms, Smooth Line relentlessly bamboozled our poor susceptible market with an array of ploys and subterfuges that would make an earnest rival like me yearn for the intervention of a special prosecutor—if it weren't for the fact that even their most egregious behavior fell neatly within the law. Once, when they somehow failed to sign up the leading lady in a spectacularly publicized CIA missile laundering scheme, they set their army of killer bee agents relentlessly on the phones for three days non-stop, spreading a rumor that the woman was gravely ill with a rare (and reportedly contagious) disease. I can't say I was sorry to see the squelching of such an igominious career, yet it was just that sort of unbridled spitefulness that kept me awake nights worrying what they might do if—oh happy day!—Frankly ever mounted a real challenge.

Last season (a "season" runs the academic calendar, beginning in summer's waning sweetness and plowing through the winter into spring), Smooth Line damn near cleaned out the market, first by offering one of those confoundingly silly gimmicks that every so often seizes the public fancy, an "intellectual weight loss program" for those who suffer from "heavy thoughts," following that up with a major tour by an alleged KGB defector, a beautiful blond woman no less, whose tale of dastardly sexual espionage was absolutely impossible to corroborate. The Soviets protested that they'd never heard of her, but try telling that to your average college activities chairperson.

The plague that nearly blighted the minimal harvest which remained of our season was their sweepingly successful tour by the former Secretary of Defense, paroled from his conviction on fourteen counts of graft, speaking out on the techniques of stress management and creative thinking he developed while incarcerated.

"You've got to be kidding," I howled when I first heard about it. "You've got to be kidding!" Why has that phrase become the recurring incantory cry in the dark of so many who wade waist-deep in our culture? It's as if we desperately yearn to disbelieve, to feel genuinely baffled and confounded and dismayed at those witless idiocies garnering such gaudy popularity, when in the harsh realism of our hearts we know better.

I'm no naïve idealist. Perhaps I once was, but I stand upright in adulthood ready and willing to salute the incontrovertible supremacy, even the cosmic appropriateness of that venerable, ironclad standard: the lowest common denominator. And yet the question still gnaws at me: must it always be quite that low?

At any rate, Smooth Line was hot, and in a market as narrow as ours, when one agency gets hot it's a big drag for the others. Hot consists of topics that are trendy and individuals deemed important, either by virtue of accomplishment or momentary newsworthiness. Hot makes office life exhilirating and sparked with promise. *Not hot,* as I said, is a drag.

We did our best to hang in there by offering a versatile line-up of jobless progressive politicians, middle-brow journalists capable of moderately informed commentary on virtually anything happening anywhere, a controversial lesbian attorney, a cluster of social reformers vaguely remembered from bygone crusades. When student activities directors and program chairpersons came at us with the inevitable query, "What do you have that's hot?" I instructed the staff to go on the offensive by gently reprimanding the campuses for superficiality and short-sightedness. My strategy was to direct challenge the value system off which the buzzards from Smooth Line were feeding.

Whereas Frankly Speakers has a generally laudable reputation, we were not taken very seriously. A booking agency urging programmers towards social relevance and intellectual subtlety is regarded with the same skepticism as evangelical churches which require a cover charge at the door. Many of those churches, of course, are wildly successful.

We were struggling, but we stayed afloat. On the few occasions when our preposterously groovy accountant, Rex Apple, attempted to alert me to the thin ice on which we skated, I simply hit the speaker-phone button on the lower left of the phone console, leaned back and read the sports page while he jabbered away. For a small business, a periodic accounting is like psychoanalysis, stripping illusion away from reality. Who's got time, or the heart, for that?

Businesses have an antagonistic relationship with time. Time gone by without demonstrable improvement in a variety of meaningful indices feels like defeat at the hands of time. The fact that Frankly Speakers stayed afloat thus counted for very little. We'd made no appreciable headway in such elemental matters as market share, public profile, and gross dollars. Life (as we know it) had not improved. Marion the steadfast and spunky office manager did manage to get away for a one week cut-rate excursion to Aruba, seven days and six nights of gambling and sunburning, but she failed to connect with a guy, or at least one she was willing to talk about. Kenny, our crackerjack booking agent, did well enough on his commissions to purchase several new outfits of designer threads, but he looked no different to me stomping around his cubicle like a rock star twirling his extralong phone cord like a lasso and crooning into the receiver. Piper, who sits across the cheesy burlap space divider (it actually smells like shredded cheddar) from Kenny, used her meager savings to attend an Aspen, Colorado, workshop given by a legendary Tibetan healer. Piper was still trying to get pregnant after years of marriage to a philandering house painter named Alec. No last name—just Alec. She does a tolerably effective job as an agent, but I've had a clear apprehension that nothing but the proverbial pink little bundle of joy will achieve "hot" for her.

Then there is Mona. She had been with me the longest, knew me the best, and, though she railed against my every shortcoming with a fury that often seemed more rooted in early childhood trauma than whatever the nominal case of her complaint, she remained a stalwart employee. Mona's deepest longing (or so I thought) was to be the sort of fashionably breezy, prosperous, carefree career woman featured in slick monthly magazines like *New Woman*. One of the singular triumphs of Frankly Speakers was that we had somehow managed to sustain her blazing self-image.

The mundane facts of my situation (white male, mid-thirties, vivid dreams, dubious accomplishments) are hardly the classic stuff of an epic struggle. Usually I'm averse to melodrama (unless it's in the service of a worthwile promotional campaign) precisely because its passionate sweep relies on personalities and events that are a million miles from anything I've ever experienced. Yet here I was, feeling as though my life were down to some bottom of the ninth. A layer of desperation was sucking slowly in on me, like an oxygen tent collapsing, although there was no tragic loss or wrenching heartbreak or cold injustice I could point to. Could it be nothing more than the first chill fear that life might turn out more ordinary than grand?

Mona took our recent setbacks quite hard. My attitude was that the tough times were partly attributable to a temporary cultural conservatism that would soon run its course, and before long we would be right back . . . right back where? That seemed to be her point. The glow of nurturing a nice little business had given way to the gloom of maintaining a nice little business. And of course the persistent issue of time. The whole world was a few years older.

The big kick in the groin came the day Mona informed me that she'd been offered a job by Smooth Line. Thirty percent, guaranteed, above what she was making at Frankly. Bonus incentives to beat the band. All relocation costs to the Big Apple covered. Access to exclusive insider networks for finding an apartment not situated in the far reaches of boroughs she'd only read about in gruesome crime stories. Options to participate in a moveable feast of publication parties, premieres, and glitzy soirees that would virtually assure, given the odds, periodic appearances in the strobe-lit backdrop of *People* magazine celebrity snapshots—in short, a well compensated acceleration onto the fast track. They were flying her to New York for a weekend discussion.

"Is that what you really want?" I asked in my father-knows-best Socratic voice. "Is that truly what you're all about?"

"I could have kept this offer a secret. But I feel obligated to inform you." Mona when she's on the high moral ground is someone you'd like to strangle. "We have a very positive working relationship, Danny, and you know it means a lot to me. You gave me my start in the business world and I'll always remember that. But I'm at the crossroads where I have to think of my future. I have to look ahead. I have to face facts." With a giddy sigh, she raked both hands in a fluffing motion through the thicket of her newly poodle-coiffed, still reddish hair. "And as guys like you always like to tell us, a girl only lives once."

I certainly had never said that to her. And if it is a line I'd employed with other women, Mona had no way of knowing it. But this was not the moment to nit-pick. I held my tongue.

On that bleak Friday night in bleakest January, Mona flew off to be courted by the scoundrels from Smooth Line. I was angry but I couldn't blame her. Agency life is not a search for spiritual enlightenment. The point is to move forward and progress. The point is to surmount time, not wallow in it. Face the facts.

After closing the office, I stopped off at The Grotto, a nearby boîte that features the sort of transparently phony tropical beach-front decor that, at the end of a week of neurotic wheedling, is almost as refreshing as the real thing. In point of fact, a direct transition from a compacted office workday to an actual exotic retreat would be a seismic shock to the sensibilities of all but the schizophrenic. Places like The Grotto function as halfway houses, particularly for those who are going nowhere.

The bar was still uncrowded. The sibilance of business people exhaling their anxieties was not yet deafening. Visibility was about five feet. What dim lighting existed seeped up from the corners in purple and amber whispers. A bartender, overeducated like most in the district, once told me his theory that a patron's proximity to the source of muted light provided unconscious clues to his inner motives for being in the bar. I pretended to be impressed: at last we had a methodology for deducing why people go to bars. My own reasons were hardly mysterious. The apartment that, as an alternative, I might return to was a depressingly cluttered, coffee-stained, uncomfortable garret, more a barracks than a home. I was a single male administrator of a faltering enterprise. My most valued colleague was off to explore employment elsewhere, with scumbags no less! My boyhood dreams of glory and frolic were suffocating beneath a thick topsoil of upper back and neck tension. I needed a drink.

Midway down the long varnished driftwood bar, which was overhung by a thick rope fishnet that had succeded in snagging a paperback copy of *Megatrends* and a floppy disc, I spied not only an open barstool but one with women seated on either side. I couldn't tell if they were escorted, but there would be ample opportunity to investigate that. A few stockbrokers tumbled in behind me, their silk neckties pulled loose to project an allegiance to frontier boldness. I scooted for the barstool.

"Is this taken?" I asked of whichever would answer.

A narrow-faced woman with oversize purple horn rim glasses balanced on her pixie nose gave me an impressively instantaneous once-over (I was dressed, for me, with passable propriety, in corduroys and sweater) before answering, "Yes." However, the woman on the other side of the gap, with longish hair and broad shoulders from the back, replied, defiantly I thought, "It's free."

Here was my opening to be witty without being obnoxious, a rare chance in such places. "You, madam," I gloated, directing all my attention to my benefactor, who still had not turned to face me, "have that special quality of someone I can believe."

I straddled the stool. The bespectacled pixie swiveled away to resume conversation with what I now observed to be two girlfriends, each dressed similarly in plain dark female adaptations of the Wall Street uniform. No doubt they had hoped the stockbrokers would get my parking space. Unwittingly I had taught them yet another hard lesson about assertiveness and survival.

I tried to make eye-contact with my sponsor, but she continued to hunker resolutely over an iridescent blue cocktail that glowed like a prop in a magic act. She probably felt she had extended herself enough in my direction; it was now left for the gentleman to crawl on his belly the remaining distance.

"What are you drinking?" I asked innocuously. "Sure looks dangerous."

Whammy! As soon as she looked up, I was stunned by her eyes, which were dark and haunting and deep like ready graves. I don't know what it was; they harbored some troubled territory, not threatening but sad like my mother's. I felt like a silly child transfixed by a deformity. I stared far too intensely for a first encounter, and could feel the unease of her self-consciousness. I wanted to pry my glance down to her mouth, which was affable and alive, or to her hands, which toyed with the slender stem of her turquoise drink. But I was clutched against my will by her eyes.

At such moments of disconcertedness, one functions on instinct, and conversational instincts tend to follow the standard stock prattle of television sit-coms. "You look familiar," I managed to state, hoping to buy an extra moment to collect myself, like a boxer on his knees taking a nine count. "Don't I know you from somewhere?"

"We slept together once." She said this with such nonchalance that it didn't even occur to me that she meant it.

This was not a situation I wanted to be in. My attempt at glib cordiality was being transmuted into a wholly unintended insult, one of the rudest in the male repertoire. Worse, I'm no Lothario who takes libertine pride in being too casual to remember, if, in fact, she was someone I once slept with.

"You're Danny Frank," she said, looking not at me but across the increasingly busy and festive room.

I wanted to tell her she'd have to produce more evidence than that before I pleaded guilty.

"University of Illinois." There was an ex-smoker's husky melancholy in her voice. "You wrote for the college paper. You wore sunglasses indoors before it was fashionable."

I nodded my head in affirmation. That was more than a dozen years ago. The fact is, those were prescription shades. Without them I couldn't have seen the blackboard.

"People knew who you were," she continued. "You were an iconoclast. You wrote editorials about spending too much money on a new football stadium. You said it was as wasteful as the government spending tax money on bombs."

I shrugged. "It seemed to be true at the time."

"You lived in a first floor apartment of an old frame house. In the basement was a saxophone player who stayed up all night. Your place smelled like an exotic land. I didn't know it was only incense."

Now it was coming back home. Her eyes were dark and fascinating even then, only not so haunting. She had liked me a lot. I had liked her. The rest was pretty foggy. I groped for her name, and miraculously retrieved it. "Nina Hallet! What are you doing in Washington?"

Remembering her name seemed to lift some yoke, and she gave me a half-smile "Research."

I too began to feel revivified. It's exhilirating to discover one's memory intact. "It was," I sheepishly asked, "only one night, wasn't it?"

Now she looked straight at me while sipping her magic potion. "It should have been more."

Probably she was right on that count also. After downing her drink, she told me she had to get home to feed her kitty because her roommate, who normally assumed the evening responsibilities, was in Barbados on a fact-finding mission with the Congressman she worked for. My options were to remain in The Grotto, return to my hovel, or latch on to Nina's sympathies.

"Do you live far from here?" I asked.

If a woman answers that question by mapping out such complex instructions for getting there that a dogsled trek through Siberia might seem more accessible, then you've received a subconscious hint. Nina's response, onthe other hand, was all encouragement: "Just the other side of the Circle."

Nina occupied the first floor of a brownstone row house in a neighborhood that was making a lightning transition from poverty to posh. After diligently unlocking several clumsy steel contraptions, she ushered me into the living room which had high ceilings and a triptych of impressively tall windows forming a concave bulge towards the quiet street. The centerpiece of the space was a sprawling semi-circular sofa swathed in gray corduroy. I was told to make myself comfortable while Nina fed dinner to little Hamlet and fixed us drinks.

The profoundly conflicting odors of the single professional woman's life washed over me: the sweetest Parisian fragrance and the back-alley stench of kitty litter. How often the two go together. At least bachelors like me are consistent with our coffee-stained kitchen linoleum and our subliminal designer's musk.

Nina Hallet had been a much better student than I, and the business manager of the student newspaper. She had the kind of consummately serene and empathetic demeanor that almost seems like a bygone era. We did spend the night together once, after much deliberation (that too, a bygone era). Her hair was cut short then, prim and efficient to care for. Now it flowed, so boldly out of synch. I couldn't quite put my finger on it, but there had been some reason why once was enough. It might have been something about her; it could easily have been something in me.

Nina sauntered into the room and set down a twin glasses with a dark vermouth currently being featured in an expensive television ad campaign depicting vignettes of single women employing the liquor to overcome the vexations of very handsome, fey men. I'd like to think she bought the stuff prior to the media blitz.

She sat down. We toasted and drank. I couldn't find the stereo speakers—they might have been concealed behind the fat waxen leaves of the rubber plants—yet we were listening to the seductive mumbling of a jazz deejay. The evening was a tribute to Ellington; I couldn't tell why. The only illumination was the amber mist from the anti-crime vapor lamps in the street.

We kissed and pulled close and soon we were harmonizing in short rhythmic breaths. Buttons and hooks and zippers released to welcome patches of dewy flesh. I squirmed towards horizontal and she sank back to accommodate my maneuver. Her hair smelled like springtime. It was where I wanted to be. My nimble fingers crawled over a swath of skin that was smoother, tighter than the rest, embroidered by a ridged seam. She flinched.

"An operation?" I asked, only to calm her, not because I cared to discuss it. My hand continued its mindless journey.

"It was a mole. You don't remember?"

Now I did. She'd had a mole, big as a hand with bristling hairs, on the inside of her upper thigh. That was it! What a prig I was. Had I once actually believed that unmarred perfection was going to be an option in this life?

"I had it removed," she continued, inching back to an upright position. "You were one of my first lovers, and I hated the fact that it bothered you. I hated the fact that such a small thing, which never bothered me, was such a big deal to a man."

My hand went still and cold. The street outside was silent. The only interior light was the soft greenish glow from the digital clock on the VCR.

"It didn't seem fair," she added sadly.

"It wasn't," I readily agreed.

A long vacant quiet fell over us. This night was not to be an easy release from my nagging worries. I closed my eyes and made a dear desperate wish. May all our dreams come true. Let no one of us bear the burden of quenching another's hope. May kindly Nina find a transcendent fulfillment to banish all the tarnished past. May Frankly Speakers not take a nosedive, not just now. Let Mona not be corrupted by those undeserving vultures. Please allow me, for just a while, to explore my destiny without all this bewildering interference.

Not only were my fingers now cold, they were balled into a tense fist. I couldn't blame Nina for rotating away.

"What are you thinking, Danny?" she asked with a note of concern. "A penny for your thoughts."

I have never yet been thinking what a woman wants to hear as a reply. Correction—I take that back. The few times I've thought it, the question wasn't asked. The eerie green clock blinked forward another minute. I considered saying nothing. "Tell you the truth, I was thinking of offering one of my employees a five per cent raise. It's the most I can afford."

It wasn't what she wanted to hear, but I was too strung out to lie.

Mona returned mid-morning Monday and I immediately summoned her to a private conference in my office. The Frankly Speakers suite is a cramped, low-ceilinged, overpriced space on the third floor of a 1930s WPA building that once housed some of those New Deal offshoot agencies that would administer America into an egalitarian Utopia. The current owners, a syndicate of Iranian exiles with financing from offshore banks, had set about renovating their new acquisition in accordance with the principles of mitosis. Walls are thin constructs of two-by-fours and blueboard, dandified by artful skim-coating and a peppy paint job. Where once existed expansive conference rooms that allowed voices to echo while mapping out a better world, now we have maze-like interior half-wall partitions which could be used to play a hell of a game of hide-and-seek.

For two years we have rented space here, making us veteran tenants. Most of the others are fly-by-night consulting services, ephemeral political front groups, P.R. start up ventures. Washington is a city of subdued tones unless someone is making a pronouncement. Countless times I've tried to eavesdrop for snatches of revealing conversation from behind the flimsy, makeshift corridor walls, but so far the only thing I've picked up has been the loud jangle of an old-style phone slammed down and once a howled curse, in an Arabic tongue.

Mona entered my box of an office sporting a stunning purple velour blouse that shimmered of Manhattan. I closed the door behind her, and bid her to sit on our Goodwill couch.

I first met Mona seven years ago when I was working as an accountant assistant at the reputable Arthur Velvet Agency, a P.R. outfit that specialized in a form of job placement for defrocked government officials. Mona was someone who appeared around the office one summer, dressed in a breezy fashion not typical of a career-track young woman, performing various types of phone tasks under the direct authority of old Velvet himself. It was rumored that Mona's father knew Velvet from way back, which could mean Brooklyn's Flatbush, World War II, the NBC advertising department, Ft. Lauderdale, or numerous way stations. Mona's function was described as "helping out," a camouflage for all manner of lassitude and aimlessness.

I had come to Velvet from a brief stint as a news reporter on a suburban Maryland community weekly, a job I was good at but had no patience for. It wasn't that chronicling the deliberations of the zoning board of appeals or summarizing the educational philosophies of the new high school principal were wholly inconsistent with my secret desire for a significant life; rather, I felt condemned to a painfully slow progress. I guess I've always had a struggle with time.

Mona was entering her senior year at the University of Virginia and one of her tasks was to organize and respond to lecture invitations for Velvet's clients. Old Arthur was receiving big bucks from elsewhere, from book deals, endorsements, criminally lucrative consulting contracts, pocketing as much as a third off the top of whatever he could negotiate. The meager dollars that might be garnered from a booking agent's commission were not, to him, worth the potential indignities.

I learned this information during my first face-to-face discussion with Mona, at the coffee maker in the lobby, late one muggy July afternoon. I was bored, as usual, and even if she wasn't a little exotic looking, with wavy reddish hair and a colorful forest flower print dress just loose enough to conceal a figure of almost any dimension, I would have struck up a conversation just to revive myself.

I told her what I did, adding a touch of glamour to the parts that were just toadying and paper-pushing. Account assistants, really, are just white collar butlers.

She told me her major (Women's Studies) and confessed she had no idea what the hell to do after graduation the following spring. She said she had been quite busy the past few days because Velvet's newest client, a Supreme Court nominee who'd been rejected because his forefathers had once run a fluorishing slave trade, was being deluged with speaking requests.

"You wouldn't believe how much money these places offer," she informed me while dribbling some powdered creamer into her cup.

"How much?" I bit.

She started to answer, then halted. It was the hesitation of Eve. Mona's facial expressions have the range and malleability of an actress. The difference is that no one but she knows the script. She stirred the dissolving granules of creamer, brushed a non-stray hair off her cheek, shot me a twisted, patently insincere, deliberately half-baked smile, and replied, "I'll have to get back to you on that."

She could not have been thinking that I was a person with designs on starting a lecture agency, because at that time I had no such thought. Over the remainder of the summer she trickled me tidbits of information, xeroxes of incoming speaking requests, seemingly casual revelations of this and that over by the coffee maker. My newfound interest in the business potential of a lecture enterprise was in no smallway whetted by the jigsaw puzzle manner in which pieces of data were being parceled out to me. Some mild flirtation might have passed between us but, like low intensity microwaves in the atmosphere, it was diffused and largely undetected. Before returning to Charlottesville for her senior year, Mona coyly wished me luck and noted that she'd be back in town job-hunting over New Year's.

Shortly before New Year's, I launched Frankly Speakers. I should probably have come up with a better name, but I was in a hurry and convinced that in time good works would add resonance to the bland moniker. In a few months I was sufficiently solvent to hire someone. Mona was the only person who came to mind. Why not put your life in a corked-up bottle and see where the oceans carry you?

Returning to my swivel chair, I explained, "Whatever is said here, I'd like to keep it between us. Even if we get a little worked up, let's try to keep our voices down."

Mona has the most intense abhorrence of instruction of anyone I've ever known. When she whispered, "Fine, Danny, whatever you say," I grew alarmed.

I folded my hands atop my desk, a stern but sympathetic pose. "I've done a lot of thinking, Mona, this past weekend about our situation. We've worked together now—how long is it?" I wanted to draw her into the dialogue, but she sat placidly silent. "Enough time, at any rate, for you to know how valuable you are to the operation. As I've said, I've done a lot of thinking. About who I am, where I'm going, what it is that I want from this life . . ."

I thought I detected her stifling a yawn. Standing up, I moved ponderously to my one puny window, which looked out upon a dingy alley and a squat dumpster bulging with billowing plastic garbage bags. No inspiration there. I faced her and continued, "And it struck me that you too must be undergoing a similar type of introspection. And I was thinking that before you make your final decision about Smooth Line—and I will do my best during this discussion to refer to them with professional respect—it would be useful for you to know a little more about what my plans are for Frankly."

What I did next was not my finest hour. I felt like the guy pledging undying eternal love just to get laid. I rolled out for Mona's consideration a very recently devised long range strategy by which Frankly Speakers, ragtag and moribund as it may appear, was actually the perfectly architected cornerstone to a projected vertically-integrated conglomerate of intertwined satellite enterprises, each feeding off the other's virtues in brilliant synergy. Six months, twelve at the outside, was all that was needed to solidify the base and begin implementation. Christ, I was really winging it! Yet it sounded okay, and I thought I noticed Mona starting to pay heed. The voice that was speaking through me was a new one, but it appeared to be working.

"What I'm saying," I emphasized, "is that you, Mona, are essential to these plans. Of course we don't live in a world where reality necessarily conforms to one's plans, but I thought it was important for you to know exactly what's being contemplated here. The Big Picture, as they say. Now my resources are limited, but I'm prepared to offer you . . ." I sucked in my stomach and straightened my shoulders to enunciate the gravity of this, "a five percent raise in commission."

With deliberate fluidness, lest I reveal my tension, I eased back into my swivel chair to await her reaction.

First, she located a stray glitzy thread on her sleeve to twist and tug and finally lean forward to chew off. Then she discovered something amiss in the rear roof of her mouth, and with a probing forefinger and undulating tongue set out to remedy the irritation. Finally, Mona looked me straight in the eyes. "Do you have any idea how many computers they have at Smooth Line?"

I was determined not to be provoked. "Several?"

"One for every agent, and more. Do you know how many support people they have?"

"I'm afraid I don't."

"Three and a half. One just to make travel and hotel reservations. Actually one and a half. Their offices are located on the thirty-fourth floor with a corner view of the East River."

'What happens if the elevator gets stuck?"

"Don't be so defensive, Danny. You know whose picture they have hanging in their lobby, right above the receptionist's head so you can't miss it? With his signature blown up to ten times its normal size in the lower right?"

I shrugged with exaggerated disinterest. "Quaddafi?"

"Gerald Ford."

"No! The former leader of the free world? You don't say!"

Mona let go with a full giggle, and I immediately relaxed. No matter how rich their offer, they couldn't force her to take Gerald Ford seriously.

"You would have been proud," she continued. "I just stood in their lobby looking up at the picture with this blank stare, like 'Who is that guy?' They acted like I was just the dumbest person in the world. They told me next week he would be in town to have lunch with the staff. I actually think I spit a little to keep from laughing."

I felt buoyed, but I wasn't ready to press her for a decision.

"I have to tell you, Danny, I had my eyes opened. They have files for everything, for letters of recommendations, for newspaper reviews. Everything can be cross-referenced. Each time they need a piece of information they don't have to go rummaging through piles of junk just to find it. Everything is neat and in its place and easy to find and a person doesn't have to get herself into a ridiculous frenzy just to do her job. Business hums along. They live normal lives. They take real lunch breaks. They don't have pizza crust rotting in the corner."

"Come on," I protested, "neither do we."

With a rotation of her blazing eyes she guided my focus over to the door where, sure enough, a partially eaten pizza wedge lay.

She cleared her throat. "And they've just signed a speaker who's going to clean up, no doubt about it. I know this market by now and the campuses will be banging down the doors to get this one. Take a guess."

"Chairman Mao."

"Dead!"

"That wouldn't stop Smooth Line. They won't inform the poor dumb students until the last minute, and then they'll provide a substitute."

Mona couldn't resist a chuckle. "Actually, you're warm . . . Get this. Maharaja Jo. The ten-year-old Tibetan Guru!"

"The pudgy little kid who collects Rolls-Royces?" It struck me as absurd, but most of our competitor's ideas strike me that way, even after they succeed. "Does he even speak English?"

"Berlitz. The tour doesn't start until fall."

I scratched my scalp in bemusement. "Ten years old. My, my."

"They're thinking of offering one-on-one spiritual counseling sessons to the first ten callers. They've even worked out a campaign to defuse the age problem. The kid's program will be titled, 'The Wisdom of Youth.'" Mona shook her head in admiration. "You've got to hand it to them, it's a great idea."

"Aren't there federal laws involved? Child labor? False advertising?"

"The kid's immune because he's a religious leader. At least that's what they told me. They think of everything, Danny. They're like chess masters. They have a board of directors with guys from Harvard Business School who know how to do studies, and use data to make decisions, instead of just pacing the floor and hoping to come up with ideas." Mona leaned forward to pick a paper clip off the floor, and began twisting it into a curious pretzel shape. She looked at me beseechingly, and I thought she might cry. "Why are things so chaotic here? Why, even when we do something right, is it always at the last minute and only by the skin of our teeth. I have nightmares about how messed up we are. I'm getting too old to be lying alone in bed at night worrying if some speaker got his airline tickets. There's more to life than this kind of anxiety. When I'm home alone I want to inhabit a different space. I want to be drawing my bath and getting in touch with my romantic and spiritual side. I want to be dreaming about exciting mysteries and interesting people—men, perhaps—not tearing my hair out fretting if we remembered to send a contract or some other dumb thing. I want life to be orderly, Danny. I'm distressed, can't you tell? While I'm still young I want a life that's more than this. I'm not the most stable individual and, well, this disorganization is too much for me. I get too agitated. You, on the other hand, don't get agitated enough. I sometimes wonder if you have a blood circulation problem. Things don't seem to worry you as much as they should. It really amazes me. You're like a sloppy teen-ager, except you're not in your parents' den anymore. People are always taking advantage of you and you hardly ever notice. It was me who caught that printer on the Environmental Decay brochure billing you twice. You would have paid him again rather than take the time to check your records. Of course it takes an archaeologist to find anything in your so-called files. Do you want to know what commission Smooth Line operates on? You'd weep if I told you. You know what else? They get airline bonus miles from the trips their speakers take? They get to go places, exciting places, free. Don't ask me how. They have a pension plan, profit sharing. They have profit! They cut better deals, they study the market. They . . ."

The poor mangled paper clip snapped in her hand. She lifted her moistened eyes to look up at me, remorsefully shaking her head in sympathy like a mother to a feeble, helpless child. She pulled a deep breath and sighed, "I turned down their offer."

I couldn't believe it! I jumped to my feet and thrust my fist in the air like a hometown fan at the first crack of a long fly ball. "That's great!" I hollered, reaching across the desk to congratulate her.

She made no move. Her demeanor remained grim. Her upper lip curled in disdain. "Don't you see how this proves what I've been saying?"

I didn't.

"You didn't have to offer me that five percent. Oh I'm taking it all right. Every damn penny of it. Don't you see? I'd already made up my mind. You made a dumb, thoughtless, unnecessary proposal when you could have gotten what you wanted for less. Christ! This is the grown-up world. When are you going to learn that?"

I was far too delighted to get flustered by this onslaught. Frankly Speakers was not crippled, not just yet. Joyous with relief, I couldn't resist asking her, "Why?"

"Why what?" she snorted.

"Why did you decide to stay?"

With a spastic ferocity she hurled the twisted paper clip fragment over toward the pizza remnant, and shot me a cold scowl. "Oh, what do you care, anyway?"

Chapter 2

No sooner had the staff gathered in the tattered executive suite for our regular Monday morning confab and seance than the phone rang. Actually it chirped. One of the triumphs of modern technology has been the almost seamless reorientation of our Pavlovian ear to this simple shrill noise that once upon a time meant only that a cricket was trapped somewhere in your tent. Early capitalist man had originally been conditioned by the jangling metallic ring-ring, first cousin to fire bells and burglar alarms, a sound akin to that which might be made if a bucket of silver dollars were tossed onto the pavement from a second story window. The brisk, crystal ring-ring awakened in us the vibrant hormones of impending event—a beau phoning up for a date, a customer looking to buy, a melodrama reported in the dark of night. But we creatures adapt. Now it is the Age of the Chirp.

Since my feet were propped executive-style on my desk and my state-of-the-art flexichair (my only material indulgence) was tilted as far backward as the owner's manual permitted, any sudden move forward would have been daredevil. Thus it was gracious of Mona to pop off the sofa and grab for the phone. Since she tended to be surly and even hostile on Mondays, I interpreted her assistance as a hopeful omen.

"Frankly," she answered in a sing-song upbeat, an elbow propped on my desk corner.

The rest of us, Kenny, Marion, Piper, examined our cuticles and shuffled papers to kill a few seconds while Mona dismissed the call.

"You're calling from where?" we heard her sweetly inquire.

Technological innovations have added new dimensions to the formerly flat functions of the telephone. Mona poked one of the square key-bulbs at the lower corner of the phone console and *presto*!, amplified over the office intercom, we all heard the adenoidal, uncertain words of the caller.

"This is . . . uh, Gary . . . uh, Jones . . . from Minot State."

"Excuse me," Mona broke in, "How do you spell that?"

M . . . I . . . N . . . O . . ."

Mona interrupted rather aggresively. "Not the school, your NAME. How's that spelled?"

It was the old adolescent sport of putting someone on, jazzed up by new telephone mechanics. Pick some poor unsuspecting bimbo and bait him into idiocy before the assembled listeners. It's a game usually played in the office along about Thursday afternoon when nagging pressures have made us demonic. I shudder to guess what kind of weekend Mona had if she's playing it first thing Monday morning.

"G-A-R-Y." He spelled it slowly. With such an elemental name it probably has been a long while since anyone asked him to spell it out.

"Was that a Y?"

"Yes, m'am. My last name is J-O-N-E-S. I'm calling cause we're needing a speaker for Democracy Week, which is something we have every April, only this year it's moved to February on account of President's Day, which is in February and our advisor thought it'd be neat to combine them, you know, to make it more meaningful and the like."

"Gee, that's a superb idea, Gary." Mona's voice was beyond unctuous and had crossed into that hallowed terrain of fraudulent coyness occupied mainly by high school actresses struggling to portray hookers. With an exaggerated wink signaling us that this one might be fun, she inquired, "Have you talked with any other agencies about this?"

"The lady from some company out east supposed to call at ten. I dunno, my advisor might have talked with some."

"You're not being unfaithful with me, are you Gary?" Mona shot us a lascivious smirk which, given Gary's demonstrable naïveté, struck me as slightly demented.

"How's that, m'am?"

"Only kidding, Gary. Tell me, what other lecture programs have you done, so I can get a picture of your . . ."She groped for the diplomatic word. "Your concerns."

"Back in the fall we had a guy, I think he was from Texas, who talked about college life."

Another feature of this modern phone system is that, like the proverbial two-way mirror instrumental to so many smutty roadside gas station jokes, punching the lowest button on the left enables the primary party to talk to others in the room without being overheard by the caller. Mona lashed out with her forefinger and jabbed the two-way mirror button. "Can you believe it?" she exclaimed to us with no fear of Gary overhearing, "Why not a lecture on how to tie your shoes?"

Deactivating that function, to Gary she cooed, "College life—what an interesting topic."

"And last year," Gary prattled on, "we were fortunate to be able to bring in President Ford."

"The president of Ford?"

"Ha, ha. No, m'am. Gerald Ford. You know, the guy who was president."

"Gosh, he does lectures? What did he say?" Mona's eyes, in mock astonishment, lifted upward like helium balloons.

Gary struggled for an answer. "Well . . . you know, how this is a great country, cause we're free. And having goals in life. And being strong, and standing up for what you believe. I dunno, but it made the TV and all."

"Any three car highway collision makes the TV!", Mona yowled to us. To Gary she noted, "That must've cost you the farm."

"Weren't cheap," he replied. "Some alumni helped us out with it, though. My English prof wrote a letter to the *Gazette* complaining how the money shoulda been used to hire a teacher for an entire year. But Dr. Rosen, he's the sort who's always analyzing things, trying to figure out better ways."

"Unlike President Ford," Mona stabbed the function key and snickered. Releasing the key, she smoothly asked, "What's your budget for Democracy Week . . . roughly?"

"Maybe four thousand. Plus expenses. Maybe more if the alumni get involved again. We've been thinking it'd be a good idea to get a lady or a minority person."

To us: "Anything besides an impotent middle-aged white male." To Gary: "Someone like Bill Cosby or Nancy Reagan?"

"They'd be great!" Gary was getting worked up. "We can't get them, can we?"

"No."

The staff meetings are supposed to be a combination rehearsal and pep talk for the week ahead, which I would like each employee to treat as seriously as an athlete playing for a team entering the last leg of a pennant race. I was itching to get on with it and signaled with an emphatic circling of my forefinger that Mona should wrap it up or reel it in.

"I want to do a little research for you," she told Gary. "I've got someone in mind, but she's tied up in negotiations at the U.N. until late in the afternoon. Let me take your home phone number, Gary, and I will give you a call, probably after eight tonight. Maybe I'll take a long hot bath and call you while I'm in the tub. I've got a phone cord that stretches and then I'll be nice and relaxed."

Mona took down his home number, hung up, and for a moment

we gawked at her, as sometimes we glimpse ourselves, in awe and disgust. The meeting resumed.

Kenny had prepared a veritable laundry list of "new ideas" for this meeting. It's harder than one would think to discover a speaker who is a) not already represented by a rival, b) not too obscure to command the hefty minimum honorarium from which we extract our commission, or c) not too wealthy, preoccupied, or senile to give a hoot about the sizeable income supplement. I have offered a variety of bonuses and rewards in order to inspire the kind of imaginative thinking that can produce an idea that is hot. I started with a dinner for two, any restaurant of the winner's choice. The results were disappointing. I raised the reward to a weekend in New York, again for two, hotel and transportation paid for. An eccentric former astronaut who found corroboration of the Bible while in orbit was the best anyone came up with. The carrot presently being dangled was a round-trip ticket, for one only, anywhere in the continental U.S. I believe there was some fine print on the bottom of the ticket restricting its use to a narrow span of time between Christmas and New Year's when it's hard to reserve a flight anywhere too costly, but I'd cross that managerial crisis when we got there. The fact that Kenny so enthusiastically seized the bait at least in theory proved the wisdom of my strategy.

"Captain Kangaroo," was his first suggestion, which he read to us off a sheet of notebook paper in the rich tremolo of a class president hosting the high school awards banquet.

I chewed pensively on my lip and emitted an audible murmur to indicate that, unlike most offerings, this one would not be immediately dismissed. Bolstered, the staff began cross-examination.

"What would he lecture on?" asked Piper, who is predisposed to like anything that harkens her back to those years predating her marriage.

"Anecdotes from his TV show. Principles of education." Kenny scratched his boyish yet balding temple, a scientist brooding over a complex equation. "Maybe the Captain is a warehouse of radical social theories and is just waiting for someone to ask his opinions."

"Is he alive?" asked Mona.

"Don't know."

"That's rather primary, don't you think?" One of Mona's office hobbies is maintaining a list of deceased personalities still being promoted by other agencies. Her favorite is the coast-to-coast mass mailing announcing a limited tour by the Scarsdale Diet doctor which arrived just a few days after his shocking and highly publicized murder at the hands of a jilted lover. "Dead speakers," Mona stated categorically, "just aren't worth the trouble."

I nodded to Marion, who, God bless her, had actually been taking notes. "Let's check it out. If he's alive, see if he's interested, and how much he wants."

Without glancing up from her notepad, she sought clarification. "Should I ask if he's got anything to say?"

"Oh, yeah, that too."

Kenny moved on to another suggestion. "Now don't react immediately to this one. Let it sink in." Using a shopworn method of building suspense, he paused to whet our curiosity. We were all pretty jacked up from caffeine and vaguely suspicious of his rather uncharacteristic outburst of enterprise. Kenny usually preferred elucidating the ideas of others to proferring his own. "The head of Scotland Yard," he announced.

"Not bad," I commended. "What's his name?"

"Does it matter? It's the institution that counts. The image, the myth."

"What's the topic?" I followed up.

"Mystery. Crime. Delicious stories with surprise endings."

Mona was wide-eyed. "You thought of that yourself?"

Kenny smirked and accepted what appeared to be a compliment with what appeared to be a curtsy.

The phone chirped and Mona pounced on it. "Mr. Frank is tied up in conference," she told the caller. "Send another invoice. I'll see that it's taken care of."

"The printer?" I hoped it wasn't.

She nodded smugly. "Pay by Friday, or you'll be deported."

Our margin of solvency was frighteningly thin. If our lesbian attorney took seriously ill or if Chet Janko, the foe of environmental decay, finally suffered the savage rub-out that for years he had claimed (at my urging) he was being threatened with, Frankly Speakers would be reduced to panhandling to pay our monthly rent. We were getting by, but were in no position to sustain the merest of setbacks. And the mood around the office recently was commensurately precarious. It's shocking to acknowledge that the rhythms of the spirit, one's roots in the aesthetic dimension, are bound up with matters as mundane as gross earnings and accounts receivable. For the prescribed hours of the working week, we are, sadly, who and how much we sell, and our relationship to this vast and wondrous world becomes accordingly happy or sad. After hours, we may partake of scintillating friendships, whirl away to an assortment of challenging hobbies, romp to dreamland in lustful romance, yet our moods will remain fundamentally sour if all our phone calls go unreturned and the few speakers out on tour are drawing paltry crowds.

The goal is to find something hot. Hot clients, to office life, are an aphrodisiac. Incoming chirps transform our plasterboard cubicles into an aviary. From bedraggled, shlumpy Willie Lomans we take on the bright polish of cultural curators. In tough times, agency life is like cultivating crops in sandy soil: your throat is parched and religion begins to make sense. But when a speaker is hot, the basic laws of energy have reversed: you become spirited, lithe, stimulated, inspired. Drug addicts are familiar with such vicissitudes.

Kenny rattled his sheet of paper. He had more. His eagerness to claim the airline ticket was disgustingly transparent, but that's what management by motivation is all about. If it takes the lure of a freebie to Key West or San Francisco to jump-start our little enterprise, then that's no weirder than a craven corporate v.p. busting his arteries in the hopes of retiring to Tahiti.

"Walt Disney," he trilled.

"Dead," Mona snapped.

Kenny retaliated with a venemous glance. His lips trembled and his eyes welled up. After collecting himself he managed to whimper, "Disney? Gone?"

"But not forgotten," I jumped in to buoy the situation. I couldn't tell if Kenny was being theatrical or if he was truly upset. The fact that he's ferociously allergic often makes him appear to be tottering on the edge. "I do believe Walt Disney passed away a few years back. But if it's okay with you I'll have Marion double-check."

As Kenny withdrew behind a veil of wheezes and sniffles, I rambled on with my usual proclivity to vastly overdo conciliations. "A personality who is a beloved part of our collective childhood is, regardless of what we find out about Mr. Disney, an excellent concept to focus on. I think you're definitely onto something, Kenny. The lecture circuit is so dominated by issues of strife and chaos, a speaker who takes us back in time as if we were little children being held by the hand, back to days of simple innocence and straightforward, basic..."

I was rudely interrupted by the heavy drumroll of Mona's fingers on my desktop. She has an antsize patience for my theoretical eludications, unless they zero in on essential subjects like money and sex. Just in case I missed the hint, she yawned and daintily patted her mouth.

"Any other suggestions? I inquired. "Last call."

It's weird being in a business where a right and timely idea can be so efficiently and expeditiously turned into money. One day it's at best a latent, subconscious, insubstantial, conceptual germ with no possibility of existence beyond the walls of your cranial cavity; the next day it has a name and that name occupies center stage in legal contracts committing each signer to serious endeavors or face grave consequences. The germ has more than sprung to life; it influences life. Lo and behold, by means no more risky or strenuous than the aimless pacing of floors, the habitual scratching of one's scalp, and the contemplation to the very brink of hypnosis of the proverbial lint in one's belly button, a golden transformation has occurred. It is as if the Lord has responded to a fervent prayer. When a good idea emerges out of nowhere it is every bit as wondrous and unfathomable as the heavens.

As my spirits were too low and vulnerable to face the gloom of ending this session, I tried to keep the ember of hope glowing with an offering of my own: "The guy's not well known and his credentials are a little murky but what he's got to say is, in my opinion, pretty astounding."

I gazed around for a response but no one was biting. My office notoriety for coming up with suggestions considered hopelessly idealistic and intellectual was, I felt, an unjust caricature. Sure, I felt that Frankly had some responsibility to educate and uplift our constituents, but did that necessarily brand me an ivory tower dreamer?

Trying another approach, a personal one, to enlist their waning interest, I added, "He's a guy I actually knew slightly back in college, a year ahead of me. He'd heard about us in my alumni newsletter—you know the junk they use to fill up those things—and he sent me a whole packet. Seems he's spent the past decade delving into . . . sort of researching and trying to figure out . . . well, who runs the world. I mean, you can't exactly fault him for trivial pursuits. Anyway, he thinks he's finally got an angle on it and it's a pretty astonishing rap. What he does is trace the current powers-that-be—the President, National Security Council, CIA director, that Defense Department con man Smooth Line's representing, certain key bankers, the owners of some of the international media conglomerates, an Asian drug lord, even—Christ!—a syndicated columnist!—he traces them all in this fascinating way to a group of Nazis who escaped after World War II with the direct assistance of the Pope and then this gets you deep into this weird, mysterious relationship between medieval secret cabals within the church and latter-day practitioners of the occult. Oh, I almost forgot the Mormons. He ties in the Mormons and Watergate." Something told me that my time had expired. "It's pretty far out stuff," I added lamely.

It was an office tradition, born of a desire to keep her from drifting off, to allow Marion to ask the obvious questions that were on the tip of everyone's tongues. She trudged at me, "What're his credentials?"

"He's been working on a doctorate in Religion. I think he supports himself as a cabbie."

I could feel their frosty skepticism. As agents we are but conduits for the distilled sensibilities of a general populace that tends to be suspicious of anyone avidly pursuing something other than money and fame, the only goals that make sense under the current regime. Still, I firmly believed, or at least fervently hoped, that a market niche could be found for someone proclaiming a controversial, if arcane, interpretation of the world order.

Mona redirected us to the heart of the issue. "Has he been on any shows? *People* magazine? Ever indicted?"

"In college," I recalled with fondness, "he was busted for pot."

Piper tried to be analytical. "I can't see a handle. How do we promote him?"

"Simply that we have a speaker who's onto something big."

Piper was dubious. "But is he a reporter or a professor or anything?"

"No. It's kind of his hobby."

"Figuring out world politics is his hobby?"

Put that way, it sounded pretty preposterous to me too. There is a priesthood to the public discussion of global issues and if you lack the imprimatur of a Ph.D, L.L.D., M.D., by-lined newspaper clippings, or—as a last resort—a highly publicized indictment, forget it! Alas, I empathized with where they were coming from. There was no point continuing to play devil's advocate; I knew the score.

"O.K.," I conceded with some bitterness. "I'll write back, tell him to get a blockbuster book out on the subject first, or make a few guest appearances on Geraldo."

"Speaking of Geraldo," Mona responded with a terrifying burst of enthusiasm, "did you see that guy on '60 Minutes' last week?"

Churlish at the insensitivity to my proposal, I sniffed sarcastically, "What the hell does that have to do with Geraldo?"

"The guy on '60 Minutes' was Latino, okay? Like Geraldo." What is this, a sixth-grade quiz?"

"Sorry. Proceed."

"Zapatú was his name, the mystic revolutionary. He's alive because I saw him on TV. He speaks English. He's in exile somewhere in Central America. He could probably use the money and the change of pace. And so could we."

Whatever kind of weekend Mona had, it had put her in touch with deep truths. I rotated my gaze to encourage feedback. Marion, the coward, pretended to be taking notes. Kenny was exempt from participation until his sniffling subsided.

Piper, who views Mona as a role model in a variety of ways too convoluted for my meager psychoanalytic skills, was wide-eyed. "Let's go for it," she enthused, her round face bright as a bubble.

"Just think of it," Mona added, "A real honest-to-god revolutionary, not some hoax of a dumb little ten-year-old kid who's only interested in Rolls-Royces, but a man of passion, a man of vision. Have you ever seen pictures of the guy? He looks like Springsteen with a handlebar moustache."

"There might be visa problems and all kinds of red tape," I warned. I take no pleasure in being the voice of reason. One of the irritants of adulthood is having to occasionally abdicate the thrilling treehouse of speculation for reality's grim plateau. "We're going to have to deal with the State Department, foreign embassies, customs, the IRS. And that's only if we manage to find the guy and he's into it."

"How will we ever know unless we go for it?" urged Piper.

I couldn't resist one more stodgy interjection. "What if we track the guy down and discover he's already signed an exclusive with Smooth Line?"

Mona, exasperated with my cautions, had a ready response. "We leak to the press that Smooth Line is promoting communists, and then we return to the same dreary business."

Around six-thirty, I headed out with the intention of stopping by The Grotto. Mona was also getting ready to leave and I asked, as a courtesy, if she wanted to join me.

"Give me a minute to go to the bathroom," she answered, to my mild surprise. Mona usually has her evenings scheduled many weeks in advance, even Mondays.

Mona's minute in the bathroom stretched on and I wandered about the empty office, killing time. In front of Kenny's cubicle I stooped to pick up a wadded scrap of paper. Mindlessly I straightened it out and found myself reading a handwritten draft of what appeared to be a job application. Now *Kenny?* I worried that I was growing paranoid. Probably it was a response to a personal ad. Above Kenny's desk loomed a giant black-and-white poster of Marilyn Monroe struggling against a gush of air to keep her summer dress from billowing up her thigh. Kenny longed for immortal drama, and his chances were no worse than the rest of us.

It was Mona of the Night who emerged. Her eyes, which are naturally large and comical, had been reset into haunting caves of purple mascara slashed at savage angles. She looked disturbingly fierce, and slightly ridiculous.

"You look great," I told her, and from the way her lips pursed into a sneer I could tell that she wholeheartedly agreed.

The Grotto was uncrowded, with most of the dozen or so patrons distributed along the driftwood bar. The pet parrot over by the cash register scratched at the seed-strewn floor of its cage, pecking for some lost part of its past. Recalling my last visit, I wanted no encounters with my own.

Midway down the bar I spied, sure enough, a fellow I knew back at the Velvet Agency. His name was Davis Reynolds, and had some connection to the famous tobacco family. Interestingly, he was in approximately the same position as when I last saw him more than five years before, chatting up a pretty woman.

I began to steer Mona down the bar in that direction and was given immediate feedback that I had overstepped my bounds. She stopped dead in her tracks and peeking over the shoulder of the nearest male, a nicely tailored scotch drinker, she asked, "Your name isn't Larry, by any chance?"

Rather than hover like a neutered chaperone, I made my way towards Reynolds. A pale, bony, ascetic-looking man, women were wild for him. It took several nights on the town with him for me to realize his simple secret: he was wild for them.

"If it isn't the estimable Davis Reynolds?" I saluted, sliding into that space between barstools which functions as a breakdown lane. "And looking more . . . more whatever than ever."

I'd caught him off guard at a bad angle. As he swiveled to better confront his accuser, I stole an uninhibited glance at his ladyfriend. She was more fleshy than what used to be his preference. Yet Reynolds was always flexible, and five years can be crammed with enough tumult to alter even a person's sexual equilibrium.

"Well, well, what'd you know? Davis gripped my arm a little too firmly. "A shadowy figure from my murky past."

There are places in the world where it's something of a faux pas to ask straightaway about someone's vocational status; Washington isn't one of them. "What the hell are you up to?" I asked.

"Aide to a Senate committee, if I do say so myself." He straightened the knot on his silk tie to dramatize the point. "but don't get alarmed, we were denied subpoena power. And yourself?" I ran into Mindy Lantz a few months ago and she told me you'd become a venture capitalist."

"Hah. I hope you didn't believe it."

"These are strange and trying times, Danny. How many of us are what we wanted to be? Anything's possible."

"I run a lecture agency."

"Christ, you must know Jake Deaver over at Smooth Line." Reynolds sounded disgusted. "You're in that business?"

I threw up my hands, innocent of the accusation. "I've never met the guy. We compete with him—that's the extent of it. Why? What's he like?"

Reynolds screwed up his face like he'd swallowed rancid milk. "Unfortunately, he's the sort who will inherit the earth. The guy is not a pretty experience—unless he's on your side."

Reynold's ladyfriend performed a slight tensing of her neck muscle as a means of prodding him to get on with the overdue introduction. They must indeed know each other well forher to employ such a subtle signal.

"Lisa, meet Danny Frank. Danny, Lisa Franklin." Davis took a stiff swallow from a tiny glass. "Sounds like a nursery rhyme, your names."

I reached to shake her hand, which had a warm, snug fit, and held it overtime for one portentous moment.

Reynolds continued. "A lecture agent, huh? Wasn't old Velvet dabbling in that field?"

"Dabbling was his business. Did you read in the *Post* recently where he was named to some commission studying . . . the impact of TV cartoons on political values, or something like that?"

Reynolds twisted on his stool, already bored with this discussion even though he'd started it. He always had a minimal attention span, and women seemed to like that about him also. My own proclivity to seek all information, probe all emotional history, has usually been a turn-off. Most people are happier as the recipient of a quick, hot flash of superficial intrigue than they are with a deeply thoughtful inquiry. Too much curiosity is considered kinky.

"Still single?" Reynolds asked me while shifting his gaze around the bar.

I nodded. "You?"

"It's in arbitration. Lisa here is the best friend of my ex. In fact, it was her good counsel that made us come to terms with the error of our ways." Reynolds grabbed another swallow. "The error, of course, was being married. I tell you, Danny, I've come dangerously close to being snagged by the old rat race. Sometimes I think back on that period at old Velvet's. We really thought of ourselves as a new generation about to take over, didn't we? It's shocking how little has changed. Remember that work stoppage we staged to protest the pardon of Nixon?"

We both laughed. We had been so earnest in our revulsion at that disgusting encore to the Watergate scandal, whereas our boss, poor old Arthur Velvet, was by turns confused, irritated, and finally apoplectic at our obtuseness.

"Arthur Velvet was from the old school," I explained to Lisa. "We were the young turks, Davis and I and a few others. We were so pissed off at the pardon. We felt every citizen should take a stand. I vividly recall all of us sitting around discussing it—Arthur was not big on people sitting around—and at first he was very sympathetic. 'Politicians are all rug traders,' he said. 'Of course, it's a scam. What'd you expect, parliamentary procedure?'"

"It was absolutely incomprehensible to him that the staff actually contemplated doing something about it," Reynolds elaborated. Since he and I already knew the story, we found ourselves in that delightful situation of reminiscing for the ostensible benefit of an indulgent, unobtrusive, and attractive third party. "Velvet was a firm believer that a sort of caste system applies to public life: people who appear to do things, like politicians and entertainers; and people who promote the appearance that things are being done. Telling him that we wanted to take a stand on a national issue—he gawked at us like we were Martians."

It was my turn. While Reynolds tried to flag down the bartender, I described to Lisa how we designed a huge banner made of bedsheets which a secretary went home to get from her apartment during lunch hour. When Velvet returned from his lunch, he saw a crowd of people gathered outside our office building staring up at the huge makeshift sign suspended across three sets of windows, stating, in bold red paint, "Pardon All Mass Murderers."

"I thought old Velvet was going to call in the National Guard," remarked Reynolds, rejoining us. "Remember how he started climbing out on the ledge on his rickety little knees to rip it down?

Danny here begged him to wait at least until the photographer from the *Post* arrived. When Velvet heard that he almost took a leap."

"The *Post* in fact did take a photo," I told Lisa. "I've got it in my scrapbook. Right alongside my Little League team picture."

"Little League again?" A familiar female voice, husky with bravado, blasted me from behind. "It usually takes you several drinks to get all the way back to Little League." Mona proceeded to prop her forearm on my shoulder in an expression both of kinship and disdain.

Well, that was the end of the Arthur Velvet reminiscence. Mona is definitely not the patient, indulgent third party type. Besides, she'd already heard this story.

Davis Reynolds had left the agency before Mona's time, so introductions were in order. "Meet Mona," I announced to both Reynolds and Lisa. "We're colleagues." I once introduced her as "working for me" and suffered a week's worth of feminist diatribes for the transgression.

In the hand not weighing down my shoulder, Mona held a tall turquoise drink, which she wordlessly tipped like a regal scepter, first to Reynolds, then to Lisa.

"Davis is a crony from the Velvet Agency, and Lisa is a friend of his," I explained to Mona. "I batted nearly .400 in my final year in Little League and I thought they deserved to know about it."

"That guy I was just talking to," Mona nodded toward the front of The Grotto," what a first-class jerk-off. He couldn't shut up about how much money he's made in the past three weeks. He asked me if I wanted to go back to his condo to check out his tax statements. And he wasn't kidding! Whatever happened to higher consciousness?"

Mona can really put on a show. The last time I employed the term "higher consciousness," she reproached me for using empty rhetoric to mask my organizational ineptitude.

Reynolds had an insight. "The guy might actually be a poor poet just pretending to be what he thought you wanted."

Mona eyed him intensely. Then she popped the sort of conversation-halting question that's her trademark. "Are you two a couple?"

Bucking my shoulder to rid it of her hand, I addressed them, "Mona is doing a survey. You need not respond."

Reynolds was intrigued and I could sense the old juices starting to flow. "Lisa is my ex-wife's best friend. And we work together. That's a pretty heavy relationship, don't you think?"

Mona slid away from me towards Reynolds. "Then do you want to dance?"

The Grotto has no dance floor per se, except a dimly-lit no man's land just past the jukebox on the way to the lavatories. With the exception of uniquely celebratory occasions like St. Patrick's Day and the Summer Solstice, I don't believe I've ever seen anyone dancing there. A couple of times I've felt like it. But never have.

Reynolds was game, however. Lifting from his stool, he extended his hand to Mona in a courtly gesture, as if inviting her to waltz. There was an endearing absurdity to this, as the music jangling down from the speakers was a raucous calypso with a pulsating bass line. Together they sauntered off towards the jukebox.

Lisa and I were confronted with the vexing decision of whether to take a stab at normal conversation or abandon ourselves to simply watching the unfolding duet.

She surprised me by declaring, with no prodding, "It's okay with me if you'd rather just watch."

For a sweet instant I felt that soothing inner glow of believing the vast world contains a woman who can intuit my needs. "Will you watch along with me?" I asked.

The formless improvisations of unsynchonized touchless dancing can be naked expressions of character. Is there a wooden, rhythmless dancer who is not in some more fundamental way a stiff? Or a mannered, self-absorbed skater who is not a shameless narcissist? Reynolds evinced the affability and tasteful restraint of Astaire, though impeded by a limited range of motion suggestive of a stultifying lifestyle. For a woman, Mona is minimally graceful yet so joyous about any form of tension release that a heartfelt flow leaps forth. We watched her bend at the waist to twirl her butt while Reynolds trotted about in an incongruous hip-hop soft shoe.

I couldn't think of a thing to say to Lisa, even though she continued to demurely project good vibes. When our eyes would occasionally meet, there was no tension or self-consciousness, yet words would not come. The situation was ripe yet strangely infertile. I shuddered at the realization: I had become one very complicated organism.

I wanted to hold her hand, kiss her on the forehead, lavish my fingers on her soft swells. I wanted us to swoon in a euphoria that never subsides. I yearned to soar in wonder and vitality, and for those magnificent hopes which incubate in the rich depths of my bewildering soul to be born during this life, and to thrive.

But it would have been impossible to convey all that to an unfamiliar woman. The best I could do was to ask good-naturedly, "Would you like to dance?"

And I liked her even more when she politely declined.

CHAPTER 3

When I arrived at the office in the morning, Marion had already taken a phone message from Mona. "She told me to tell you that her meeting ran overtime," Marion dutifully reported. "She'll be in a little later."

I didn't flinch, lest I fuel office speculation that I harbor a repressed interest in Mona (which I don't believe is true) and that I allow her to walk all over me (which may have a basis in fact).

"What do you say we start smoking out old Zapatú?" I said to Marion with melodramatic determination. "Any idea where to start?"

Marion is bright enough, but she has the type of intelligence that has been overtooled by educational institutions. Her approach to all problems is to proceed along the logical pathways that usually achieve high marks on formal exams but do little to penetrate the chaos of real life dilemmas. On the other hand, she is the only one in the office who can find a bottle of white-out when you really need it. "We can look him up in *Who's Who*," Marion offered."Maybe call the State Department."

This was an approach that would get us nowhere, but I tried to restrain my impatience. "Yes, we should definitely pursue those," I assured her. "But we need to keep in mind that Zapatú is one of those people who lives outside the law, so we might come up short by relying only on our normal reference channels. The challenge of this project is to create new avenues of tracking him down. I've been thinking that the thing to do is to somehow circulate the word along the underground that we've got something to offer him."

Of course, Frankly Speakers has no connections to anyone in the world of subterranean politics, domestic or foreign, and I was hoping Marion would show enough alertness to call me out on this point. Instead, she diligently jotted a note in the notebook she keeps perched in her lap and with a placid demeanor concealed her true thoughts, whatever the hell they were. Marion was not about to zealously enlist for this investigation.

Still, it was her job to hear me out. I proceeded: "Let's review what we know about Zapatú. He's wanted by the authorities in his homeland, so we're not likely to learn much from official channels there. The U.S. supports the government there, which means that if his whereabouts were known to anyone in our government, like the State Department or the Congress, they would have turned the information over. The *Times* and '60 Minutes' each interviewed him, but you know the fetish reporters have about secrecy: they're all hoping to go to jail to protect their sources and then go on the lecture circuit to boast about it. Still, we should try to contact them. And wasn't there a group of writers and Hollywood types who sponsored a campaign to grant him exile here? It was called the Committee for Concern, or something like that. They might know something. It shouldn't be that hard to locate them, if they still exist." Marion had been vigorously taking notes, which by no means verified that she'd been listening. I slowed the cadence of my speech for emphasis. "I want this to be a priority. I've got a hunch this is a vital project. At a vital time. You know what I mean?"

Marion peered up from her notepad and with a blatantly artificial vigor replied, "Oh, definitely!"

Around eleven o'clock, Mona blustered in, slamming the outer door, whacking her overstuffed tote bag into the Xerox machine, and with these amplified gestures announcing that she was in no mood to be messed with. Fine with me. I was on the phone with Apple, the accountant, and thus exempt from the need to acknowledge her distemper or chastise her for tardiness.

"You haven't deposited your employee withholding?" Apple strained to make his inquiry more than rhetorical.

"I must have slipped up. I'll get right on it."

"And the quarterly payments? I gave you prepared forms. All you had to do was sign and make out the checks."

"Geez, I forgot. I've been so busy lately."

I felt under siege. The fact is, for an entrepreneur discussions with the accountant are indeed like psychoanalysis: the alleged benefits are both bitter to swallow and too remote to provide gratification.

Rex Apple is something of an eccentric. He plays the bagpipes for spare change in DuPont Circle on summer weekends, has the high-octane verbal energy of a salesman, and enjoys a semi-annual fluctuation in bodyweight of at least one hundred pounds. Clients who only see him in the spring personal tax season know him as a pudgy, jovial father confessor. Year-round users of his service, like myself, know his thinned-down, more scornful nature, the side that is ever mindful of the tough trade-off which must be negotiated between order and fun. This was February and Rex was mid-stream in his seasonal metamorphosis. "Danny," he asked, "are you becoming an anarchist?"

"I promise, I'll get right on it."

A woman's voice, not over the phone, responded, "That's your answer to every problem."

I cupped my hand over the receiver and addressed Mona sternly, "I'm talking to Apple. Disappear!"

Mona plopped herself down on my Goodwill sofa, and let me know through a system of fidgety gestures that she was intent on sitting there, however impatiently, until I hung up.

I reiterated to Apple my vast guilt and vowed to immediately remedy the malfeasance. Turning to Mona, I asked, "Have a nice evening?"

She stared abstractly at the ceiling while toying with one of her earlobes. "You left without telling me."

Like a chess strategist theoretically playing out a series of contingent countermoves, I saw all the ways I would be thwarted if I even attempted to respond. Had Mona wanted me to stay last night? "New earrings?" I asked her.

In a huff, she snapped up to leave. On her way out the door, she nearly blind-sided Marion who was bustling in with uncharacteristic verve.

"I've got news," Marion declared, breathless with urgency. "Ready? The guy from CBS is away in Israel till next week, but I reached the *Times* reporter who interviewed Zapatú. Just like you said, he wouldn't tell me anything. Except he did mention that I could try a Spanish literary agent in Spain, and I called her. Her name is Consuela Vasquez."

I felt like applauding Marion's effort, but feared she might interpret it as sarcasm. "You habla espanõl?"

She was beaming with pride in her accomplishment. "Si, señor. Señorita Vasquez said—and I quote—there must be a design muy grande to this chaos we call life. Apparently she'd just received a message last week from an American professor who'd somehow met Zapatú, she wouldn't say where. The professor told Señorita Vasquez that Zapatú has written a manuscript, a memoir, or at least some chapters, and was looking to publish it."

"Who's the professor?"

"She wouldn't say."

"Why not?"

Marion shot me a look of mild rebuke. "Would you, over long distance telephone to a stranger?"

This whole culture has watched too many espionage episodes on the tube, myself included. I pondered the loose ends. Zapatú writing a memoir? A traveling college professor? A tip from a reporter at the *Times*, publicity organ of the powers-that-be? A Spanish agent claiming grand design? It was all too neat.

"So where does that leave us?" I asked.

"Señorita Vasquez wanted to know more about us, so I gave her the standard line: exclusive agent for prominent political figures and media personalities. When she hears back from the professor, she'll contact us."

My fingers were tapping with spastic vigor on my desktop, and my posture had shifted from spineless slump to red alert. "We've got to get to this professor. I don't like waiting on another agent. They're too slick, too mercurial. Did we learn anything else about this professor? Can't we get to him on our own?"

"He's balding."

"What? How'd you learn that?"

"She just mentioned it in passing."

"I thought she's never met the guy."

"Good point. I could call her back and ask."

"Naw, that would just make her suspicious. Balding? I don't get it. How was her English? Was it hard to understand? Maybe she was saying he's . . . I don't know . . . maybe she was cursing the cucarachas."

For an instant I was awash in the delicious vicarious sensations of distant lands and colorful customs—Barcelona at twilight, Zapatú of the dark eyes hiding in the jungle, taco sauce and castanets. Not bad for a guy doomed to spend the remainder of a dreary day in a cheesy office overlooking an alleyway dumpster. Already this project was paying psychic rewards. Hard cash would be the next goal.

I strode to the window, and propped one foot on the sill, The Thinker: "A balding college professor . . . hmm . . . she might be hinting that he's a leftist. That would make sense. Zapatú is usually escorted wherever he goes by a band of armed guerrillas, according to press accounts. I doubt that this professor just stumbled into him. It must have been prearranged. How would an American teacher arrange such a meeting? Through Castro? The Soviets?"

I noticed that Marion had begun chewing the tip of her pen and was no longer taking notes. Her thoughts had drifted to more mundane matters, like dinner with her sister or the faulty flush mechanism on her apartment toilet.

"Great work," I commended her. "Let's confer later."

She sprang to her feet. "Yeah, definitely."

A few days later. It was one of those depths-of-March mornings where the dankness drives straight to the heart. It took me several minutes to wriggle out of my soggy overcoat, my gloves, wool scarf, extra sweater, all of which I flung to the floor in disgust. At my window I peered down to see a carbuncular mound of ugly sooted snow like a primitive totem rising up to ward off evil with the threat of worse evil. A wino was unzipping to take a piss. In utter despondency, I turned away to find Marion waiting patiently in the doorway for her boss to finish his meditations.

"I've got news," she announced. "No thanks to those pricks at CBS."

She was hopping with vim. I waved her into our hovel of an inner sanctum.

She continued, "Yesterday, before I left, I managed to speak with that CBS correspondent I'd been trying to reach. He was really snooty and difficult. He gave me a lecture on how hard he had to work, weeks and weeks, to track down Zapatú and then I had to listen to all the reasons why the free world depends on reporters like him protecting their sources. I just said, 'Fuck you, Jack.'"

"You told him that?" I was proud of her.

"His name was Jack, Jack Spence. So last night after aerobics I was in the sauna and I really started giving this some thought." Marion finally plunked down on the Goodwill sofa, but only on the edge.

"And?"

"This professor—what do we know about him? We know he's probably left-wing, 'cause how else would he get to meet Zapatú. And we've got a good idea that he met him recently, possibly over the Christmas holidays 'cause that's when professors get time off. So we can start by narrowing this down to left-wing college teachers who traveled to Central or South America sometime in late December or early January!"

I stood up abruptly and walked behind my desk, careful not to glance out the window to the squalor below. "O.K. I'm following you."

"Well, I'm thinking the State Department. I'd bet they keep track of those kind of things."

This was the Marion I knew. For a moment I thought she had been thunderstruck by genius. "The problem with the State Department," I elaborated, slightly crestfallen that her brilliant deductive reasoning had dwindled down to such a hapless conclusion, "is that there's no chance they'll ever tell anything to the likes of us. They don't even give straight answers under oath to Congressional committees."

"You're always so cynical," she whined.

"Doubting the integrity of the State Department is cynical?"

Marion chewed on this for a moment. Cynicism is not just a psychological style, like contentiousness; it's an often valid perspective on life. The problem with it is that it can squash all motivation.

I realized that I had misplayed my managerial role. I tried to rekindle Marion's zeal. "We are zeroing in. Good work. Let's think this through. We're getting there, all right."

She nodded her head in snappy agreement, a sure sign that I was being tuned out. She stood to go, a look of barely concealed dejection on her sweet round face. From the outer office came a horrible clatter, like a packing crate being repeatedly kicked. Mona had arrived. A woeful gray hopeless day stretched before me like a barren tundra.

"Wait," I called to Marion. "We've got plenty of leads to pursue. there's an organization of leftist teachers—Union of Radical Educators, or something like that. And give a call to Bernstein. We get him enough lucrative gigs. It's about time America's most acclaimed investigative reporter helps us out. And I've got another thought—right-wing groups. They monitor these kinds of people.

Tell them you're a true believer, make up a cover story. Zapatú, here we come!"

My chest heaved with hyperventilation: I had been ranting. Marion furiously scribbled a last note to herself and, performing a snappy salute, marched off to do battle.

Although the sun was not exactly breaking through, a few layers of cloud appeared to be dissipating. Light of a happier kind issued in from the terrible alley.

By the next morning, Marion was able to track down the Organization of Progressive Scholars (OPS), but their phone number in Ann Arbor, Michigan, yielded only a tape-recorded message announcing an economy class group tour to the USSR, featuring meetings with Soviet officials as well as political dissidents.

"I left my name and number and said I was interested in more information about the tour." Marion looked flushed and energized by her newfound ingenuity. She was perched almost acrobatically on the sofa's threadbare armrest. "I just thought to myself, if I left my real reason for calling they'd figure I was undercover FBI or something."

"Very good move." My own voice sounded lifeless and rote, like a computerized phone message.

"Then I reached the Coalition for Liberty and Freedom, here in town. They were very friendly and open. I spoke with a young Korean woman. Just a second..." Marion thrashed through the pages of her spiral notebook, unsuccessfully. "Well, I've got her name somewhere. I told her that I was doing a report for my college newspaper on how communist professors actually assist guerrilla revolutions in the Third World. And did she know any way I could get a list of teachers traveling to Latin America?"

I was bowled over. "That's unbelievably excellent!" Now I sounded like a high school assistant coach.

"She told me she thought my request was—quote—doable. I'm supposed to call her back late this afternoon, and she might have something for me. I asked her to make a particular check if any professor had ever assisted the famous Zapatú. I told her, God bless you."

If we had the resources, I would have lavished a bonus on Marion. Instead, I stood to extend a hearty one-man ovation.

At that moment, Mona strutted in raising a tipped finger in humble acceptance of the applause. "Thank you, thank you, one and all," she nodded. "I hope you're not too enraptured to deal with the fact that one of our speakers is snowed in at O'Hare."

Emergencies are Mona's natural habitat. She always puts on a grim face but it's hard to believe she isn't loving it. Hurriedly she filled us in on the details. The speaker was Marge Holman, the lesbian attorney and poet. The engagement was at the University of Southern Mississippi, air service to Laurel, and even if the Chicago airport cleared up immediately, there were no flights that could deliver Ms. Holmar in time.

"I still haven't talked with the people in Mississippi," Mona said. "I've left word at their office, which they're never in, their dorms, the dean's. This one is pretty cut and dry. Nothing we can do: the Lord's work."

Each contract for a speaker contains an "Act of God" clause stipulating a rescheduling of the event if necessitated by illness, foul weather, unavoidable breakdown or delay in transportation systems, or an outbreak of war (deemed, legally, to be an act of God). It's one of those commonly used catchphrases that make you want to stop and think. This, however, was not the time.

Kenny hollered in from the outer office, "Call for Mona on line two." Marion took the opportunity to slink out.

Mona leaned across my desk to pick it up on my phone, gesturing for me to stay seated. She punched the broadcast key.

"Jimmy Roy Ethridge," came a homey twang. "I'm the advisor. What's up?"

Mona's specialty, like all agents, is students of sub-average intelligence who can be manipulated like poodles at obediance school. An advisor, no matter how dumb, tends to present a different set of dynamics. Patiently and without condescension, she explained to Jimmy Roy her deep and passionate regret about the blizzard raging across the Great Plains, where Ms. Holman was flying from.

"Shoot, it's like summer down here today," noted Jimmy Roy. "Just yesterday I was swimmin'."

Mona didn't mince words. "I'm afraid we're going to have to reschedule. How's your calendar in April?"

Jimmy Roy replied with alacrity. "Probably we should just can it. Things are too busy, what with spring orgy and all. What'd you say this gal's name was for tonight?"

"Marge Holman. On Women's History. You've got an obligation to reschedule."

There was a pause while Jimmy Roy ruffled something that may or may not have been his calendar. Finally he answered, "After orgy we got Alcohol Awareness week, then it's practically final exams. Shoot, there don't seem to be no time left."

Mona grimaced. Her eyebrows thickened like a squall amassing on the horizon. "Are you familiar, Jimmy Roy, with the act of God clause?"

"Yes, m'am."

"And you understand how it applies to situations just like this?"

"God means something different to each one of us. That's the whole point of a pluralistic society."

To me, Mona snorted, "Someone's putting words in this dickhead's mouth." To Jimmy Roy, she can conciliatory. "You have a legitimate point. However, I've had considerable experience with these types of situations and discussions with numerous lawyers..."

"Lawyers!" Jimmy loudly interrupted. "I thought we was discussin' matters of theology. Shoot, if you're talking legal matters you probably be wantin' to speak with our attorney, Mr. Wyatt Davis."

"Lawyers!" Jimmy loudly interrupted. "I thought we was discussin' matters of theology. Shoot, if you're talking legal matters you probably be wantin' to speak with our attorney, Mr. Wyatt Davis."

Mona's face was the twisted picture of wrath, for Jimmy Roy, for Attorney Wyatt Davis, for lesbian feminist attorney-poets, for the entire south, and the midwest with their infernal snowstorms, indeed for all of life that is not methodical, smooth, and organized primarily by her will. Amazingly, her voice emerged soothing as cough syrup, "Tell you what, Jimmy Roy. Give me a home number where I can reach you tonight. It'd be best to try and work this out when we're not so pressured. I'd like to go home after work, draw a nice hot bath, stretch the phone over, and give you a ring. About nine? What do you say?"

"Sure enough, m'am," is what Jimmy Roy said.

After she hung up, I tried to bolster her. "The act of God clause doesn't have a thing to do with theology, the little weasel. They'll reschedule."

Mona grabbed a paper clip and in two seconds twisted it into a precision figure eight. "Who needs this grief? I don't know why I put up with it."

Oh Christ, I thought, do I once again have to delineate, in homilies which demean my aesthetic standards, that suffering is the inseparable counterpart to joy, that success is only achieved throughtoil, and that if business could be performed free of hassles such as Jimmy Roy the already marginal demand for our services would be dangerously reduced?

I was spared by Marion, skipping through the door and brandishing her little notebook like a pep rally flashcard. "Guess what?" she chirped.

"You met a heterosexual unmarried male," sniffed Mona.

"I found the professor! Or at least how to reach him." With a jaunty windmill motion, Marion spiked her notebook against her ample knee like an exultant wide receiver—touchdown! "I'm getting kind of good at this, if I do say so myself."

She flopped happily down on the sofa beside Mona and proceeded to trace her path to glory. The Coalition for Liberty and Freedom indeed called back to refer her to an aide to the Senate Foreign

Relations Committee who keeps a file on leftist academics traveling abroad. She gave the aide her line about writing an article for her college newspaper and with no hesitation beyond a cursory request for anonymity he treated Marion to a small dissertation on the devious ways of international Communism. He explained that many professors enjoyed so-called consulting relationships to underdeveloped Latin American nations, and that invariably there was more than met the eye. In reality, according to the aide, what masquerades as humanitarian assistance to the great mass of oppressed peasants is little more than an influence-peddling outreach program directed from Moscow and/or Havana. Just before hanging up, the aide suggested that Marion might want to research the activities of a certain University of Virginia sociologist recently returned from the country of Belize where, he added in a final note, the Marxist revolutionary firebrand Zapatú was rumored to be in hiding.

I couldn't believe it. "Zapatú? That's tremendous!"

"Virginia, my alma mater," sighed Mona as she busily pretzeled another paper clip.

Marion was gloating with pride at her accomplishment. I wanted to hug her in congratulation, a move that would be readily misperceived as both sexist and another dodge from paying a bonus.

"And you got the professor's name?" I asked excitedly.

She glowed with exuberance. "Yep. I told the department secretary that I had met one of the profs in Central America and he had left a book behind that I wanted to return but I had lost the slip of paper that his name was on. 'You must mean Dr. Hoffman?' That's the name the secretary said. Dr. Andrew Hoffman."

"Is he in the U.S. or still down there?"

"I'm still checking that out." She thrust her fist triumphantly at the low corkboard ceiling. "Geez, I really scored!"

I stretched across my desk to slap her a high five. Perhaps once we were a pioneer people, but what we've become is a nation of sports fans.

Mona stretched her spine and yawned loudly. "Search no further."

We had been rudely ignoring her. I knew her game. "Can I help you?"

"Search no further," Mona repeated in droll deadpan.

The game called for me to commence a detailed interrogation for the meaning of her cryptic remark. This, however, was no time for games. "Out with it," I snapped. "Whatever IT is."

She hung her head like a distracted child over her new little paperclip sculpture, this one a corkscrew. "When I was in college at Charlottesville, Andy and I were rather close."

"Close? What is meant by close?"

"Please, Danny, Let's keep this professional."

"Proceed."

"Put it this way: if Andy knew I as trying to reach him, he'd respond. Promptly."

"Were you a student of his?" I was genuinely curious.

"Daniel, please." With delicate fingers she undid and re-hitched a large purple ceramic earring, then glanced up with wide-eyed insouciance, as if to ask what everyone was waiting for. "By the way, if I can get through to Andy and get his help, what do I get?"

I was keenly aware of Marion's hot displeasure with this shift in focus. "Dammit Mona, we're a team. Everyone does what they can to help us win." It sounded hollow but I hoped Marion would perceive me as not caving in.

Earring readjusted, Mona said, "Another question. Do you think there's a chance you'll be going to this Belize or wherever, to meet with Zapatú?"

I was thinking that it might freshen my soul to spend a few days in the tropics, spiced by adventure, tax deductible. "Possibly," I replied.

Mona finally looked straight at me, eyes sharp with ummasked directness. "If you go, I'd like to go with you."

Marion had remained placid, but I could feel the rumblings of her scrutiny. I was enraged at Mona for boxing me into such an awkward corner.

With a chief-executive-style clearing of my throat (more a tepid little cough than an authoritative harumph), I lifted myself up to demonstrate that our gathering was about to enter a new phase. "You've done a great, wonderful job, truly all-star," I told Marion, loathing my transparent unctuousness. "Now I need to confer with Mona on a limited access basis."

It was facile, meaningless phrase but Marion thankfully took the hint. I felt bad for her, another sad chapter in the eternal saga of the plodder being eclipsed by the hotshot.

When she'd gone, I turned in anger toward Mona. "I don't know what you're driving at. Zapatú represents a great opportunity for us. Why can't you be a team player and just goddamn help like the rest of us?"

"I just wanted to know if there's really a chance you might go down there to meet them." She was a little girl, in coy voice asking daddy for a lollipop. "Is that so bad of me?"

"Mona, it doesn't please me to remind you that we have great difficulty tolerating each other's company for more than an eight-hour workday. And we don't even know for sure if we'll ever even contact Zapatú."

She broke into a wide, joyous, silly smile, ear to ear like a drunk. "Those are my terms, take it or leave it."

Take it or leave it? Suddenly I felt a rush of fondness towards Mona for the sheer simplicity of the choice, even if I didn't completely understand it. I was so overtired of calculating, negotiating, strategizing, anxiously dissecting the vast expanse of existence until my worldview had dwindled to a squinting examination of meaningless numbers in capricious columns. Take it or leave it? What a grand approach!

That night, Kenny and I attended a local lecture at the University of Maryland by one of our speakers, Chet Janko—Foe of Environmental Decay. For me this was a good chance to see how Janko's presentation had evolved since the last time I saw him three years ago. For Kenny, who booked the date, it was a chance to meet face-to-face the Maryland lectures chairperson, Sissy Ransome, with whom he'd had an intensely flirtatious phone relationship since last fall.

Since our office is only an hour's drive from the campus, I had always been a bit puzzled as to why Kenny and Sissy had never gotten together. To overhear their telephone chatter you'd swear that wild horses couldn't keep them apart.

As we maneuvered from the parking lot across a diagonal walkway to the auditorium, I asked Kenny, "What do you think Sissy will look like?"

"Big teeth, long face," he said without hesitation, "wide brown eyes bulging out to greet the world, not set deep. She and I have described our physical features to each other in great detail. I don't even think we have to meet."

I wanted to ask him if he'd told her he was gay but I kind of knew the answer already. The fact is, gayness fit Kenny, whatever that fit was, and I certainly had no trouble accepting it. I knew that his particular ceaseless chatter and unquenchable urge to engage, connect, reach out, touch and be touched would suck all the oxygen from the breeze if it were driven by heterosexual urges. Gay, he was, to my mind, okay.

"How did you describe yourself to her?" I asked.

He gazed down as we gingerly forded a rivulet of mud seeping down from a thawing slope. "I can't exactly remember. It's not an easy thing to do."

"You're a handsome enough guy. It shouldn't have been that hard."

"You've never been in my situation," he scoffed. "How would you handle it?"

My description would no doubt fluctuate drastically according to my assessment of who was hearing it. Even when I look into a mirror I rarely see a picture that will stay fixed long enough to capture.

We had come to the top of a hill and were faced with a rotund red brick structure fronted by those sturdy white columns, thick as giant redwoods, which serve as international symbols of serious intentions. At the very top of the steps, dwarfed beside the center column, stood a long-faced, gangly, big-eyed girl who had to be Sissy Ransome. I wondered if she had enough information to recognize us.

Dozens of students were pouring up the steps. They carried books, basketballs, knapsacks so bulging that one might think a mass migration was in progress. At least we wouldn't be the only ones who showed up. My worst fears had been quashed.

With an agile scamper, Sissy began to skip down the stairs towards us. I could only conclude that Kenny had provided her a serviceable self-description. Good for him. A better man than I.

Her big teeth gleamed like a Holiday Inn highway sign, and with impressive verve she thrust a handshake straight at me. I was dumbfounded: Kenny had provided her a description of me!

"Sissy Ransome," she introduced herself.

I tried to catch a signal from Kenny, but he was a few feet below busily scraping mud off his shoes by grating them across the lip of the auditorium step.

"How's the crowd?" I asked her, stalling until a solution came to mind.

"You look just like I thought," gushed Sissy. "Maybe not as tall."

I wanted to collar Kenny and make him confess, right on the spot.

"How about me?" Sissy asked, with a humble girlish downcast to her gaze. "Kind of what you thought?"

I might be able to sustain this charade for another ten seconds, at most. Students were streaming by us, in clumps of two and three. Sissy awaited my answer. Kenny, the little turd, stood awaiting my answer. I did also. "A little taller. And prettier." My tone was far from sweet. I turned to Kenny with great irritation. "I'm sure you won't be the only one in the damn hall with mud on your shoes. Let's go get a seat."

Like a fidgety horse, Kenny made a few rapid backward scoffs of his hoof before heading in. I could tell Sissy was disconcerted by the cold reception, but in due time she would understand—understand more than she wanted.

The auditorium was an old, wood-floored barn of a building with an overhanging balcony that was already creaking from the stampede of students filling it up. Sissy led us down the side aisle of the main floor, and it became immediately apparent that she was a woman of local stature. Everyone seemed to know her, hooting out with a variety of clipped, cryptic salutes, almost like jungle animal calls. A girl with purple hair gave her a two-fingered whistle. A boy in military fatigues simply grunted "Ha, ha" as though she would know exactly what he meant.

Undaunted, Sissy gave a friendly wink. "I've saved you seats. Right in front."

"No, no," I halted her halfway down the aisle. "It's important for us to feel the pulse of the crowd. Right over here would be fine." I gave Kenny a none-too-surreptitious elbow, to emphasize that it was about time for him to come out.

Sissy energetically chewed on a wad of gum, which had the effect of organizing her conversation into staccato cadences. "Take. Any seat. Be back in five."

I stopped her. I was fed up. "*Kenny* here should probably go backstage with you, to let Mr. Janko know that we're here."

Sissy stiffened into an old-style, vaudeville gape-mouthed double take. Her bug eyes seemed to lift outward like upturned hands for an explanation.

Kenny shot me a ferocious scowl, but dutifully trudged off behind Sissy as she tromped sullenly toward the stage. Well-wishers continued to hoot at her, but she pushed icily past them. She and Kenny would have time to thrash it out. I was confident that he would come forth with some explanation for his litlc subterfuge, and eventually she would like him all the more for it, once her pique had subsided. He would soon be back to his loosey-goosey free association telephone banter—Prince Kenny. And she would feel like a queen.

My seat was one of the old flip-down types, made of varnished bowed pine, comfortable only to those who are mightily at peace with themselves. After a couple minute's experimentation with every conceivable permutation of leg, back, and butt position, I resigned myself to discomfort and resolved to move on. An unexpected span of time alone can be a propitious opportunity to benignly assess one's place in the cosmos. What I wound up doing was watching girls.

Prancing up the aisle on my left, having already traipsed the hall's circumference like thoroughbreds preening about the paddock, were a trio of young women: a tall, thin, sway-backed girl, not unlike our Sissy; a butterball, all breast and pelvic expanse; a preternaturally voluptuous Amazon with cheekbones so rosy they looked like individual smiles. Each had hair that was radiantly clean and meticulously maintained. You would think grooming was a cumpulsory activity. And their skin was clear and unworried like rainwater. The boys also were fit and brimming with hormonal urges: smooth-cheeked even when attempting beards; with taut, primal voices that bleated and croaked like barn animals; their super-active hands slapping backs or self-consciously massaging their own trim tummies and puffed up biceps. There was enough combustible energy in the old auditorium to cause an explosion.

And as I halfway feared (and halfway hoped), they came rushing back to me—my own utopian undergraduate days. Every speech or rally I went to made me believe the world could be changed for the better, not just by the slow machinery of evolution, but through the deliberate acts of inspired people. And every warm smile exchanged on the garden path towards a hot midnight kiss was a step closer to perfection. I participated in a sit-in once at the university president's office to protest the awarding of a grant to the Physics Department for nuclear research. More than participated—I had written a series of columns precipatating the protest. For three days and nights a few dozen of us refused to be moved from the office lobby. Oh what a glorious feeling to completely disrupt your routine (especially when there are no serious consequences) in the name of a righteous cause. *Time* magazine published a photo of the incident, and I still have it, right in with the Little League team portrait and the clipping of the Ford pardon protest. There we are, crammed togther in the candlelit corridor, men and women sprawled nearly on top of each other, scraggly and disheveled, raccoon eyes blinking in the camera flash like immigrants in the hold of destiny's ship.

Kenny plunked down beside me, and declared, "Everything's cool."

Snapping up from my reverie, it took me a moment to guess what he was referring to. "And Sissy?" I asked.

Kenny brushed me off with a fey swat of his hand. He was telling me that I should quit acting so silly. Fair enough. I resumed watching the students milling about for vacant seats, coolly scouting for friends, performing their last minute parade for the hordes of prowling eyes.

Sissy Ransome emerged on stage to a raucous clatter of applause, both appreciative and mocking. She appeared quite calm, tall at attention, heels clicked together, head high, spine straight. The large crowd was her triumph; her few moments at the microphone constituted her victory lap.

"Before we bring on tonight's distinguished speaker, I have a few announcements." Sissy has a husky vibrato in her voice and one can imagine her, with the slight prodding of a tinkling piano, breaking into the opening bars of an old chestnut, like "Blue Moon." I could easily understand what had attracted Kenny. "All next week is the university blood drive. Medical professionals will be set up in the main lobby of the administration building, noon to five, Monday through Friday. On March 12, the rock band Thing will be performing in the Union. They're branching into some new material, reggae and blues, so even if you've heard them around town you'll probably want to check out their new repertoire. One final note—the radical feminist mime troupe, Shut Up!, will be doing a roving performance at various points around campus next Tuesday. They're really worth checking out. Don't be scared."

Sissy then launched into a nicely paced, very articulate and thoroughly laudatory capsule biography of Chet Janko, foe of environmental decay. The fact that she was reading verbatim from a hype sheet I had authored in no way tarnished my pleasure in hearing it.

Mr. Janko was raised in Akron, Ohio. His twin brother had died of leukemia at the age of nine. His father, a lifelong emphysema sufferer, finally died of asphyxiation during a wave of bad air in July 1972. Mr. Janko's childhood goal was to be a police detective and write suspense novels on the side, in the genre of Stephen King. It was his passionate interest in survival, both for himself and his fellow man, that drove Mr. Janko to research and speak out on the perils of environmental decay. His hope is to return one day to a log cabin, in a green meadow, by a fresh running stream, and sit down to write a suspense book...

"Less chilling than what he has to present to us tonight. Please welcome, Mr. Chet Janko." Polite applause. Sissy turned over the microphone to Janko, a tall guy who wears cowboy boots to accentuate his height and lend a bow-legged, John-Wayne-come-in-to-clean-up-the-town, gunslinger swagger to his demeanor. The houselights dimmed, then accidentally brightened, then finally dimmed.

I have talked in the past with Chet about what I perceive to be problems in structure and emphasis. He listens patiently to my criticisms, even goes so far as to nod in tentative assent, then proceeds to point out to me that he is a man with a mission and cannot be primped and pruned like some fledgling Congressional candidate. My major complaint about his presentation is that I feel he gets too heavy too soon, and bludgeons his audience into a kind of intellectual numbness. Chet responds that bludgeoning is exactly what the situation calls for. I notice a Catch-22 to that, but there's only so far you can push a point. My job is to book the gigs.

Chet blasted off with a depiction of the state of the natural world in the year 2000, if current trends continue. In what I interpreted as deference to my advice, he started with the "lighter" stuff—

dumping of industrial waste, pollution of the fresh water supply, accumulation of non-disposable garbage products. He wrapped up this portion with a vivid depiction of some tranquil little bay near San Juan, Puerto Rico, where a mountain of illegally dumped and non-biodegradable automobile tires had grown so large that the local tides, previously subject only to the influence of the moon, were substantially altered.

I sensed the audience getting impatient. Chet sensed them thirsting for more. He sailed into his showstoppers—depletion of the ozone layer which preserves our delicately balanced ecosystems, intensifying of the sun's rays precipitating epidemics of fatal melanomas and a melting of the polar ice caps, gross distortions inthe oxygen content of the air we breathe, floods and suffering and massive death. Chet had removed his sportcoat and undone his tie, and he stalked about the stage looking as desperate and pained as the last man left on earth. He clutched the portable microphone like a stoneage aborigine clinging to a sacred bone.

"In conclusion," he warned, straightening himself out and reinserting the mike in its upright stand, "you in the audience, the next generation, will inherit a natural environment that is under siege, from forces both overt and hidden. I strongly urge you to . . . to heed these dangerous developments . . . and remain vigilant and concerned . . . and don't commit the sin of sticking your heads in the sand. Thank you, thank you very much for your attention."

There was a moment of stone silence followed by a polite yet uninspired applause which expired soon after it began. Chet Janko nonetheless took a sweeping bow as if humbly acknowledging a phantom ovation, then informed the audience that he would be happy to field any questions.

None came. People looked around, nudged their neighbors. I hoped for the sake of the university's collective honor that someone would think of something to ask. An agent of the old school, which I was not, would have thought to plant a few. I felt bad for Chet. He meant well. It wasn't entirely his fault that students go comatose at the prospect of catastrophic destruction. For a brief instant I considered raising my hand, to alleviate the awkward embarrassment. But the only questions I could think to ask with a straight face concerned business details, like when he was going to reimburse me for the promotional literature.

With the adroit timing of an old vaudeville emcee, Sissy dashed out and hastily announced that a reception for Mr. Janko was being held at the student union function lounge, where it would be possible to discuss these vital issues in a more relaxed context. With great relief, the audience lifted from the creaky wooden seats and filed out, subdued and murmuring, some to themselves. I got the distinct sense that over the next few hours, more than a few cozy suitors would be whispering into lovers' ears that our future on earth is brief and uncertain, that moments of pleasure must be seized while time remains.

As soon as the audience rose to leave, Kenny bolted for the stage to intercept Sissy. Less in a hurry, I slowly made my way forward against the flow and found Kenny pressed to the lip of the stage, on his tiptoes, thrusting up towards Sissy who still stood imperiously at the microphone.

"Please come to the reception," Sissy pleaded.

Kenny, back to his old cocky self, blew her a hasty show biz kiss. "Gotta run," he crowed. "Buzz you tomorrow."

CHAPTER 4

Our Air El Salvador flight dipped beneath a pillowy strata of threatening gray clouds, then glided in low over a landscape of tangled green mangrove and dead brown swamp. Already the passenger compartment had become muggy and thick with foreboding. A fat black fly had somehow been trapped in the cabin, and buzzed spastically from one seat to the next, occasionally careering at full tilt into one of the double plated plexiglass windows. It's curious how one can become thoroughly absorbed with a minor nuisance like a fly while completely tuning out the vastly louder and immensely more significant grinding of the propeller engines, which groaned laboriously onward.

The plane made a graceful starboard tilt, and for the first time I caught a full panorama of this jungle outpost. To the west were thickly forested hills, uncarved by roadway or any aspect of development, disappearing into the low gray mists. Stretching south, in the direction we were heading, was an endless savannah of scrub trees and silent muddy pools. The turquoise sea was supposed to be somewhat beyond and I leaned far forward for a glimpse, almost nibbling the neck of the priest who sat in front of me. But we were too far inland. All I could see was the sprawling carpet of vegetation.

Mona had pretended to be asleep ever since we took off from Miami. It was her way of impressing on me what an exhausting week she had put in at work and how, as I was told, she "didn't get a wink of sleep last night." When I had failed to ask the logical follow-up questions concerning who she had been out with and exactly why a night's sleep had been sacrificed, she slammed shut her eyes, leaned back, and pretended to be napping. However, I knew she was awake because her neck tensed up whenever the fly came buzzing around.

As we zoomed in over the jungle, I muttered an occasional "Ooh" or "Aah" to let her know that there was scenery worth seeing, if she would just give up the charade. Mona knows that I enjoy sharing my observations, even if it's only empty banter. Her resolute silence carried a sting of retribution.

In the distance, straight out from the wing, I noticed a compound of huts with rusted tin roofs huddled at the curl of a stagnant bayou. I felt the urge to make a remark, some appreciation of the strange world we were entering, some homily like, "Their lives must be so peaceful down there."

Instead, I muttered another "Ooh," hoping to rouse her.

Mona didn't budge.

I was getting frustrated. "All right, Mona. I'm all ears. Who was it you went out with last night?"

She steadfastly held to her slumbering pose, although I detected a slight involuntary creasing at the corner of her mouth.

"I really hope it wasn't that nerdy guy with the headphones and sun visor who sells flowers in the Circle."

Her eyes remained shut, but her chin quivered.

"Everyone knows that you're the only one he takes the earphones off for. Just last week he asked me your name."

Her right eye squinched down a little too tight.

"And when I told him 'Mona,' I thought he was going to cry with joy."

Her eyes popped open and she clucked, without the usual nastiness, "Don't you ever shut up?"

"See those little huts out there?" I tried to point but there wasn't enough room to extend my arm. "Can you imagine how peaceful their lives are?"

"More peaceful than mine."

The plane leveled, then dipped still further, shaking and lurching, rattling and creaking, then leveled again and bounced and hiccupped its way to an eventual rest by a one-story cinder block building that looked like a truck stop. On the side was a Volvo with a goat chained to the front fender.

As the plane, rickety enough to make landing suspenseful, came to a halt several passengers broke into applause. Most, however, were too limp with relief to do more than relax their death grip on the arm rests. Passengers on the aisle seats began to straighten up and warily edge out to where they could grab their overhead luggage. Handbags, packages, knapsacks festooned with bright decals came tumbling down. When the plane's door opened, a warm gush of pleasing sour air filled the cabin.

"What happens now?" yawned Mona.

"Now . . . now, we improvise."

She pretended to be too sleepy to complain.

"Immigration" was a process of having our passports superficially scrutinized by a roly-poly coffee-skinned man with crescent-shaped sweat stains spreading from the armpits of his thin cotton dress shirt. When each of the deboarding passengers had undergone "immigration," it was time for "customs inspection," a process conducted at the other side of the room by the same roly-poly man. A radio from outside loudly broadcast a speech whose only discernible phrases were the frequent sing-song proclamations of "independence" and "liberation." Our inspector, now perspiring profusely, proceeded to slap, squeeze, rotate and unzip approximately every fourth piece of luggage. He found no contraband. It was past four o'clock by the time we were released into the tropical afternoon. The sun had finally broken through the low ceiling of gray. Bright yellow hibiscus smiled at us in the light.

Our ultimate destination was a nameless offshore cay, a couple hundred kilometers to the south. We were supposed to take a cab into Belize City, and from there catch a bus which was supposed to run four times a day to the coastal town of Juanita. At Juanita we were to find a boat to ferry us to our offshore rendezvous with Zapatú. Mona claimed to have worked all this out in precise detail with Professor Hoffman, or "Andy," as she referred to him.

The "taxi pool" was simply a lineup of local vehicles owned by drivers enterprising enough to meet the afternoon plane. None of the autos, mostly Toyotas and Datsuns, all dented and somehow damaged, carried a formal "Taxi" identification. The drivers hovered in the shade by the hibiscus, slapping palms and exchanging money with each other. Some kind of game was in progress.

"Taxi, mon. You come with me!"

We looked around and, sure enough, the remark was directed to us. One of the drivers had sauntered over to his auto, a Kelly green compact, and was holding the door (it was only a two-door) open for us. Before we could compose ourselves, he had our bags in the trunk and us wedged in the back seat, where a lethargic fly crawled across the dusty upholstery.

Mona had been slow in coming to life, but I could see that she was now regaining her form. "Do you have a license?" she confronted the driver, as he sidled behind the wheel. "Are you registered to operate a taxi?"

The driver, a tall, thin, snaggle-toothed man with pitch black skin, turned to us and laughed. "No, mon. No license. No registration. But dis car get you where you going."

Mona was not prepared for such an unrepentant response. "Sir, could you say that again?"

"You hear me, mon. I take you where you going. Why you fuss?"

I kind of liked his style, but this was going to be one long, trying journey if I didn't display some solidarity—pronto! "Hey, the lady has a legitimate question," I interceded, sounding like the law school weenie that lurked somewhere in my recessive genes.

"Yea, mon," the driver replied with a sing-song sarcasm totally devoid of contrition.

"We're catching a bus to Juanita," I asserted. "Can you get us to the bus terminal?"

He chuckled, slipping the car into gear. I wasn't so obtuse as to think that a country whose national airport is the size of a three-car garage would boast much in the way of a central bus terminal, but I figured I'd play into the driver's predisposition to caricature Yankee travelers. In remote cultures, the new visitor can either feign familiarity with local customs, which is usually preposterous, or submit to a demeaning awkwardness in virtually all endeavors, which can be equally preposterous.

"The bus terminal?" the driver sang. "No problem."

We rambled off in a funnel of dust. My inclination was to pump the driver for information. One of our speakers, a former one-term Senator who was held hostage for three days by Middle-East terrorists, begins every one of his lectures by relating an anecdote he allegedly hears from a cab driver on the way into town from the airport. It's always the same anecdote—something about how a farmer's wife learns to distinguish liberals from conservatives. Still, there's no doubt that cab drivers can be good sources of local intelligence. On the other hand, they ask a lot of questions.

"You from the States?" We were hurtling down an unlined blacktop strip at 60 m.p.h. and the driver had actually turned his head all the way around to look at us.

I nodded, not wanting to encourage him.

He took a peek back at the road. "What part, mon?"

"The east."

"Is a big country, the U.S. You here for business?"

Mona and I had concocted a cover story for our trip down here. We were to be tour operators specializing in those week-long get-the-wits-scared-out-of-you adventure trips into wild and ungovernable places. We were in Belize to scout out locations. We traveled with no business card or formal letters of introduction out of a wish to encounter the region in a fresh and unadulterated way. What we were searching for was nature in a raw and overwhelming form, provincial hamlets unaccustomed to seeing pale skin, featuring rumors of lawless marauders and smoldering volcanoes.

"Just traveling," I told our driver.

"I never met American who travel to Juanita," the driver turned around and chortled.

"Just watch the road and drive!" Mona lashed out.

Silence took over.

The cabbie veered to a halt at a storefront pharmacy with a tattered canvas awning, where a thin young boy squatted on a red-and-white soccer ball. It was a wide unpaved street of small stucco buildings painted as if by a child, in simple blues and pinks and whites. Hardly anyone was about. A stout woman sloshed a bucket of water into the gutter. Several emaciated mongrels dozed in the shade of a stripped down '74 Duster.

The cabbie turned to savor our reaction. "Bus station. Bus come any time."

As he loped around to open the door for us, I tried to recall what our budget guide book had stated about the estimated cab fare from the airport into town. I think it said two dollars, Yankee money. I was determined not to get fleeced, especially in front of Mona.

After helping us out and handing us our bags, he said, "Two dollars. Gratuity included, mon."

Mona gave me a nudge. "That's not enough," she whispered.

I wanted to kick her shin. Instead I fished into my pocket for a floppy bill of local currency, big as a napkin and decorated with bright pineapples. At the Miami airport I had exchanged for a hundred dollars' worth. The problem was, I had no recollection of the exact exchange rate. I believe what I gave him was worth fifty cents. but it might have been five dollars. Or worse.

He rumbled off, leaving us alone beneath the awning with the young boy. Mona whispered, in a voice loud enough to be heard the length of the street, "How much did you tip him?"

"A quarter, approximately, depending on what Wall Street did today."

"Good," Mona commended me. "That's about the right amount."

Soon enough a billow of dust emerged at the end of the street, rising and enlarging, and the bus heaved to a halt directly in front of the pharmacy. Several school children in ironed white blouses and blue slacks hopped off, followed by an arthritic old East Indian, a rolled blanket slung across his stooped back.

"A Juanita?" I asked the driver.

"Climb aboard," he answered.

Mona hoisted herself onto the first step. "This does go to Juanita, doesn't it?"

The bus driver threw out an indolent frown, letting her know that he was not going to indulge that line of questioning. "Si. Juanita."

We shimmy-hipped our way down the narrow aisle, looking for two vacant seats. The bus was only half-filled. We found a pair of seats together, right behind a burly woman with a caged hen on her lap and in front of an American couple I recognized from the plane.

The bus coughed and rolled out, and I found myself growing uneasy about the American couple. Where did they get on board? Why would anyone besides us be going to Juanita, which was hardly known as a tourist attraction? We were going to have to watch what we said.

Belize City has little exurban sprawl, and within minutes we were chugging past virgin tracts of unpopulated jungle and swamp. With the low sun streaking through the roadside thatch of twisted vines, twinkling prisms of light sifted through the bus's dusty half-open windows to dance on its rusting metal ceiling.

"Damn," I exclaimed to Mona, barely able to contain my excitement at entering a world apart from my worries. "This is the real thing."

Her eyes were again closed, but the soft contentment in her features led me to believe she might actually be at rest.

The bus hummed along, its fat, bald tires peeling across the steamy asphalt. In the distance was a footpath curling through the undergrowth, and as we pulled near I could trace its lazy ascent all the way to a lone hillside shack where a woman was hitching her wash to a line. I longed to follow her routine movements, to vicariously inhabit the peasant simplicity of her life, but the bus rumbled on.

Suddenly the vehicle jolted, as if an axle had snapped, and choking clouds of dust billowed in through the windows.

"What the fuck?" Mona snapped into consciousness.

Up and down the aisle, people struggled to shut the windows. Apparently we had come onto a stretch of dirt road.

"What the fuck?" Mona reiterated.

With the windows shut, it soon grew very hot and rank. The honest sour fecundity of life lived close to nature's loins permeated the stagnant air. Mona is fetishistic on the subject of deodorants and if it had been possible to blame the smell on a particular individual, I'm sure she would have stomped right over to have words with him.

Instead, she turned to the people behind us, the American couple, and asked, "You know how long the ride is to Juanita?"

They were an unlikely pair. She was short, pale, pudgy, a little meek about the mouth and eyes, while he was a burly black man wearing a preppy polo shirt and a big gold watch on his muscular forearm.

"They say eight hours," answered the woman. "But that is subject to many factors."

"Like the wind or clouds," added her companion in an unexpected deadpan. "Or whether the driver has a girlfriend en route."

Before Mona could disengage, the woman asked, "Weren't you on the plane this afternoon?"

Mona gave me a surreptitious nudge in the chops, presumably to warn me against revealing too much.

"Why didn't you just pick up the bus at the airport?" asked the guy with the gold watch.

Mona raked me with a chilling glance.

"We had an errand in the city," I lied.

The bus hit a wallop of a bump, and the disturbance was all the excuse we needed to swivel forward.

I couldn't resist remarking to her, "I wonder why old Andy routed us to the pharmacy. No doubt he has his reasons."

Mona was not feeling playful. "Eight fucking hours," was her last utterance.

The road was deeply rutted and followed the course of a particularly eccentric river which corkscrewed down from the rising hills of the interior. A recent rain had tamped the dusty road down to mud and puddle. We were able to open the windows again, admitting a rush of cool sweet jungle air. In a low gear as laborious as an Alpine funicular, the bus began to gradually climb. Squat shrubs gave way to towering trees with leaves as big as water lilies. There was movement in the murky river below, ripples around a rock and swelling at a bend. The groaning machinery of the bus engine subsumed all external sounds of nature, yet I could almost hear, singing from the gnarled thickets and sweeping, tangled vines, the haunting caw of prehistoric birds, the twitter of acrobatic parakeets.

"Wow," I exclaimed to Mona. "Can you imagine the..."

She was dozing, mouth open, her breath coming in rhythmic, dry, guttural snorts—just another animal in repose. She really can be a pretty woman, when silent and still.

I watched her, along with the darkening forest, until all light drained away. Then I was left alone.

We were awakened with a start when the rumbling stopped. The bus had pulled into a sort of roadside restaurant. A few picnic tables were arranged beside a low adobe wall. A mega-watt bulb buzzed high on a utility pole, casting a harsh light on this pebble and dirt patio.

The guy from our flight stood up in the aisle, yawning and cracking the knuckles of his outstretched hands, "Rest stop," he announced, clearly for our benefit. "Food here is okay, if you stay away from the beef. Which is probably dog."

Mona straightened up. "Where the hell?"

"We've landed in Oz," I informed her.

She gazed out at the floodlight illuminating the newly churned dust, and scowled.

Our neighbor, in contrast, bristled with alertness and bonhomie. "Why don't you join us?" he suggested, in a theatrically rich baritone. "We're bound to be here at least an hour."

Our new companions made a bee-line for the far picnic table, and we trudged after them, carefully toting our knapsacks. Others from the bus fanned out across the gravel courtyard or into the lone cinder block building, from which a scratchy radio blasted, at maximum volume, a lively ditty about amor.

Their names were Sims and Patricia, and they claimed to be from Chicago, although they were careful to point out that there was really nowhere they could honestly call home. Unprodded by an inquiry from us (since we were wary of provoking any reciprocal questions), Sims explained that he and Patricia were representatives of an organization with headquarters in Switzerland that attempts to eradicate world hunger by combining organizational know-how with spiritual forces.

"That sounds interesting," I said matter-of-factly, with no intention of following up.

A young girl, maybe ten, in a white cotton dress, appeared at our table and slapped down a laminated menu. She looked us over with her big dark eyes, then drifted away.

"Where you from?" Sims asked, good naturedly I thought, considering the tacit insult of our unresponsiveness.

Mona grabbed for the menu, forestalling a reply. I couldn't remember if our neat little cover story included details about a home residence.

Prolonged silence was going to create more suspicion than a wrong answer. "Washington, D.C.," I finally responded.

Patricia came alive. "In government?"

"Hardly," scoffed Mona, coming to the rescue. "Danny and I travel quite a bit and I suppose we are often thought to be State Department, or something like that. In Bali the proprietor of our hotel was so sure that we were government officials that he even tried to bribe us to get a U.S. visa. We tried to explain to the poor guy that we were simply travel tour operators. Which is what we are. Of course he assumed we were just hiding behind a cover story, and insisted we take the bribe anyway. Remember that, Danny?"

I was in awe of the complexity of her performance. It confirmed a theory I have about the imaginative genius hidden in each of us, waiting—sometimes forever—for the right chance to be born.

"That was sure something," I stammered. "We actually did take the bribe. But mailed it back. From Jakarta. With a note of apology."

"Not taking a bribe," Mona added with a flourish, "pretty much proves you don't work for the government."

Everyone laughed.

The young girl in the cotton dress returned to take our order.

"We're with the bus," Sims instructed her. Pointing to a column on the menu, he asked, "Which of these won't take long to cook?"

Her dark brown eyes inspected each of us. "The bus," she replied, as though she knew something that wasn't worth explaining, "it will wait."

Wait indeed! We had time to eat and digest a bounteous meal of tortillas and beans and squirmy local vegetables, and hear from Sims a fascinating and well-told account of his Peace Corps experience in pre-revolutionary Nicaragua. We had time to visit the washroom, which featured bona fide plumbing and enough pine-scent deodorant to conjure Christmas in the Canadian woods. Then we strolled the circumference of the little courtyard, nodding to our fellow travelers, few of whom had been dining. The woman who had been seated in front of us had her hen out of its cage, and the thing was scratching around in the gravel and dirt. I asked her if she had seen our driver, or if she knew when we would be departing. She gave me a helpless shrug, as if I'd asked if she knew when rain was next expected.

We had entered a culture without clocks, beyond time. That we were all traveling somewhere, and would prefer progressing in that direction to idling here indefinitely was a fact that counted for very little. That our driver had not been seen since we pulled in was a fact that appeared to trouble no one. The night was warm and tranquil. Dawn would greatly resemble dusk. Tomorrow would most likely be similar to today. Only we gringos, with our inward notions of time, cared to monitor the nuances.

The outpost town of Juanita awakened in a slow, peaceful unfolding, an ancient ritual which Mona and I had the opportunity to observe from box seats—literally. In the pitch dark, we sat on slatted fruit crates with our backs propped against the corrugated tin wall of the general store, which would not be open for another hour or two. Or three.

On the store's padlocked front door was posted a tattered bus schedule. Despite our lengthy layover at the roadside cantina, we had arrived in Juanita pretty close to the appointed hour. The system managers of the bus line had apparently factored in some of their organizational idiosyncracies.

Sims and Patricia had left us a couple hours back, in a town called Whitehall. They claimed to be meeting other "project organizers" there, and we believed them as much as they believed us. Strangers met along the way are, like characters taken up in a novel, forever subject to reinterpretation.

We had been deposited in Juanita along with several lumpy burlap sacks, and the woman with the hen. There was nothing to do until dawn. Mona and I tried with great difficulty to make ourselves comfortable on the fruit crates. The hen woman perched on one of the burlap sacks, humming sweetly to herself, or possibly her poultry. Her lilting soprano was all that we heard.

Slowly I noticed that the darkness was lifting. I could discern pockets of shadow along the street, implying nearby structures. There was a ruffling in the air like the draught from a suddenly opened door, and the night was punctuated by the restless cackling of faraway roosters. From somewhere along the street, a baby whined, then giggled, then cried. A man with a gruff voice admonished someone or something. In remote alcoves of the dark, dogs howled out to each other. An ill-tuned auto engine sputtered to life and motored off in a direction opposite from us, its headlights dimly seeking a path through a maze of shanties. The auto ascended to what at first looked like a cloud bank, but now appeared to be a lavender ridge.

I informed Mona that I was going around back to take a leak before it got too light.

"What about me? Guys have everything easy." She was already the loudest thing in Juanita.

"Do you have to go?" I asked her.

"I think so."

"Momentito," I told the chicken woman, making a stupid gesture towards our bags. "We come right back."

I held onto Mona's elbow as we gingerly baby-stepped across a craggy weed patch. There appeared to be a couple of low trees separating us from a neighboring shanty, where a radio could be heard from behind wooden shutters. The most secluded area was seemingly the space between one of the trees and the corner of the general store.

"Me first," I said. "Then I'll guard for you."

I knew Mona didn't like this sequence, but even she recognized the folly in wasting time debating. She lurked impatiently in the dark shadows, as I unzipped and happily began to pee.

Zipping up, I moved toward the tree. "Your turn. No one will see."

"Promise you'll turn your back?"

"I can't even see the ground, it's so dark."

"Do you promise?"

"Yes." I looked away as she squatted by the store. Down the shadowed lane of shacks, a donkey whinnied and got loudly slapped for some misdeed.

Mona announced, "I can't go. Are you sure you're not watching?"

"Go already!"

"I can't. You're making me tense."

"Do you want me to leave?"

"Don't you dare!"

The horizon had become a luminescent blend of crimson and blue, and the twinkling stars in that part of the sky faded one-by-one into the soft blush of encroaching light. A creature slithered through the damp weeds.

"What was that?" Mona's voice vaulted from the shade. "Did you hear that?"

I wasn't going to indulge her. "Are you finished yet?"

"I haven't started. I need to hear running water. Or have something simple to read."

"Maybe we should try this later. In a real bathroom."

"But I have to go NOW!" The old nastiness was creeping into her tone. "And I'd rather go out here than in one of those disease holes."

"Then go already."

"Danny," she cooed. "You know what might help?"

I did not reply.

"If you would whistle something. Or sing. Do you know 'Yesterday,' by the Beatles? That usually works."

I hummed softly up and down an improvised scale to find the right note to start. Moments of true absurdity, I thought to myself, are the ones that do the most to make sense of this life.

"Love was such an easy game to play,
Now I need a place to hide away
Oh I believe . . .

Soon my song was accompanied by the warm patter of pee on the landscape. The world was moist with relief. Mona called out, "You can stop now."

With less trepidation due to enhanced visibility, we traipsed our way back to the front of the general store. Everything in me was alive. There was rapture in the bounteous calm of dawn, and indeed I felt like singing.

"Why she had to go,
I don't know,
She wouldn't say.
I said something wrong,
Now I long . . .

"Knock it off," cautioned Mona, suddenly the keeper of quiet.

"I can't," I confessed. "I long for yesterday-ay-ay."

CHAPTER 5

Carlos Zapatú's turbulent career in politics began almost a decade ago as a graduate student in history at the national university where the first protests against the military took place. Until that time, he was an obscure middle son of middle-class parents. His father managed a Coca-Cola distributorship. If he showed any exceptional talent or skill as a youth, or impressed any of the community elders with the scope of his promise, no one is on record as remembering it. A grade school instructor recalled him being "pretty normal." His closest friend admired Zapatú merely as "a decent fellow, the sort who's never too busy to be on time."

At the university, something changed. It is impossible to discern what set it off—hormones, ideology, circumstance, or, as they say on the exams, all of the above. He learned to play the guitar and once gave a performance in the campus's main open plaza, where a girl named Isabel looked on with affection. Nothing extraordinary about that. His name first became known to the academic community through a series of cryptic letters-to-the-editor decrying acquiescence to state censorship and Catholic notions of sexual morality. Maybe the fact that his letters were impressionistic (and exceedingly vague as to the specifics of his complaint) struck the right chord among the ever rebellious youthful intelligentsia.

Eventually when it was time to stage a rally (for whatever purpose), Zapatú became an integral part of the format.

I had learned all this from the background news articles and feature commentary Marion was able to dig up prior to our departure. I had assiduously combed through these clippings with the fervor of a scholar about to write a biography. I wanted to understand Zapatú, to know and feel as much as possible about his passions and motivations, so that ignorance and cultural differences would play but a minimal role when we finally met. A U.S. tour by Zapatú loomed as critical to salvaging Frankly Speakers—and its president.

Unfortunately, the press accounts were oddly unsatisfying. The picture that emerged was sketchy. I wasn't getting a detailed portrait so much as a stick-figure cartoon. Hell, I knew guys like Zapatú at Illinois, and might have masqueraded as one myself if... if circumstances were reversed.

I was particularly frustrated by the apprehension that Mona had learned additional details about Zapatú in her communications with "Professor Andy." On the bus she'd made a quip about Zapatú's chamelon nature, but clammed up as soon as I pressed her for more. It had been quite exciting for her to withhold information and filter it to me on this mysterious need-to-know basis.

The *Newsweek* report was probably the most useful: "A slight, almost frail, bearded young man stood atop the marble base of one of the library's majestic pillars, holding a megaphone. As soon as he began to speak, the boisterous throng fell mystically silent. Even the shrouds of smoke from the still-smoldering vandal fires seemed to temporarily clear away. This was Zapatú."

The article went on to discuss the week of riotous demonstrations and government crackdowns that preceded the rally. "Zapatú's words soared through the crowd like an anthem," *Newsweek* reported. "Blasts of gunfire crackled from several directions, transforming the assembly into a blood-splattered chaos. The giant orange and black Popular Unidad banner was strafed by automatic fire. As protestors scurried for cover, Zapatú clung to the bullhorn and shouted the words that would certify his fame, 'Never more the darkness; blind them with light!'"

All news accounts from this point on tended to confuse him with Che Guevera. Maybe he did retreat to the mountains with a band of zealous compatriots, one of whom was a raven-haired beauty whose lusty figure was accented by the ammunition belt she wore angled across her breasts. Maybe they did live like nomads, trooping through the night and spending their days huddled in the jungle plotting some spectacular return. Perhaps the military did receive sporadic sightings of Zapatú, attending an agrarian harvest festival, addressing a surreptitious labor assembly, fishing for snapper off a Cuban trawler. Certainly ordinary human lives can suddenly turn dramatic, yet there was something disconcerting about how these accounts tended to imitate TV scenarios.

It's not clear how Zapatú made his way to Belize. The military rulers were probably happy to permit his escape. What arrangement he enjoyed with the government of Belize and, by proxy, the United States, is a question I would have liked to ask the good professor if Mona had allowed me to speak with him.

The plan to connect with Zapatú was devised by Professor Hoffman and Mona. I learned the details only as we went along.

At dawn, we made our way to Juanita's small, ramshackle harbor, and inquired (according to instruction) after a "Manuel."

"Isn't that a rather common name?" I had asked Mona.

"Don't worry," she reassured me with the aplomb of a veteran guide. "They'll know who we mean."

At a windowless hut at the end of a pier, a burly man with gold-capped teeth nodded in seeming acknowledgment to our question about Manuel. He said we could catch a ride to the cays from a Frenchman named Claude.

Manuel squinted into the early sun, already baking hot, and pointed out another shack, painted silver, on the opposite rim of the harbor. "He right there, mon."

Claude may or may not have been French, but he did seem to be expecting us. His fourteen-foot outboard was swabbed up and fueled. He instructed us to sit in the middle, and we unsteadily hopped in over the gunwale.

Claude cautiously puttered past a flotilla of launches, barges, floating fruit stands, and bobbing scraps of styrofoam refuse. The harbor appeared to be in a perpetual traffic jam. Once we were nearly blind-sided by a sort of motorized gondola. I waited for the shouting and threats to begin, but Claude just saluted with a hearty laugh, and veered away.

Eventually we hit the open waters, and Claude opened the throttle. We skipped like angels across the turquoise sea. Carving into a series of uninhabited spits of mangrove, Claude cut the motor and we glided perfectly into a dock that was nestled out of view in the tall sea grass. Up on land we could see thatched roofs peeking between clusters of palms.

Claude told us to go to a bar run by someone named Manuel. There we were to ask for Dora.

We hoisted ourselves onto the dock. Claude revved his motor and rooster-tailed away.

"Dora will take us the final leg," Mona explained to me.

I was starting to feel that the operation had been made needlessly rococo. Also, I was getting very tired and irritable. "Why the hell couldn't Claude do it?"

With sisterly assurance, Mona took my arm. "Really, Danny, the less you know, probably the better." Her tone couldn't have been more cloying.

The bar we sought was little more than a circular canopy providing shade for a double-tiered shelf of bottled liquors and a Waring blender. Manuel was there, a teenager sporting a Pittsburgh Pirates baseball cap. Dora was away, he didn't know where. He bid us to come with him.

"Perfect," Mona whispered, as we trudged behind Manuel back to the dock. "Just as planned."

Her sheer delight at the unfolding of these minor stages was starting to wear on me. I could feel a crossness, a bad attitude, welling up in me like a gas pain. But then the warm sun laid its healing hands on my pale face and the sweetest thought came to mind:

It was Monday morning. I might be back at the office, already knotted up in some aggravating nonsense. How much better it was, even if it meant enduring Mona's games, to be skimming merrily across the dancing turquoise sea.

Manuel cut the motor as we skated past a breakwater of coral. Ahead was a horseshoe cove, with a crescent of sand beach, mounted by a rising tier of palms. The long fronds waved and flapped in the wind like cheering spectators in a ballpark bleachers.

As the grinding drone of the outboard motor diminished, our ears could detect a lively bass rhythm pulsing across the bay. There was a big league sound system somewhere on this outpost. Closer in, we could see a windsurfer effortlessly gliding the shoreline and a swimmer, favoring his left arm, performing a languorous crawl stroke in an uneven arc away from the pier. On a bright purple beach blanket in the sand, two mulatto women sunbathed topless, oblivious to our arrival.

"Siesta time," Manuel explained as we docked without fanfare. "Always siesta time."

Manuel doffed his Pirates cap to the sunbathing women, who paid no attention. We followed him across the beach to the palm grove. Set back just deep enough to be hidden from the sea was an entire compound of precisely crafted octagonal huts with thatched roofs propped upon half-walls of porch screen. Thumping reggae music was blasting from a huge open-sided tabernacle. I couldn't help thinking of the Jonestown massacre.

"Where is everybody?" I asked.

"Last night a big celebration," Manuel answered. "People just waking up."

"What were they celebrating?"

Manuel shrugged.

The lack of sleep was starting to catch up with us. Our modest backpacks weighed heavy and it was a struggle to keep up with Manuel's loping pace. If anyone watched us schlepping ponderously along they might mistake us for fellow outcasts limping in from our own craven exile.

Manuel paused before a hut that was off to itself, surrounded by tall flowering bushes that smelled like honeysuckle.

"This all yours. Make yourself a home."

I was already half-asleep, but I remembered my purpose. "And Zapatú?"

"Maybe tonight." Manuel graciously opened the screen door for us to enter. "Everybody friendly. Just ask if you need."

I watched him amble deeper into the palm grove, where he entered a distant hut.

Mona had been quiet—until now. "Christ! I specifically told Andy separate rooms. Damn." She dipped backward to slip off her knapsack, then heaved it onto one of the army cots.

Collapsing onto the other cot, I slumped against my knobby pack, too beat to remove it.

The room was spare, but clean, with a nightstand between the beds, a kerosene lamp, a fishcoil for insects, a water jug, and an empty bookshelf as a dresser.

Mona scowled. "I want your bed."

I jerked to attention. My eyes had fallen shut.

She was vehement. "Yours is farthest from the door. It's safer."

I was just alert enough to point out the obvious. "They're exactly the same distance from the door."

"If someone was sneaking in during the dead of night, in the pitch black darkness, due to the angle of the door they'd head for this bed first."

I groaned and struggled to my feet. Dropping my pack, I fell onto the other cot. Within minutes I was deep in sleep.

The usual transition time from heavy slumber to functional awakeness is greatly protracted in environments which are hot and muggy. On the other hand, such climates breed vast phyla of many-legged crawling creatures whose sudden appearance on one's skin, particularly the neck or face, can radically accelerate the waking process.

About an hour earlier I thought I was getting up, but apparently I didn't move. Groggy and supine, I was starting to sit up and assess my circumstances—this hut, the tropics, Zapatú—but the next minute I was drifting along the outfield grass, chasing down a flyball fast as my skinny kid's legs could go, sprinting, stretching, lunging out to grab the spotless white orb with its perfect stitched seam.

Unconsciously I lifted my hand to scratch my lower lip. The source of the itch scampered to my cheek. I rubbed my cheek, and it scurried to my throat. Clawing and swatting, I bolted up, short of breath and shivering. I glanced around. Whatever it was was gone. So was Mona.

I slipped outside. A violet light wafted toward me off the bay, silhouetting the tapered trunks and kindly fronds of the palms. The sky above was darkening. I had seen this idyllic panorama before in romantic Technicolor movies, always with music swelling. Indeed, I heard music, and stumbled towards it.

The scene on the beach was like a church outing. A dozen men and women encircled a crackling fire. A thin bearded man, Christ-like in a loin cloth, strummed wildly on a guitar. Against the purple horizon, a scissor bird coasted on the breeze. I scanned for Mona.

There was a woman, not facing me, with Mona's tangled fall of red curls. But the woman's back was naked and she was swaying to the music with the abandon of a native. I approached by an elliptical route to get a better look.

A dim ember was being puffed on and passed along the circle, hand to hand. A wineskin was extended to the guitarist who momentarily paused for a gulp. The woman with the naked back danced forward to stir the high blazing fire. It was Mona, all right.

She spotted me and put her fingers to her mouth in what looked like an expression of fright. Then she let loose with a shrieking sailor's whistle, the type directed at curvacious lunch hour secretaries by construction workers straddling steel beams ten stories up. All music and talking stopped. Only the fire, with Mona standing beside it, crackled.

She was wearing a small bikini, and obviously felt at home. "Mi amigo Danny," she announced to the stoned gathering. "Did you have a good nap, Danny?"

I knew better than to answer immediately. Who knows what she's told them? I waved hello, like a political candidate entering a banquet hall, then walked with studied nonchalance to a nearby gap in the circle, where I plunked down in the sand to reach for the joint, which was conveniently coming my way.

"Happy to be here," I declared, drawing a deep drag. I exhaled, "don't stop the party on my behalf."

I had situated myself between two women. In the leaping light from the fire, their faces blazed with intensity and passion (although firelight has the ability to cast even the most vapid face with characteristics of brooding determination). What struck me most, now that I could breathe easier and survey, was how the seating placements were arranged in alternating boy-girl-boy-girl fashion, like a summer camp recreation outing. Where were the rocket launchers, the khaki and beige camouflage fatigues, or at least the vodka?

"My name is Rosa," a dancing orange oval face leaned at me. "You are here to meet Zapatú, no?"

"Yes I am. Is that him?" I pointed to the folksinger.

She smirked, having found my remark funnier than she wanted to let on. "No, no. Not that."

The woman to my other side piped up from the shadows, "You will know him when he appears.That is his way."

"But it is not so simple to learn his ways," rejoindered Rosa. "He is the sea—much depth, many moods and colors."

The other woman inched forward to access my peripheral view. She was hauntingly thin, yet young and fit—taut would be the term. "I will tell you about the first time I met Zapatú. I was a medical student at the university and he was just another hot young man. There were so many. In my country..."

Rosa abruptly interceded. "That story perhaps should be told at a later time." The force in her tone did not encourage rebuttal.

The other woman acquiesced silently back into the shadows. I was on the verge of a moment's peace when I saw, from across the bonfire, the guitar player loping toward me.

He squatted directly in front of me, his loin cloth looking more like a diaper hanging on his smooth, almond torso. "I am Pepe. Your Mona has told me all about you and your mission. I think it is a very brilliant strategy. You have my respect."

Pepe was almost classically handsome, like a chiseled actor in a Grade B television movie. His dark eyes radiated a ferocity too piercing to project anything remotely real. His mouth was thin and determined. His chin was square yet perfectly dimpled at its geometric center. It was hard not to see a man too easily loved for his looks to have ever grappled with worldly strife.

"In this life," he continued, "on rare occasions it is possible to meet total strangers who are so familiar, so intimate, so wise in the ways of the soul that the only rational explanation is that this person is not a stranger at all, but a messenger of some grand design." Pepe's eyes bore down on the opaque night. He was a master of the squint-eyed, faraway stare. "Such a person is your Mona."

I thought, boy, do I have some evidence to the contrary! But it crossed my mind that the anecdotes I would offer to discredit Mona might only reinforce Pepe's high esteem. He seemed to be that kind of guy.

I decided to play straight man. "Tell me about Zapatú. How is he holding up?"

Pepe feigned distraction, chuckling cryptically.

I played along. "Did I make a joke?"

"No, Danny. No joke. My mind was just drifting. Zapatú you ask? He is well. He is a chameleon. When it is time for action, Zapatú is the lion. When it is time for planning, Zapatú is the owl."

"Also the giant turtle," added Rosa.

Pepe's cosmic stare narrowed down to a derisive sneer. "Too much ganja for you, Rosa. Zapatú a turtle? Now that is a true joke. He is not old, or slow."

Rosa was too pleased with her metaphor to back down. "But Zapatú is wise. Old means wise. And slow means steady. Zapatú is wise and steady."

"And you are too high." Pepe turned to check for Mona, who was still fussing with the fire.

"Will he be here soon?" I asked Pepe.

"Zapatú comes when the time is right."

"Exactly like the turtle!" Rosa quivered with delight at her breakthrough. "Has anyone ever seen the giant turtle when the time is wrong?"

"Time," I couldn't resist noting, "is never wrong."

They both hushed. Pepe shot me a wary but respectful sideways glance. Rosa murmured assent. It has been quite a while since I'd scored any points with that kind of quip.

From the darkness behind me, a male voice, mild and unassertive, remarked, "I hope I'm not too late for supper."

Carlos Zapatú stepped into the firelight and stood unobtrusively at the perimeter, much the way I had done. He made no attempt to call attention to himself. He gave no proclamation, nor asked any indulgence. As if oblivious to the presence of the group, he bent over to fuss with a strap on his sandal, spending several minutes readjusting its position across his ankle.

I had seen several news photos of Zapatú, yet in person a different image was presented. The gap between photogeneity and reality is often profound. We represent one speaker, the attorney Marge Holman, who so little resembles her publicity photos that the student welcoming committees usually don't recognize her at the airport. They wind up having to page her over the terminal intercom, only to suffer the embarrassment of realizing she's the one who's been impatiently stalking around for the past fifteen minutes. The solution, of course, would be for Frankly Speakers to issue more updated, accurate photos, but that would not, in Marge's case, be sound marketing practice.

What I noticed immediately about Zapatú was that he was of middling height, not tall; his complexion was not the swarthy bronze of his comrades but sallow, almost jaundiced; his piercing eyes were pale, myopic, and watery, as if allergic or irritated by contact lenses; his hair was as richly black as the pictures, but rather than being wild and leonine, it was neatly trimmed and fell in a logical part. In a vague way, he looked a little like me.

His sandal strap finally adjusted, Zapatú glanced around, then walked backward toward the palm grove, into the darkness.

The struck me as peculiar. "What gives?" I asked once he was gone.

"He is pondering a big project," Pepe replied matter-of-factly. "Such men as Zapatú—they often are absorbed in thought. I hope, Danny, that you were not expecting to meet a politician like your gringo president, always smiling and shaking hands."

Mona pranced over. "What that him?"

She looked fit in her bikini, so at ease among these campers. I had anticipated being received in a more business-like manner and I was starting to feel irked, alienated, alone. "Tell me, Mona," I taunted, "is this all part of your game plan?"

Pepe, the handsome phony, answered for her. "This is no game. And only Zapatú knows the plan."

"Of course." I squared off against Mona. "Where'd you get that outfit?"

She glowed. "Surprised?"

I was perplexed as to what she was referring to, but I remembered the correct answer: "Yes."

CHAPTER 6

"Now that's the sort of dream a girl likes to have at night!"

Mona's improbably perky voice zapped my slumber like an electrode shock. I tried to ignore her, but in rolling onto my side I caught a furtive glimpse of her sitting straight up on her cot, her salmon night shirt dappled by the morning sun.

"I actually dreamt a happy dream," she crowed.

Reluctantly I mumbled, "Tell me."

Oh . . . oh nothing!"

Usually I awaken in a good mood. This put me in a foul one. "Did the burgler stalking you have a pistol that misfired?"

"Ha, ha."

"Did the werewolf that was about to pounce get preoccupied with another victim?"

"Very funny."

Finally I sat up. "Maybe the snake coiled around your throat got bored and slithered away?"

"If you must know, I dreamt about sex and love." She hopped off her cot and began rifling through her backpack. "Don't you ever dream about sex and love?"

"I'm too concerned about business."

"When was the last time you got laid anyway? That little nurse hasn't been calling recently."

"How would you know?"

"Girls have ways." She yanked a snakeskin makeup bag from her pack. "It's common knowledge that office vibes improve when the boss is getting laid."

"Oh, is it? Did you read that in one of your magazines?"

She extracted a pocket mirror, and settled in for a long self-study. "Actually, I'm thinking of writing an article on the subject."

I stretched out my arms and realized how stiff my neck and shoulders were, probably from that long bus ride. "So what do you make of the scene here?" I asked.

She moved the mirror slowly like an electric shaver around the circumference of her new morning face. "I really wouldn't mind staying a few weeks. I'd be a tiger back home with that kind of tan."

"And how about Zapatú? I can't figure what's supposed to happen?"

"That's because you're so uptight. Loosen up, Danny. See the big picture."

She was treading close to a very sore spot. "The big picture . . ." I lowered my voice while retaining an emphatic edge to indicate I'd be shouting if I didn't fear being overheard. "The big picture is that I'm down here on a business trip and am being dealt with like some dufus tourist on a package excursion. What the fuck did you and this professor discuss? That's the big picture I want."

"I told you, I can't reveal more than you need to know."

"*I* need to know?" I howled.

She peered over her mirror and gave me her poor-poor-baby sympathetic sigh, one of the most obnoxious gestures in her repertoire.

"To tell you the truth, Mona, I don't think we're being taken very seriously."

"Are we serious, Danny?"

I gazed up at the thatched ceiling and addressed it, as if it were a jury of peers evaluating the folly of my predicament. "I am down here at great expense to recruit a potentially valuable speaker to bolster a faltering lecture agency. Many of the arrangements have been made by a longtime and trusted colleague, yet I have reason to believe that the deal is not coming together in an orderly fashion. If the deal doesn't come together, I waste a lot of money. If I waste a lot of money, the faltering business could terminally falter. There are very grave consequences if that happens, very grave. So I suggest to this colleague that we're not being taken seriously and she replies . . ." I lowered my gaze from the jury box to Mona, who, with the aid of the pocket mirror, had detected something invisible on her chin. "Tell me again, Mona. What was your reply?"

"Are we serious?"

"Dammit, yes!"

A brisk morning breeze blew across the palms, transforming the jungle stillness into a busy percussive clatter. A nearby bird twittered in syncopated soprano accompaniment. Mona snapped shut her makeup mirror and announced, "It's a gorgeous day. I'm going for a swim. Do you mind waiting outside while I change?"

It struck me that I had grown half-curious to see her naked. The sensation was titillating yet discomforting. As Mona herself had so indelicately pointed out, my much professed romantic tentativeness might be nothing more than a common type of psychological avoidance, concealing, even from myself, troublesome emotions. Maybe so, maybe so. For all the scruff and scrape between Mona and me, a tingling of affection (no different, perhaps, than that which normally develops between warm bodies in close proximity) had grown noticeable, at least to me.

Did she feel any of this? I was fairly sure she liked me, even though I fell drastically short of her (or anyone's) idealized vision of the heroic Superman. Even at my best I was destined more to be the Clark Kent incarnation of that legendary dichotomy.

I loped outside into the underbrush for a discreet pee. It was a gorgeous morning. The sun danced low through the palms, splashing the day with its brilliant light but none of its heavy heat. The compound was quiet. I kept thinking of Jonestown.

Just as I was zipping up, I heard a voice call "Hola." Manuel, the boat guide, was ambling our way.

There was an inexplicable relief in seeing him still alive. "Howdy," I called.

We intersected outside our hut. He was dressed the same as yesterday, cut off shorts and a white t-shirt, but a Chicago Cubs cap with the big red "C" had replaced the Pirates.

"Comfortable last night?" he inquired with a lascivious wink.

"Sí."

"And the lady?"

I nodded toward the hut, a thoroughly ambiguous gesture. "Tell me, any idea when I get to meet with Zapatú?"

"That is what I come to tell you." Manuel craned his neck to peek into our shack. "He wishes to see you soon. This morning. You will go . . ."

Mona popped out wearing what looked like a G-string and pasties. She certainly knew how to pack for a business trip. "Hola," she clucked.

It would have taken a gunblast to divert Manuel's stare.

I tried to return to the point. "You were telling me about meeting Zapatú?"

The poor kid was smitten. Without taking his eyes off Mona, he mumbled in a zombie monotone, "Go to big house. There you will find him."

Great news, but I wanted some clarification. Zapatú is expecting me? Is that what you're saying?"

Manuel was stone silent. You'd think he'd never before set eyes on a pale-skinned girl in an abbreviated bikini.

Mona coyly inquired, "Is it safe to swim right off the beach?

Manuel was agog. "Sí, Señorita. I will show you."

"And how about meeting Zapatú?" It disturbed me to have to keep reminding everyone of our purpose.

Mona radiated a cheerleader flippancy. "You go do your business, Danny. I'll do mine."

The way to approach business meetings is like first dates back in high school. You know what the other party will look like, but you have no control over how he or she will act. All you can do is, as they say, be all you can be. And hope that the chemistry is right.

Nervously ringing the girl's doorbell, I would recite to myself the reasons why I was a choice specimen—this did not take long—and brief myself on my objectives—this took even less time. When she emerged all perfumed and coiffed, aglow in some sleekly alluring pastel outfit, I quelled my rampaging insecurity with that last straw grasped for by all proud yet downtrodden peoples: my day was coming yet!

Weaving my way through the palms to the big house where I was to meet Zapatú, I found myself fixating on my inadequacies: white, middle class, gringo imperialist; questionable courage; marginal physical conditioning; spiritually aimless; politically irresolute. What I needed to recount were my strengths: keen sense of promotion; effective sales force (I hoped they weren't screwing off in my absence); decent market position; commendable business ethics; flashes of insight.

There was no need to ring any doorbell. Zapatú stood waiting on the verandah in thin, loose cotton drawstring pants and a Grateful Dead t-shirt. He welcomed me with a hearty wave. "Let us go," he shouted as though I were a trusted comrade, "before the day turns hot."

Zapatú descended the porch and turned toward the interior. Dutifully, I fell in behind. He toted a canvas knapsack that had a thermos protruding from its open flap. When I started to speak, he briskly nixed me off with an emphatic backhand gesture, a universal signal to keep quiet.

The sandy path quickly dwindled into a maze of weeds and bush and drooping fronds. After fifteen minutes, all I had learned about Zapatú was that he had narrow hips and an easy, purposeful gait. He had learned nothing about me, except that I can take a hint and keep my mouth shut.

At an unremarkable spot that was neither clearing nor lookout nor distinguishable in any way from the undergrowth we'd been traversing, Zapatú halted. He threw his face back to catch the early sun, and I noticed small welts of fatigue cupping his eyes. "Now," he said, removing his pack, "we can talk."

My instincts were to be chatty, convivial. Somehow I managed to say nothing, and that seemed appropriate. My time would come.

Beads of sweat bunched on Zapatú's brow. As soon as he wiped them off, new ones, bright like baby pearls, sprouted in their place."Don't get me wrong," he quickly added. "I have absolute trust in all my . . . comrades. But I have learned that in some matters I am doomed to be alone in this world. Therefore, I choose to conduct my business alone. Does that make sense?"

I liked him. Adulation had not completed its inevitable taint. "That a reasonable tendency," I readily assured him.

"And when it becomes appropriate to inform others, of course I do so."

I enthusiastically concurred. "Otherwise you have to explain yourself before you're ready and you wind up in long discussions before you even know your own thoughts."

"Exactly!"

"And thoughts need peace and nurturing. They're like seeds. They don't need discussions and arguments."

"Exactly." Zapatú's moist eyes relaxed.

Finally I felt at ease enough to ask, "Is there somewhere in particular we're heading to?"

An orange and blue bird zipped up from a nearby shrub and darted towards the sky. "Perhaps we should follow the birdie," Zapatú answered with a faraway gaze. After an awkward lull, he added with a sigh, "It is refreshing to be with a gringo. My comrades would already be tracking the bird."

Zapatú twisted open the thermos, unleashing the brisk, civilized aroma of brewed coffee. He took a swig. "In answer to your question, there is nowhere special we are going. Just a hike. To learn each about the other."

We resumed uphill, to the east, where a bald promontory jutted above the palms. Gradually the plush green growth gave way to dusty scrub and spiney cactus. It was an exciting and oddly fortifying experience to be following the path of someone else who hasn't decided where he's going.

The wind kicked up and the air was dry. It was lovely and warm, with the quick breeze blow-drying our skin as soon as the heat moistened it. It suddenly seemed all right to get straight down to business, here with glorious nature to cushion us.

"I assume you've been told something about why I'm here, and you're interested in knowing what kind of opportunities exist for you in the U.S.?"

He halted, and again fished around to his pack for the thermos. "A gringo professor gave me a note on one of those days when I was open to suggestion."

"Professor Hoffman?"

"Andy, yes. What an odd duck."

"What's he like?"

Zapatú swigged some coffee, then offered the thermos to me. It was painted red and white like a barber's pole. "He is a middle-aged child. Makes everything more complicated than it already is. When he starting telling me about you, I said fine, whatever, tell the guy to write or come on down to talk. But no, he insisted on channeling messages through second and third parties. He was like a boy playing games. I told him, Andy, if the imperialists want to nail me, you can be sure there's nothing I can do to stop them."

It would be too complicated to let him know how gratified I was to hear that. "Did Professor Andy get into any specifics?"

Zapatú shrugged me off, like a baseball pitcher nixing the sign. "Later for business. Tell me about yourself."

I recalled the nimble way Kenny had misled Sissy, but I resisted. "I'm a businessman."

"That's all?"

"Sure there's more." I was uneasy with what he was getting at. "There's always more."

"For example. Are you good to your friends?"

My answer surprised me. "I believe so, but I don't have many."

"And the girl? Mara?"

"Her name is Mona."

"Like the word? She 'moans' with love, eh?"

"Just a coincidence. It's spelled differently."

"And she is your woman?"

This wasn't what I wanted to discuss. Our pace was lagging even if we had no particular destination. "She is an associate. That's all."

"I don't know the word. An ass . . . what kind?"

"A comrade. A colleague."

In my irritation, I had scooted several paces ahead of Zapatú, and now he scampered to catch up. "But she is nice looking and so friendly," he hooted. "Maybe I do not understand your culture. Are you married?"

"No."

"And you are not interested in her? Pepe has told me good things. You do not find attractive her hips, her smile?"

The uphill grade to the bald promontory had steepened and we chugged now at half-pace. The sun was rising and we suffered under it.

"She and I work together," I puffed. "All my concentration is on work. If I get distracted, my business will fail. For sure."

"And the goal of your business is to make money?"

"Right."

"And the reason you want money?"

Anyone could tell where this was leading. Yes, we are born into situations which often make no sense.But philosophical continuity is not the goal of life's struggle. The depressing irrationality of our workaday routine is best shunted aside like the discovery of a benign cancer, on the assumption that at least we won't die from it.

Finally we arrived at the point, an arid mound overlooking a precipitous drop to the pebbled beach below. A maverick wisp of cloud briefly shielded us in a welcome patch of shade. We both were breathing heavily. My jeans clung damp and heavy to my tired legs.

Gawking at the rugged formations of clay and craggy rock jutting down to the rolling surf, I felt slightly dizzy. "Is there a way to get down? I asked.

He dangled his pantalooned leg over the precipice, letting the wind billow out the light cotton fabric. "Is that where you want to go?" he asked me.

What I wanted to do was get down to business, but I gave a non-committal shrug.

"Follow me," he said.

There appeared to be two options: an incremental downslope along the jungle perimeter, intersecting the shore much further to the north, or a quicker, shorter, more difficult descent straight over the edge. Just as I had begun to think of Zapatú as a guy I could relate to, not so very different from myself, he proceeded to inch himself over the ledge. I was quite surprised. Surprised, and mortified that I would have to follow.

There was no path to speak of, yet there was a run-off sculpted by the rains that provided horizontal footholds at frequent intervals. At a glance, it seemed feasible. It wasn't K-2 or the face of the Eiger. Undoubtedly many had done it before.

Zapatú lowered himself cautiously, for the dirt was sun-baked and brittle. I stayed several steps above. When he came to positions with no firm spot to plant a foot, he judiciously backtracked and tried out an alternative route. He impressed me as both nimble and wary, two excellent traits.

"How are you doing?" Zapatú called back to me. He was on a perch too narrow to permit swivelling around.

I was groping for a quip when I saw the dust kick up, and Zapatú start to slide. His legs swung out and his torso lurched. I didn't fully believe what was transpiring until I heard him scream. It was a horrible wrenching shriek, and then his hands shot up over his head and he lurched into a helpless incremental slide, spread-eagled against the severe stone incline, his fingers desperately clawing for some crevice or protrusion to grip.

I was perhaps ten yards above him, too remote to do any good. Any hasty lunge by me would only have doubled the predicament. I watched it all unfold with an eerie inevitability, like a film in slow motion, punctuated by the sort of spastic twitches that occur when the sprockets get chewed by the projector. "Drop your pack," I shouted. It was the only aid I could offer.

Suddenly there was a great sputtering of pebble and dust, and a ghastly caterwaul of a scream that diminished in volume as it hurtled further away. Zapatú had fallen off the cliff.

I called out, over and over again. I called as loud as I could. I called so loud my whole body trembled. I tried to vent my horror with noise. I was not up to this. I had come prepared for a business discussion. I was still the boy on a first date, poking a nervous forefinger at the doorbell. I shouted out again.

I had no choice but to go after Zapatú. The question was whether to proceed down this demonstrably perilous route, or clamor back to the top and take the gradual decline. Deliberation was not one of my options.

I scrambled back up. If I could sustain a vigorous run in this heat, it appeared to be a good ten minutes down to intersect the shoreline, then a few minutes doubling back along the shore to where Zapatú lay . . . injured? Dead?

I dashed off, hurdling bushes, storming through thorny undergrowth. In a few minutes I was drenched with perspiration. Without breaking stride, I pulled my shirt over my head and tossed it aside. My eyes stung from salt. My glasses fogged. My lungs were burning from exertion. A footpath opened through the tangle. Freed from the need to watch every step I was able to find a rhythm in my running. It was probably not even ten o'clock in the morning. I should be making my second visit to Mr. Coffee, stirring in a dollop of cream, checking with Marion on some indecipherable phone memo. What a world, where on a given moment one life can be muffled in the familiar drone of office habit while far away another careers wildly down a deadly ridge.

The roaring wash of breaking waves grew louder as I neared sea level. The air was cooler. Hitting the shore, which was a picture postcard vista of palms and sand and rolling foamy surf, I pivoted for the run back up the coast. My discount jogging shoes gripped the packed sand where the tide had receded, and my legs felt newly bouncy and strong, grabbing the beach and tossing it back. It felt oddly satisfying to be sprinting when trouble must be addressed. It sure beats frantically punching out phone calls.

I realized that if Zapatú, God help me, was dead, there would be some serious problems confronting me. His comrades back at the camp certainly seemed mellow and fair-minded, not at all what you would think of as desperate radicals, yet they were unlikely to accept at face-value a gringo stranger's tale about their sure-footed leader's accidental spill from a cliffside path. They wouldn't have to be particularly paranoid to question my relationship to the U.S. government (I once worked on a congressional campaign; my office had recently placed calls to the State Department; I dutifully paid all federal taxes) and, by extrapolation, the U.S. government's nefarious relationship to the oppressors who forced Zapatú into exile. You wouldn't have to subscribe to the whole Marxist cosmology to insist on further investigation into this one.

And who knows what Mona may have disclosed? That her father was co-producer of one of the Bob Hope Support Our Boys in Vietnam extravaganzas? That in her period of adolescent blossoming she had a flirtation with a Green Beret (and who knows what homicidal passions she excited in the poor monster)? amidst the chilling tragedy of their leader's death, would it be even remotely conceivable that I was simply a sympathetic, mildly progressive U.S. citizen just trying to make a buck? Do they have any concept of how innocent an activity it can be, trying to make a buck?

My breath bleated out in congested puffs as loud as the waves. I could see the fateful promontory up ahead. The shoreline curved inwards toward a small cove. Although drained of all strength, I pushed myself faster. Zapatú would have fallen directly onto this placid spit of sand, a drop of a couple hundred feet. I looked around.

I scanned the craggy nooks along the inlet wall, the cool shady areas where a body could be expected to crawl out of sheer survival instinct. I checked the sand for tracks or footprints. Then I saw him.

Zapatú sat upright in the low surf, with his legs outstretched. Blood had trickled across his face and shoulders, and he sported a daffy smile. He looked a fright, but he looked alive.

Still wheezing and groaning, I collapsed beside him.

"Catch your breath," Zapatú advised me.

"Not . . . not hurt?" I sputtered.

He held out his hands for display. Almost every finger was crooked or mangled or limp. He turned his face, revealing a raw gash from temple to jaw. "And my vision is very blurry," he added.

For a minute I was too racked with panting to do more than stare at him in cockeyed amazement. He really had survived. The ocean waves, which curled up and broke some fifty yards offshore, reached us in gentle dribbles and swirls. There would be no martyrs today.

Zapatú wiggled his toes, flexed his ankles, rotated his torso to test his range of motion. He still wore a daffy smile. "Not a bad place, my friend, to pass the time. People wage war to claim the peace we have right here."

I only had enough air in my lungs to whimper, "So happy . . . to find . . . you."

"I was wondering where you went."

"I yelled after you. I thought . . ." My voice trailed off.

Zapatú used his wrist to push a sand flea off his forehead. His fingers were useless. "It crossed my mind that you might have left in panic. Many thoughts crossed my mind, and maybe they all will prove to be wrong."

"What happened?"

He tilted his head back to take full pleasure of the sun. "I cannot say that I remember everything. When I first started to slip, I didn't really believe it. It was a scene out of so many dreams that I halfway expected to wake up. When I finally lost my grip for good, I felt a weird calm. I was at last fully in the hands of fate, and those are very, very comforting hands. I bounced off something hard, but my mind was outside my body and I didn't really feel pain. There's some scrub bushes along the cliffside, and probably they broke my fall. I think I passed out for a few minutes."

"You weren't frightened?"

Zapatú shook his head. "I really expected to wake up from the dream. Don't we all?"

For a long delicious time we languished in mute enthrallment at the bright pulse of precious life. Zapatú was like a stalwart soldier whose brave survival of a horrid battle is rendered even more courageous by his humble refusal to dwell on the details. A long stretch of silence was what we both needed.

I unlaced my jogging shoes and stretched my feet into the tranquil lapping sea. I splashed water over my face and chest and arms. I was in that special balmy glow that comes when disaster is averted. Reality had miraculously reverted to a dimension where I had a modicum of expertise: enjoying the tropical climate; shooting the breeze.

"Is this the wrong time," I asked, "to discuss why I've traveled here to meet you?"

Zapatú groaned in discomfort but stretched out his arms in magnanimous encouragement. "Despite my little detour, Danny, that is what I am here for."

I gave him a capsule presentation. First, he would earn a lot of money, which he could put to use in any way he saw fit. I emphasized that it was my job to secure the contracts and issue him his fees, not to ask questions. On a dollars-per-hour basis, I told him, he would be earning more than a psychiatrist. I couldn't tell if he found that amusing or ironic.

Second, he would be promulgating his cause and his message. Again I emphasized that it was not my role to dictate the substance of his lectures, but I would gladly serve as an editorial consultant in the nuances of communicating with U.S. audiences. I pointed out that for all our sins and problems, the principle of free speech still abides in the U.S. and public opinion can therefore be influenced. Allowing that he knew better than I the beneficial ramifications of reshaping U.S. foreign policy, I tried to impress upon him the notion that ordinary citizens, when motivated and inspired, can actually mold such policies. My country is still young, I argued, and still growing into its more virtuous self. People are good. The best is yet to come. Crabgrass is not caused by socialists, and we need to be shown the way.

Third, a lecture tour of the U.S. would be stimulating and perhaps fun. Four to six weeeks induration, visiting idyllic university towns, urban media centers, labor assemblies, soirees of the opinion-making elite, relieved of any worry beyond the performer's ultimate duty to be at his best when the curtain goes up.

Zapatú's weak eyes were closed, but his torso swayed in imperceptible assent. "Tell me what will it be like. Hard work? Stressful? Will I be better for it?"

Usually I make this particular pitch over drinks in a bar where the light is especially dim and the social environment highly conducive to inflated rhetoric. The bright high tropical sun and soothing tides were not an optimal milieu for business negotiations. We were stripped to the waist, lounging in the nuzzling surf like a pair of shipwreck victims searching the horizon for help. It occurred to me how much better I could conduct this discussion in a bar like The Grotto.

"From bland to spectacular, it can go many ways," I answered Zapatú. "Do you want to know what it's like if everything goes very well?"

"And then I'll hear the worst case?"

I nodded. Relax and close your eyes, I told Zapatú, not just to soothe the queasiness of blurred vision but to use your mind's eye to envision this foreign wonderland. Your plane has just landed at a suburban airfield and waiting at the gate are your sponsors, your hosts, a young man and woman, radiantly congenial with eager faces fresh as apples. It is a forty-minute drive to their college where you are to deliver tonight's lecture. You have been on tour for a week and no longer are beset with tension over how your presentation will go. You are confident that you will deliver a great speech.

Your hosts ask if you want to travel the faster, more direct interstate highway route or detour along the backroads, which are slower. You choose, to their approval, the backroads. Soon you are swooping past verdant farms where fat dappled cows cluster in the shade of great oak trees, and in the distant fields weary men in coveralls stoop over bundles of harvested crops. You think to yourself, how similar the world over.

You are in the back seat. The boy is driving. The girl turns around to ask you a friendly question about how you enjoyed your flight, and you are struck by the earnest curiosity of her face, her gleaming white teeth, her calm smile so innocent of dread. The airline food, you tell her, is the most dangerous part of traveling, and she gives you back a laugh of such warm fullness that you believe you have touched on a cosmic truth. You want to make other jokes, better ones that will excite her to perpetual laughter. That is how much pleasure you get from watching this college girl laugh.

You pass a velvet green golf course, a road sign advertising tobacco products, a crossroads town where half the stores have boarded-up windows. You make a notation in the journal you are keeping. You have it in the back of your mind that a book might come out of this. Eventually you arrive in the college town and are deposited at a motel. Your room is perfectly neat, as accommodating and easily forgotten as midnight sex with a stranger. Your lecture won't start for a few hours. You switch on the color TV and marvel at the vignettes of decadence and stupidity, which may merit an entire section in your notebook. You decide to go for a walk. It will be good to stretch your legs and meander anonymously through the life of this town. Outside you detect a scent in the air, an antiquated sweetness that you've never experienced and you follow it like a forest creature, along residential sidewalks, past a row of modest faculty homesteads, into an alley where two boys toss a football. It is a musty, sorrowful smell, more like an emotion than an olfactory sensation.

The auditorium will be crowded and hushed with expectation. You tell them stories about your life, your struggle. (We can iron out the details later.) You are an exotic to them, yet real because you appear before them in the flesh. Afterward, they leap to their feet and applaud for several minutes. You have awakened something precious in them, and although they cannot fully comprehend it, they are moved to show their appreciation. Later that night, a reception is held in your honor at a professor's home. You are the center of attention, and you find this rapt curiosity at least as replenishing as it is exhausting. Always the conversation will concern issues of social change, international strife, foreign policy, Third World revolution. There will be ample wine and other provisions to buffer the onslaught. Soon the living room becomes suffocating from smoke and so many passionate opinions. From across this crowded room, the young woman, your host, catches your eye. Taking it upon herself as the one anointed to look after your sensitivities, she brazenly inserts herself into the scrimmage and requests you to accompany her outside for a view of the constellations. The coterie of avid conversationalists mutter amongst themselves as you are pried away.

The night air is cool and sweet with that same aroma. You ask her about it. Looking straight into your eyes with that uninhibited admiration one lives to see in another's face, she says shucks (a word you've never heard before), it's only dead leaves.

Zapatú opened his eyes and with great difficulty raised his knees to rest his arms across them. "Your government—they will allow me to do this?"

"Absolutely. It's free enterprise. As long as we pay the appropriate taxes. And as long as we charge money. Doing it for free would probably cause problems. That would threaten them. Capitalism has its paradoxes."

It occured to me that storybook heroes usually are presented with two clearly divergent paths representing contrasting values, and now the United States, a nation that invented itself, had come up with a third option—self-aggrandizement at no cost to one's reputation for altruism. Such a country is not likely to have a shortage of heroes.

"Worst case?" Zapatú asked.

"You get snowed in at O'Hare."

"Wha?"

"The crowds can be small. The weather might be bad. You get lonely and homesick. You get bored with what you're saying. The journal you keep gets filled with gibberish." I didn't want to draw too bleak a picture. "But each morning will bring a new place, and new possibilities. And, of course, you'll be well paid."

Zapatú groaned in pain as he attempted to reposition his hips in the sand. "I have comrades, people I am responsible for."

I had foreseen this concern. "Any acclaim you receive will make them proud. Monies you earn can only . . ."

He interrupted, "We will not talk about money in their presence. Is that clear?"

"Of course. I am your agent. All discussions are confidential between us. As I was saying, I'm sure they can withstand," and here I gestured to the sparkling turquoise sea, the splendid beach, "a couple months without you. I know that I sure could."

Zapatú laughed. "Okay, but I have another concern. People perceive me as a man with a certain world view. One of the main reasons I am respected is that I serve, in the minds of many, as a model of uncompromising commitment to my beliefs. Almost like a priest. It is not a situation I ever set out to create or encourage, but it has become a situation I cannot escape. If people come to doubt my commitment . . ."

Agents can be more like priests, acting as father confessors. I was curious. "You've never given them cause to doubt?"

He hung his head. "Yes, I have."

"And did they forsake you?"

Zapatú propped his forearm on my shoulder for support, and began to pry himself onto his feet. I threw my arm around his waist to help hoist him.

"One more question," he said. "I might meet young ladies like the one you describe?"

I tightened my hold on Zapatú's waist and we slowly began the hobble back. I chose my words carefully. "Young women indeed are drawn to men of noble purpose. On your lecture tour you will be introduced to many who've never met a man such as you."

Like a school kid, I tied my shoes together and slung them across my shoulder. The soft tide eddied about our ankles as we shuffled up the beach. We moved tenderly, as slow and deliberate as tortoises. Rosa, it turned out, was vindicated.

I readjusted my hold on him. "I've been meaning to ask you about the raven-haired beauty you reportedly are seen with."

"Ah yes. The raven-haired beauty. I will tell you a secret. She is a model and part-time actress. We pay her to be photographed. She is perfect, don't you think, for the press."

As a promoter, I was quite impressed. And sorry. "Too bad. You know how thoughts about women can get into your mind—I was hoping to meet her."

With his poor crippled shoulder, Zapatú gave me a jolly nudge. "Maybe we can hire her again. With our lecture money."

Dusk in its muted lavenders and pinks enfolded the compound like a nursery. We limped in unnoticed. The thatched huts were dark and still. Everyone was down at the bay. I was no longer reminded of Jonestown.

Firelight danced through the palms and we could hear the soft strumming of the guitar. Zapatú was in great discomfort and we paused every fifty yards just to let his pain subside. We had been half a day returning from an hour's hike. Enemy commandos intent on a raid could not have arrived with any more delicacy and invisibility.

At the firelight's outer edge, we leaned against a sturdy palm trunk. Zapatú wanted to gather his strength for re-entry and for several minutes we hovered undiscovered in the darkness, enjoying the luxury of voyeurs. On the far side of the camp circle, Pepe hunkered over his guitar. Two young men were hiking up from the pier hefting a heavy bucket hung from a pole between them. Their chest muscles vibrated in the flickering orange light. Rosa crawled forward to poke at the fire. I watched for Mona but couldn't find her.

Zapatú sensed the object of my searching and pointed his horrible crooked fingers toward the shadows near Pepe. "He is so ridiculous, that Pepe," chuckled Zapatú. "A leader like me—what can I expect but ridiculous followers?"

A dark shape was suspended horizontally between the palms where he was pointing. It was a hammock. My eyes adjusted. With a woman in it. Mona. Her feet were propped high, her pelvis and torso sunken.The brightest flickers of firelight managed to catch her face, which looked so supremely serene I thought she might be dead. Then I got the picture: she was being serenaded by Pepe.

Gingerly, Zapatú inched toward the circle. One by one, people noticed his arrival, and they gasped and rose up from their knees and clamored forward. The two men dropped their bucket, halted in their tracks. The strumming ceased. A reverent choral hush fell over the gathering.

With a vigorous wave of his crippled hands, Zapatú immodestly tried to discourage the encroaching torrent of worry. "A little accident is all, my friends. No problem. Please. No problem."

"Ay, my Zapatú," Rosa wailed. "What treachery?"

"I slipped and fell. Please, some wine.That is what I could use."

Rosa eyed me with chilly accusation. She shouted for someone to fetch some wine, *pronto!*, then implored Zapatú to sit, right by the fire, not to move.

"Calm down," Zapatú insisted. "Really. I'll be O.K."

The more Rosa pondered the situation, the more agitated she became. "I knew it. I feared this. I had a dream and you, my Zapatú, were being dragged away from us in a cage. You tried to tear through the wire cage. That explains your poor hands." She bent over and began to kiss his fingers.

Zapatú pulled back aghast. "Rosa, please. Just some wine. And ganja."

"Ganja!" she screamed out, like an emergency medic demanding a sterilized scalpel.

Pepe came over with his guitar slung dramatically across his bare chest. Others moved closer, the circle enclosing. I seized the opportunity to slink off to the hammock. I was not Zapatú's agent-protector just yet. He could fend for himself.

Mona had not moved from the hammock, maintaining the exquisitely supine pose of Cleopatra ferried by slaves on a barge.

"Am I disturbing you?" I inquired.

"Not yet."

"Gee, that's good. You look so peaceful."

"Thank you, I am."

I was disappointed she didn't display greater professional curiosity. With a demonstrative sigh of fatigue, I leaned against the palm trunk. "You know, I've had a pretty rough day of it."

"Poor baby." Her sympathy was monumentally insincere.

"We barely averted a disaster out there. Zapatú almost got killed."

"Go with the flow, Danny. You're always so tense."

This was going nowhere. Resorting to the cheapest tactic, I asked about herself? "How was your day? Did you learn anything useful from Pepe?"

"Perhaps, You and I may have different definitions of useful."

"Well, I'd say that my day with Zapatú was useful, by any definition."

Mona struggled to sit up, but the hammock just swallowed her effort. She was coming out of her alleged trance." Yes? I'm listening."

I stepped out a yard to get a better view of the last silken wisps of violet fluttering above the dark harbor.

Mona again tried to rise up, groping at the net mesh, first with one hand, then both, but found herself sinking deeper. She was making no progress. It was as if she were stuck to flypaper in some silly animated cartoon.

"Tell me already," she ranted. "Is he into it?"

"It?" This interlude had changed from irksome to mildly fun. "What exactly do you mean by 'it'?"

"Will Zapatú do the tour?"

"Damn!" I swatted the side of my head in self-reproach. "I'm so stupid sometimes. I knew there was something else we were supposed to discuss."

"*Something else*? You fool! I don't believe this!"

I hung my head desparingly and shuffled in the sand, then muttered to myself like a seasoned practitioner of discount self-actualization, "No, I'm not letting myself get down about this. Good things were accomplished, some very good things. I was able to lay some groundwork. We had a healthy exchange of ideas, man to man. I think he's come to respect my grasp of international politics, my views on life. Getting your prospective client to sit down and listen and respect you—that's always preliminary. All the books agree on that. I refuse to let myself get down over this."

"Someone should!" Her eyes boiled with disdain.

"Please, Mona. Cool out a little."

"*You* forgot to discuss the main topic and you're telling *me* to cool out? Good God!"

"The fact is..." My voice trailed off, like a deep thinker distracted by an abstract contemplation too complex for words. For a moment I languished in the bitter silence of Mona's scrutiny. A pause can be a delicious thing when one is in total control of its outcome. Nonchalantly, I added, "He's agreed to do a fall tour. Everything's set."

Too proud to acknowledge being suckered, Mona's only comment was a dry, "Nice going." No high fives.

By the campfire, Pepe had resumed strumming the guitar. The Belizean breeze wiffled through the palms above us. A magical harmony momentarily took hold.

"There's room in here for two."

At first I didn't hear her, through the clatter of pinnate branches and the tranquilizing strum of the guitar. The chords were familiar. I had been trying to identify from where.

Mona repeated, "Come on up and relax. There's room." With great effort, she managed to hoist herself up slightly to make space.

I flipped onto the hammock, intending to align myself parallel but opposite, head to toe. However, misjudging the elasticity of the mesh and my own stiffened muscles. I wound up nose-diving onto Mona. Instantly I threw my arm across her in order to push off, but it doesn't work that way with hammocks. I floundered involuntarily on top of her like a wriggling trout plopped into a new environment. It would take coordinated strategy, not reflex avoidance, to wrest us apart.

Her skin smelled of cocoa oil, her hair of fresh flowers. I attempted to pull away gradually, inch by inch. Any sudden move and we would be back where we started. My bare arms felt swarthy in the heat as I balanced myself above her. She lay still, so as not to complicate the extrication. Before prying away, I hesitated one last moment, waiting, waiting, a waiting that's endured through the history of the human heart. Distant firelight flickered like truth in her wide eyes. Finally I regained full balance and reclined backward, to the position I had initially sought.

Closing our eyes, we swayed to the still reverberant tremors of our close encounter. The song that came frome Pepe's guitar was indeed a familiar one, and it was beautiful to hear Bob Dylan's music in this distant tropical place.

Zapatú crooned as Pepe tickled the guitar:

"Hey! Mr. Tambourine Man,
Play a song for me,
I'm not sleepy and there is no place
I'm going to.

To dance beneath the diamond sky
With one hand waving free,
Sihlouetted by the sea,
Circled by the circus sounds,
With all memory and fate,
Driven deep beneath the waves,
Let me forget about today
Until tomorrow."

Mona nuzzled me playfully with her foot. "Pepe played this song for me earlier, and explained all the wisdom it shows. He thinks Zapatú wrote it."

I was becoming more and more impressed with Zapatú, although not for the qualities I had been led to expect. As a gesture of heartfelt equivocation, I squeezed her foot. "And what did you tell Pepe?"

She reclined her head to gaze serenely up at the tinkling fronds and the stars twinkling beyond. It really was the most peaceful of evenings.

"I told him what men like to hear."

Ah yes—what men like to hear. More power to Mona if she had any true insight into that.

CHAPTER 7

Our first morning back, we brainstormed. Mona had yet to arrive at the office, but I was so brimming with enthusiam about signing Zapatú that I proceeded to brief the staff without her. This was Frankly's comeback, and I wanted everyone turned on and performing at optimal efficiency. Zapatú had all the potential to be our main ticket, our salvation. It was imperative that we measured up to the opportunity. The Boy Guru was already filling up fall dates, with the calculated sham of "the Wisdom of Youth." I was not about to suffer the momumental indignity of subjugation to a pudgy, bland ten-year-old kid. *I* was once ten years old, damn it! We all were!

It was Kenny's hunch that Zapatú should be priced high, at least forty-five hundred plus expenses.

Piper believed that was too much. She has a sleepy demeanor with dark, droopy bedroom eyes which, in truth, always make her look high.

"We can always drop down," Kenny countered. "Big fees—I'm sorry to say—mean quality. It's gotten to the point, these days, when they don't believe someone's good unless they have to pay through the nose. These students are suspicious of anything that's a good deal. It troubles me, if you want to know the truth."

Kenny and Piper perched like a salt-and-pepper set on the Goodwill sofa. By coincidence, they had each worn gray wool slacks and lavendar cardigan sweaters. Marion sat in the office armchair, a deep green vinyl thing held together through an intricate swatching of electrical tape. She had already scribbled down a page of notes from the meeting, and nothing had been said.

Piper held her ground. Glaring down Kenny, who perched maybe eight inches from her face, she insisted, "Four thousand, inclusive. No one knows anything about this guy."

"What do they know about the Boy Guru?" I challenged.

"Smooth Line," she scolded, "are experts at this game. We're not."

I recoiled from thinking of this as merely a "game," where slick technique and manipulation of the rules prevailed. "Zapatú," I declared in what seemed to me a self-evident rebuttal, "is a real hero of the people who carries an important message."

Kenny eased past my remark. "I'm telling you," he insisted. "The price you charge determines what they think." He turned his palms outward from his chest. "Hey, I'm not defending it. But that's the truth. They have no respect for a speaker they don't have to pay for."

I was getting depressed listening. The tour was slated to start in October, to capitalize on the fall's resurgent energy. In college communities the seasons are transposed, with fall taking on the traditional characteristics—planting, fertilizing, hoping—that accrue to spring. It is also the season when a university's compartmentalized budget brims with unspent dollars. Six months may seem like a considerable lead-time, but if the dates aren't lined up by the end of May, it becomes a desperate predicament to fill in the gap over the generally slow summer. We had to pull together.

Piper was uncommonly persistent. "What if we just can't get that much? What if three thou is all they'll pay?"

Kenny's feathers were ruffled. "Then you're not selling him right. Three thou? Come on! They pay that much for ex-con drug addicts who've found religion."

Strange interpersonal dynamics had developed during my time away from the office. Even in organizations devoted to altruism, which this was not, jealousy can be an insidious and virulent sentiment. I had expected there to be some ramification from senior management's quick trip to the tropics. It surprised me that it was taking this form.

Mona strutted in, precisely one hour late. She wore a gaily colored Hawaiian shirt and dangling white coral earrings, to inform anyone who might not know that she had recently returned from a southern climate.

"We're brainstorming about promoting Zapatú," I told her.

She wedged onto the sofa between Piper and Kenny. Now they looked like a salt and pepper set adorned by a floral arrangement. Since everyone looked to her for a remark, she made one. "My tan is already starting to peel."

Given the particular tensions, there was a chance they might pursue the topic of Mona's peeling tan and all its metaphoric implications. I hastily summarized, "We were just focusing on the issue of fees—how much should we charge for Zapatú?"

Although she was manifestly preoccupied with one of the polished coral pendants, tilting her head to diddle with her ear, Mona did, however, find time to offer her opinion. "Much as we can get."

I briefed her on the current state of our discussion, with Kenny opting for a high fee, in the vicinity of five thousand, and Piper registering reservations. Then I weighed in with my own opinion, which was to quote high and stick to it until the situation grows desperate. "The main thing," I counseled my semi-attentive staff, is not to put your quotes in writing, unless it's part of a contract. That way, if we're forced to drop the price, there won't be any kind of documentary record of our weaseling."

"What happens if some places book at the high price," asked Piper, "and down the road others get him for much lower?"

I was all executive authoritativeness. Extending the fingers of my left hand as a tote board, I pulled back the forefinger with my right hand to indicate: point one. "First, we hope it won't come to that. Second," I moved on to the middle finger, "we hope no one finds out. Third, we blame the error on lack of internal communication and bad management. Most sins are forgiven if you blame them on procedures that you swear will be immediately rectified."

Piper squinched up her mouth is that shopworn TV sitcom expression of begrudging acquiescense. "Okay," she allowed, "so what's our rap on him? Let's say I'm Jane Doe from State University, USA. Try and sell me."

Mona jumped in with a lascivious wink. "He's Latin. He's sexy. He's hot."

Piper gasped in mock offense. "Please! I'm not that sort of girl."

Kenny teetered thoughtfully on the edge of the sofa. "Mona might just be onto something."

"Thank you, sir."

"Sexy is key. Sex and revolution. They go together like..."

Seizing the opportunity of Kenny's momentary failure to find the bon mot, Piper asked, "What does he actually look like, in person?"

Either of us could have answered, although what Piper sought was the highly refined opinion of someone renowned for her attentiveness to things superficial, not the lame attempt at objective description I would provide.

Mona took the cue. "He has dreamy eyes. When he looks at you you feel like you're in the distance, in a dream."

"What's his manner?" Marion followed up, as if this were "Meet the Press." There was a breathiness in her tone, a parody of a teen-ager's lust for any detail about a matinee idol.

"Relaxed, very cool," responded Mona in, what seemed to me, also a parody. "You want to dance next to him, slow like a samba."

"When he walks just like a samba," echoed Kenny, his voice lifting into song. "Ipanema. Jobim."

Mona stroked her chin. "He'd remind you a little of Danny here." Mockingly she added, "If Danny took better care of himself. And had better self-esteem. And had something to say."

This was getting out of hand. "Unlike my trusty colleagues," I snapped, "Zapatú's people revere him and hang on his every word. They encourage him to be... well, to be all he can be. It's a little like a cult, now that I think of it. When he's away they sit around speculating about what he's up to. They compare him to jungle creatures."

"Danny's just jealous." Mona raked her fingernails across her well-tanned forearm. Then, with consummate self-absorption, she declared, "I'm actually peeling."

Mindful of Mona's ability to focus attention on wholly irrelevant personal considerations, I scurried to assert our central concern. "And, don't forget the tightrope we're always trying to walk—that fine line between profundity and popularity. That's our goal and that's how we've got to promote Zapatú. We've got to hammer it home to them that he can pack the auditorium, plus leave them thinking new, exciting thoughts."

"Like what?"

Piper asked this innocently enough, but it took the shape of a hostile challenge. Did she think me bluffing in my claim that Zapatú would stimulate students to higher consciousness? It was clearly an area where I harbored some very touchy insecurities.

Piper sensed my discomfort. "Just playing the devil's advocate," she demurred."Sorry, boss."

"Don't apologize," I insisted. "I can respond to that. Zapatú will make people think about . . . he'll force them to consider their individual . . . responsibility for the end result of policies . . . administered by faceless bureaucrats using our tax dollars . . . Zapatú will stand before them as the emobdiment of what it means to sacrifice . . . to sacrifice middle-class comfort for humanitarian ideals . . . and in so doing inspire others, many others, to get involved and . . ."

They all were fastidiously avoiding my efforts at eye contact. Even Marion had ceased taking notes.

Mona made a diffident stab at coming to my aid. "The guy's cute. He's Latin." She fiddled with the other white coral earring. "He's hot."

During this initial stage of refining a promotion, Frankly Speakers makes a standard practice of testing out a sample sales pitch to generate some feedback. A good sales rap should be as trim, piercing, evocative and eloquent in its own way as a poem. Indeed, an anthology of the best lines, if exquisitely type-set, arranged thematically, and assigned abstract titles like "Fevered Pitch" or "Verbal Highways," could be published as an unacknowledged form of folk art, like Native American chants.

Kenny took the first crack at pitching Zapatú. Settling into my swivel chair, he punched the console button to broadcast the conversation. He dialed up Sissy Ransome. Miraculously, she was in.

"Just last night I dreamt about you," she gushed, as Kenny squirmed with embarrassment. "We were at a drive-in movie and it was a little gross. Not everyone had their clothes on and you were worried that I'd be angry with you, even though it was my idea to go there. Here's the weird part—Kevin Krass of the Smooth Line Agency pulled up next to us in a fat yellow school bus and parks right in our way so we can't even see the screen. Just when they're taking their clothes off."

Kenny was perspiring. "Uh . . . yes?"

"That's all. My roommate's alarm went off. What do you think it means?"

To us, Kenny moaned, "I don't want to know. "To Sissy, he glibly stated, "There's something profound and deep to it, but I need time to give it some thought. I'll get back to you tomorrow."

He hung up, shaken.

"What the hell?" I said. "I thought you were going to try out your rap."

Kenny shuddered with the realization. "Damn. You're right." He punched up Sissy's number.

She answered on the first chirp. "That was quick," she sang. "So what does it mean?"

Kenny stammered. "I forgot the reason I was calling."

"Sexual tension can do that," Sissy allowed.

Kenny's complexion now approximated the blush of his fluffy sweater. "We've signed an exciting new speaker," he told her in a mortified monotone. "This may be just the ticket for your campus."

Sissy's voice came back breathy and low. "I'm laid back on our office sofa. The phone is sitting on my tummy. Talk to me, Kenny. I'm all yours."

"As you should be." Kenny was pulling himself together. He stood up, placing one foot on the edge of my chair and, turning his back to us, he bent over the phone receiver like a blues singer embracing the mike."You'll be well cared for. You're now in good hands. All your sensitivities will be honored."

Sissy sighed."You know what I need."

"What a little tramp," Mona pouted.

"Zapatú!" The name leaped up and swaggered with Kenny's vivid enunciation. Now he was rocking, "Imagine yourself, Sissy, dressed all in white, something peasant-simple yet stunning in the stage-light. It is you alone before the packed auditorium who bears the responsibility of introducing the premier North American—*Norte Americano*, as they say—appearance of a virtual legend, a man not just of mystery but of heroic deed, a man who is at once . . . electrifying, mesmerizing . . ." Faltering, Kenny turned to us and signalled frantically for help, wordlessly flapping his arms like someone playing charades.

"Mysterious," offered Piper. "Sensational?"

Kenny shook his head impatiently.

"Cute," Mona suggested, moistening her lips. "Perhaps hot?"

With a sneer, Kenny turned back to Sissy. "Let me put it this way. Zapatú is going to fill the hall, maybe even the gymnasium, and get more media attention than anything short of a hostage crisis. Beyond that, he's guaranteed to really stir people up. Frankly, he's going to alter some minds. Kids will be staying up all night in the corridors of the dormitory discussing it. Little prairie fires of excitement will be lit across the campus. Now I don't want to lay too much responsibility on you, but it's true that you will be credited with sparking the entire experience."

Kenny's superb instincts, which we all could profit by observing, told him to pause here. It was important to draw a response from

Sissy, to take measure of her position—beyond reclining on a couch with the phone on her tummy.

"How much?" She'd eagerly taken the bait.

"For you, forty-five. Plus shared expenses. This one's new, so the literature is still at the printer. We'll talk dates in a few days."

With his free hand Kenny jabbed at the ceiling in exuberant triumph.

"One last question," Sissy inserted."What do you know about this Boy Guru?"

Kenny was hesitant. "Um . . . why?"

"I've been getting quite the hard sell on him."

Kenny slumped. "From?"

"Last week it was a call from the Religious Studies Department. Just yesterday it was the Academic V.P.'s office. Some really astonishing developments are happening for this kid—a TV movie, Carson show—that kind of stuff."

Kenny looked flu-ridden and despondent. "Sissy, how . . ."

She tried to soothe him with maternal understanding. "Don't you be so touchy. You know that I'm obligated to talk to others."

Kenny would not be comforted. He yelped, "The boy Guru? Please!"

"Come on now, really. I didn't mean to upset you. I just wanted your opinion. As a professional in the field."

Kenny's face was flushed, and he looked on the verge of gagging. I truthfully couldn't tell if he came by this welter of agitation honestly or if it was shrewdly manufactured. "Smooth Line," he sniffed. "Sissy, how could you?"

Once again, he had her where he wanted, gravely concerned for his emotional well being. "Please, Kenny," she pleaded. Be reasonable. Anyway, I"ve got enough budget to do both."

A whimper of hope crept into his countenace." But we're committed to Zapatú for fall semester?"

She was ecstatic to hear him on the rebound. "Oh, yes, yes, yes. You've got my word."

After hanging up, Kenny received an appreciative round of applause.

"And the beauty of it is," he expounded without a trace of distress, "I didn't even have to explain what the hell Zapatú has to say."

We had the promotional piece designed to function as a full-blown poster to be push-pinned on bulletin boards, stapled to construction fences, Scotch-taped in windows of laundromats and pizza parlors. We were still pretty much in the dark concerning the substance of Zapatú's message, so the poster's emphasis was on title ("South of the Revolution"), sketchy background information ("notorious political exile, cover of *Newsweek*, featured on '60 Munites,' B.A. degree from a university that was closed down due to violent battles between students and the goons of the Guardia Civil"), plus a provocative quote ("Whereas his style may be disarmingly unique, his message is as old as Satan"—*The Christian Times).*

Working with our regular designer, Sonya Tsen, we came up with a forceful, dominating, memorable graphic image for the poster. By means of an anguished, costly trial-and-error process, I had come to trust my instincts in the skirmishing that goes on with graphic designers. The first direct mail piece ever commissioned by Frankly Speakers turned out to be a work for which you pretty much needed an instructional manual just to figure out how to unfold it. The designer had apparently taken his inspiration from a recent exhibit of origami. When I complained to him that, of the several thousand programmers on our list, it was likely that none had ever seen or heard of origami, he just shrugged and told me what amounts to the party line when people of the arts are compelled to justify their decisions: paper manipulations date back many, many centuries and, like all elemental features of visual language, they are so deeply ingrained in our aesthetic values as to be virtually inscribed in our genetic code. I informed him that very few of our customers even knew a genetic code was something they owned.

The graphic met my approval. It was an artist's drawing done with the crisp lines and primary colors of superrealism. It depicted Zapatú in partial profile, with the outline of his features made dramatic through an indistinct backlight. As I had learned from meeting with him, Zapatú is an average-looking guy, nothing spectacular. Sonya Tsen managed to recast the chin, the cheeks, and his pale eyes in a dim, shaded way that made him appear brooding and sensitive, a grave man of barely suppressed passions. Behind this looming foreground profile was a screened panorama of a cane field receding in long, symmetrical rows to a distant smoldering volcano. We had no single model in mind in designing this except, of course, an entire lifetime of being inundated by sensationalized, melodramatic, oversimplified, insidious advertisements. Talk about being inscribed in your genetic code!

On that afternoon in April when the finished promotional piece was finally delivered, a ripple of cheer spread through the office. It was already springtime. The heavy cloak of winter had lifted. Across America, college students were fretting over the prospect of final exams, and planning their summer vacations. It's a mixed blessing, working in a business so synchronized to the carefree rhythms of the academic life. On one hand, there is a kind of vicarious pleasure from dealing with people whose schedules are so loose and easy. On the other hand, we're jealous.

We decided to hold a small impromptu party to celebrate the delivery and grand opening of the Zapatú posters. Marion went down the block for a couple of bottles of champagne. In an almost unprecedented working hours gesture, I authorized the answering machine to be activated so we would not be interrupted by incoming chirps. The dozen tightly packed printer's boxes were carted into the center of my office and stacked high, like an aboriginal totem. The room filled with the spanking new scent of printer's ink, freshly manufactured like the modern world itself. I requested the staff to sit on the floor encircling the boxes. People were so pleased at deviating from the normal routine that they complied.

I asked for a moment of silence. In the religion of capitalism, such moments as this constitute a christening. In my role as high priest, I offered aprayer:

"Oh, divine spirit who governs our fate in ways whimsical and beyond comprehension, take these semi-gloss, four-color, seventeen-by-eleven promotional pieces and deliver them by whatever magic you choose into the hands of fellow men and women who have administrative control over significant budgets plus the good sense to spend it with us. Help us,oh divine spirit, to forge the connection between our labors and material reward. And once we achieve economic stability, help us in our struggle to be productive and progressive citizens. We aspire to noble things. Our abilities are as large as the unseen spirit that infuses all mankind. Help us climb out from the rubble and ascend the glorious peaks. Life is short. We hunger to do our best. That's all we want, the chance to do our best . . ."

I had run out of steam, and was groping for a way to wrap up.

"Amen?" hinted Mona.

Yes, that's word. "Amen," I concluded.

Our brief reverie was punctured by the harsh bleating croak of the downstairs buzzer. Most deliverymen—United Parcel, Federal Express, the water cooler company—are familiar with our hours and always waltz right in. The stray door-to-door solicitor, as we all know, never observes the nicety of buzzing. Rarely does anyone make an actual business visit unnannounced. Like so many enterprises in this era of telecommunications wizardry, we function principally in faceless isolation. I prefer it that way.

Kenny, who sat closest to the vestibule intercom, scrambled over and pressed his cheek to the grated steel cup. "Who is it?"

The reply came back an indecipherable cackle, possibly female.

Not one to obsess about security procedures (after all, we had no cash on hand; the net value of our "assets" couldn't keep a sophisticated junkie stoned for more than a day), Kenny activated the downstairs un-lock buzzer. Soon we heard the snappy castanets of spiked heels traipsing up the linoleum stairs, clicking closer, closer. Kenny held the door open.

Like campfire girls at a marshmallow roast, we turned our heads in a kind of juvenile ingenuousness to gawk at the statuesque woman who strode through the doorway. Her most striking feature was an unharnessed cascade of honey-blond hair that would seem more appropriate if its owner were clad in a sequined bikini rather than the formal, though snug, navy blue business suit she wore. She projected that genteel self-assuredness of someone who is known not from personal acquaintance but through the refracted familiarity of the popular media.

I racked my brain. A game show host? A billboard vermouth ad?

Mona rose. She was dressed in her matching pink terrycloth all-purpose casualwear outfit. As she approached the woman in the doorway, I flashed on the ludicrous image of the neophyte David in his scraggly loin cloth dauntlessly facing down the mighty Goliath.

"Can I be of assistance?" Mona asked in that gruff way she has of implying that "assistance" is the last thing on her mind.

The woman glanced about apprehensively. A handful of people aggregating on the floor was apparently not what she was expecting to find. "Is Mr. Frank in?" she asked after a pause.

Now I knew! Along with the entire nation, I had watched her testify on TV during the congressional investigation into the missile laundering scandal. The probe had devolved hopelessly into a great fog of obfuscation, to the point where now the primary public remembrance was of a gang of headstrong yet sincere patriots whose zeal to internationalize American-style democracy had clumsily floundered on some arcane Constitutional fineprint. She had been a minor figure, but what a figure!

She had testified over the course of several days. As the beady-eyed chief counsel struggled to portray her boss, the smug Lieutenant Colonel, as a witting protagonist in a nearly traitorous scheme of covert dealings, she had grown bold and even defiant. She possessed a seductive way of sucking on an eraser tip before dodging the counsel's questions, and by the second day of her prime time testimony she was being offered book deals, movie options, TV guest shots, lecture appearances. For some reason none of it panned out—a fact apparently corroborated by her stately presence in our modest quarters.

I clamored to my feet before Mona said something regrettable. "I'm Danny Frank, Frankly Speakers."

Like an apparition with gleaming tresses, Dawn Hall—I think that was her name—moved across the vestibule. I was absolutely dumbounded. Media stars, even short-lived ones, don't just stroll into your office unnanounced. I smelled a prank.

Marion and Piper, still squatting like bushmen by the pile of new posters, gawked unabashedly. Kenny's mouth hung open in astonishment; you'd think he'd sighted Marilyn Monroe! Mona however, stood like a rabid Easter Bunny blocking the entrance to my office.

Sensing Miss Hall's discomfort, I scooted over like an obliging head waiter. "How can I help you?"

Her tan skin shimmered with a silken glow. Her determined gum chewing lent a muscular grandeur to her jawline. Her affable knees poked alluringly beneath her skirt. A sweet scent, like a trade wind through the Spice Islands, wafted softly our way.

She struck me strangely as a damsel in distress. Glancing up beseechingly at me—no mean feat, since in her high heels she stood several inches taller—she asked, "Can we, you know, talk in private?"

It felt suspiciously like a set-up, a divisive maneuver at this rare moment of staff unity. Still, I made an instant decision to comply. Clapping my hands like an officious camp counselor to clear the room, I announced, "Party's over. Chop, chop."

Marion and Piper slowly picked themselves up as Miss Hall entered. "Hold my calls," I told them. "I'll be in conference."

Mona, however, lingered. Her eyes were nearly spastic with suspicion. She didn't believe in surprises. To her they were simply plots whose origins remained concealed. Clearly, she thought I knew more than I did.

I motioned Miss Hall to be seated on my Goodwill sofa. Bidding Mona to the door with artificial aplomb, I tried to pacify her with a cheery non-sequitur, "Why don't you call Tsen and complement her on the poster."

Miraculously, she departed without protest. Easing down into my executive swivel chair, I looked hard into Miss Hall's perfectly telegenic bone structure and uttered the only line that made any sense: "What brings you here?"

"You know who I am?" It was a question spoken like a statement.

"I do."

"So you're probably wondering why I've come unannounced to your office."

"Yes. We could start with that."

With a magnificent gyration of her hips, she hoisted one leg luxuriously across the other, a maneuver that inched the navy hem of her suit-skirt even further up her tanned and shapely thigh. Her countenance was courtly and placid, save for the vigorous gum chewing. "As you may know," she explained, "I've been signed with another agency, Premier, here in the District. I'm looking for a new start."

I removed my glasses with the ostensible purpose of wiping off dust. In truth, I'd been told I looked better without them. "Now that I think on it, I haven't heard much about you doing any gigs—if you don't mind me using an industry phrase."

"Go right ahead, I'm a big girl. That's why I'm here."

"How come?" I pressed her. "Why no gigs?"

She gave a few casual fluffs to her leonine coiffure. Her voice quavering with a previously undetected vulnerability, she complained, "They came on so strong, with all these promises. Everyone wanted me, all the agencies, but these guys promised the moon. They had Henry Kissinger himself lobby me. Can you imagine? It seemed like a sure thing."

"What did?"

"That I would be very much in demand. I would, you know, travel all over, earn some decent money, get the chance to promote my message."

Only a desperate white-knuckle grip on the underedge of my desk enabled me to surpress the burning urge to dress her down. Promote her message? Give me a break. Concealing my irritation, I asked innocently, "Have you done any speeches?"

"Last spring. A couple commencements."

"No fooling. What did you say?"

"One of the guys from the White House helped me sketch it out. I said that America was a great country for college graduates and how they should respect their leaders and put faith in their ideals. You know, be all that you can be. That kind of thing."

"Sounds pretty good." I struggled to keep a straight face. "Why do you think it didn't catch on?"

She gave a girlish shrug, and there was something poignantly touching about the object naïveté of her obtuseness. The scandal that propelled her into the limelight had been a pyramid scheme of manipulators masquerading as fall guys. Perhaps she had been the one genuine article. There might be a thin window of promotability in that—Woman As Victim, or something to that effect.

Her heavy eyes lifted towards me." Your name was recommended to me by a guy at my health club, Davis Reynolds. I wrote you a letter and when I looked up your address in the phone book and saw that it was so close to my place, I just said to myself, you know, no more piddling around, march right over there and meet the man directly. Take the bull by the horns."

"Be all you can be," I chimed in.

"Exactly!"

"So," I asked, "What did Reynolds tell you about Frankly Speakers?"

She swept a luxuriant swath of hair overhead, from left to right. "Just that you were the best in the business," she purred.

"Nothing about our, ah, political values?"

"Only that you're honest and smart and a straight-shooter. At this stage in my career that's what I need."

Her career? To my knowledge, the most she'd been was a secretary, glorified only by her stunning good looks and her boss's penchant for nefarious dealings on a global scale. She had been pumped so full of false expectations, I almost pitied her. It's lonely out there in the realm of the big egos. I certainly didn't have the heart to tell her about the spiteful rumor-mongering campaign waged against her by Smooth Line.

Moisture welled up in her dark saucer eyes and she began to sniffle. Her misty gaze seemed to shift to a faraway focus, distant and beyond, as if she were peering deep into an unseen dimension. I swiveled a few degrees to try and fathom what it was she was staring at—my framed enlargement of Abbie Hoffman's mirthful visage, another discarded pizza crust?—but then she wheezed and sighed, ever so softly like Jackie Onassis. (Now, there was an idea! Well known, controversial. But alas, she probably wouldn't need the money.) "My contact lens," Miss Hall whined with breathless alarm, "I think it's slipped out."

Is there a more unforgiving circumstance than uncorrected myopia amidst unfamiliar surroundings? The intrepid savior, I scurried over to help.

Miss Hall arched back on the sofa to facilitate my hunt. "I think it's down there," she cooed, indicating an ambiguous zone directly beneath the overhang of her perky knees.

Having discarded my own eyeglasses, I was compelled to grovel in at ground level. Frankly's cash flow squeeze had necessitated certain cutbacks, among them our cleaning service. Fingernail fragments, a dead moth, an insolent strand of green dental floss, a partially munched M&M peanut. Stand back, I wanted to warn Miss Hall, this squalid sight is not for ladies!

A deliciously primal tickle inched across my skin. I was virtually nibbling at her toes, awash in her lilac fragrance, only centimeters from her sensuous thighs. I felt the instantly restorative balm of a steaming mineral springbath.

My office door creaked open. In barged Mona with her customary obtrusiveness, babbling a blue streak about Apple, the accountant, and some new chapter in his infernal paranoia about the Internal Revenue Service.

I froze. It took Mona a moment to discover that I was not at my desk, and an additional moment to locate my supine torso curled before Miss Hall's exquisitely clam legs.

"Christ!" she exclaimed. "That's disgusting!"

Why did I feel caught in an act that was not even close to occurring? I sat bolt upright, slithering on my fanny to distance myself by at least a few respectable inches from Miss Hall's slim ankles. Mona loomed over us, a towering Mother Superior of moral condemnation.

I wriggled up to a kneeling position. "Let me explain."

"Yeah, sure," she scoffed venomously. "Mr. Political Principles."

Miss Hall registered a demure protest. "Please, really. I lost my contact lens and Mr. Frank..."

"Yeah, right. In the old days they dropped their hankies. My, my. Poor helpless thing. Let me tell you something about Danny here; you don't have to go to such lengths. Ask a girl who knows him. Really, honey, you don't have to work so hard." Mona coyly batted her fierce eyes. "Just ask him to take a swing in a hammock with you some time."

"What is that supposed to mean?" That little episode had stirred up some strange, subconscious sensations. Maybe this was the time to get it all out in the open—depending on what "it" was. "What the hell does that mean?" I insisted.

Mona ignored me. "You certainly have a hell of a lot of nerve," she wagged an accusing finger at Miss Hall. "Didn't I read something recently about you and the entire Joint Chiefs of Staff? I mean, can't you confine your cheap hussy ways to your own kind? Or at least pick on someone a little more savvy than Danny here."

With that, she issued a snappy military salute, performed a smart about-face, and stormed out.

I limped back to my desk and slid my glasses back onto my face. Miss Hall looked ashen, but I proceeded to say what had been my intention all along: that it was doomed to be an imperfect match, she and Frankly Speakers, despite my personal fondness for the open manner in which she presented herself.

I searched for some signal that she got my drift, but she responded only with a fussy fluttering of her eyes. "Gosh," she exclaimed, "My lens! It's right here, still on my eyelid."

Shell-shocked and drained, I strummed through my Rolodex, located the desired card, jotted down the number on a scratch pad for her. "Why don't you call Jake Deaver up at Smooth Line in New York," I meekly offered. "He'd probably do better by you than us anyway."

The promotional piece went forth and multiplied. The tour filled in like a dream. Frankly Speakers found itself in that golden position longed for during all the many hours of sublimated muttering over the multitude of indignities and rebukes meted out by a marketplace normally as insensitive as a tree stump to our fragile fate. Suddenly we were, to use the industry terminology, hot.

Projected commissions fattened before our eyes. The office mood tingled with that rich delirium known mainly to cocaine freaks and Wall Street daredevils. We glimpsed, as through a knothole in a fairgrounds fence, the colorful possibilities of dreams come true. Piper talked condo, actually making appointments with brokers. Kenny talked time-share on a year round place at the beach, upgraded his health club membership. Mona seemed positively cheerful.

I overheard a conversation she had with the student lecture chairperson at Miami University in Ohio. The kid had not returned one phone call from her all year, but now he was responding with alacrity to the Zapatú mailing. Over the past year the kid had squandered a sinfully lavish budget on assorted Smooth Line scams like the Defense Department parolee, the alleged KGB seductress, and Gerald Ford. An agent like Mona prays at night for the good Lord to deliver opportunities as ripe for retribution as this.

The kid launched into a little monologue on how he wanted to kick off next fall's series with a blockbuster. He was curious about Zapatú, although he had to confess that he was probably leaning toward the Boy Guru. In Zapatú's favor was the fact that the Latin American Student Association had been lobbying for a special program and this might be a way to appease them. Depending on price.

Mona handled it with the deftness of a toreador. "Excuse me, Chester. I wasn't really listening. Could you run that by me again?"

His name was Chester Mudge, and he proceeded to run it by her again. Mona had the broadcast button on, and the kid's voice sprang out from the phone console in an adenoidal bullfrog crackle. He was working hard to sound mature.

"You're actually considering the Boy Guru?" Mona taunted.

"We need something big, and hot," Chester disclosed. "S'posedly he's been drawing thousands of people. Standing room only's what I hear."

"And from whom do you hear this?"

Chester was nothing if not cagey. "Sources," he replied.

"Fine," Mona assured him. "I recognize the need for a man in your position to maintain confidentiality. Let me pose another question. Did your source tell you what country this was in, where the Boy Guru drew these throngs?"

Chester was noncommittal. "Possibly."

Mona swooped in. "Now without compromising your source, let me ask you: Could it have been a non-English speaking foreign country, perhaps on the other side of the earth?"

Chester was not the ideal student for exploring the Socratic method. "Could be," he allowed.

"One more question, then we'll move on to Zapatú. Did your source give any indication what the hell a pudgy ten-year-old has to talk about to these thousands of attentive listeners? I hope you realize, Chester, that your constituents are red-blooded Americans and just because some weird fat kid can pull the wool over the eyes of a bunch of illiterates living in the dark ages in some mountain kingdom doesn't mean that contemporary college students will fall for it. This source of yours, Chester—is it by any chance an agent?"

The deflation of Chester's puffed-up ego transmitted through the phone console as an audible hiss. But he was nimble. "I'm looking at my fall calendar," he said. "How does October 12 look for Zapatú?"

"Looks fine."

"How much was that?"

"Sixty-five hundred. Plus shared expenses."

"Tell you what, I'm very interested. But a lot of my money is tied up because I've got an offer in on... let's just say a major act. I'm not supposed to mention names at this time. I can't offer you more than forty-five. Inclusive."

"Gosh, that's pretty low. A young man of your capabilities—I'd think you could do somewhat better than that. I don't like to get personal, Chester, but you know you haven't exactly been one of our best customers. You'd be spending that much for the Boy Guru. According to my sources."

"Probably I can go five. Tops."

"Plus expenses?"

"Can I put you on hold for a minute."

While Chester put her on hold, presumably to confer with his advisor or some authorized administrator, I played sideline coach, giving Mona a jubilant thumbs-up, a sock-it-to-em left jab, and vigorous mimed applause. To these encouragements, Mona responded with an exquisitely postured boredom and a hint of disdain.

Chester Mudge was back on the line. "Will he spend time with the media and meet with a class or a seminar?"

"Zapatú is not your run-of-the-mill performer," Mona cautioned in a superior deadpan. "He is coming to America for the express purpose of spreading his message and effecting a new age of social concern. He will do whatever possible—within limits of his travel itinerary—to further this goal. In some ways, I envy you, Chester. You're in store for quite an experience." Mona closed her eyes and sucked a deep breath, like a gymnast preparing for launch. "Plus expenses?"

"October 12, you say, is good?"

I gave Mona an exuberant high five. It really was working. We had the magic. The energy was flowing our way.

She told Chester he'd have the contract by next week. Shaking her head in disblief, she hung up. "It's amazing," she noted, "that he never did ask what the hell Zapatú talks about."

Late one afternoon, I went to the large map of the U.S.A. which spans most of the wall above our noisy, antiquated lummox of a copy machine. Outside in the corridor I could hear a raging argument being conducted in Farsi. So far from home, those cantankerous foreign entrepreneurs, yet so comfortably adapted to the lawless hustle of American enterprise. Many will swim mightily upstream for the chance to spawn in this fertile pond of a country.

On the wall map I traced the points in the tour we were arranging for Zapatú. Twelve dates were already booked. Like many a citified creature, I derive a small vicarious tingle from my regular contacts, by phone and mail, with distant places. It's a sad defeat to see one's life confined to the narrow indoor space of an office, and it's an uplift to break out, even if only in thought. I get pleasure from knowing my life can be affected by snow squalls in Missoula, union strikes in Atlanta, ground fog in central Wisconsin. Over the course of a work week, I might have legitimate cause to receive on-the scene reports about: an invasion of flying cockroaches in southern Florida; dog days of boredom in Hays, Kansas; a triple murder involving a faculty wife in Amherst, Massachusetts; a student protest held in the nude in sunny San Luis Obispo. There is a wonderful consolation in having a surrogate connectedness to the wide world beyond this little dungeon.

Zapatú would start off in Madison, Wisconsin, a hearty, progressive community where he would meet a fine reception, then onto Carleton College near the Twin Cities, out to Manhattan, Kansas, finishing the week in Ames, Iowa. There was a little backtracking built in there, but we'd done worse. The second week was a model of intelligent block-booking, starting at Case Western in Cleveland, down to Miami U in Oxford, Ohio (the other Miami, the other Oxford), proceeding to tiny Rio Grande College (pronounced rye-O), then over to College Park. Much of these stops could be reached by automobile, if Zapatú could learn to navigate gringo highways. A thought occurred to me.

From there we had him moving out west. A night in Tulane, onto Texas Tech, up to Albuquerque. A few more dates were still being sketched in. I wanted him to see the great spectacle of the Rockies, the dramatic California coast, the deadbeat sagebrush cow towns of southern Wyoming. This nation is so vast, and infinitely stimulating. There's so much Zapatú would see and experience. I couldn't help envying him.

Even though it was past six o'clock, the sun came high and bright through our dusty windows, sneaking in with the promise of summer. I lingered at the map, half-hypnotized by the topography of its countless possibilities.

"Planning a trip?" Mona startled me from behind.

I was too tired to make a smart rejoinder. "Just wishing," I sighed.

"Brad and I have been thinking of a camping trip in the Smokies. You're welcome to join us."

Brad was her new beau, a really decent guy who'd visited the office several times without rubbing me the wrong way. It was a sweet offer coming from Mona. All the same, I'd have rather spent a week doing my taxes than go on a trip with the two of them. "Thanks." I told her. "I'll give it some thought."

"Brad thinks you're pretty cool," she continued. "I told him he's wrong, but it's not worth arguing about."

"No, it isn't," I agreed.

"What do you think of Brad?" she asked.

I was still staring at the wall map. A last angle of sunlight was slanting across Marion's meticulous desktop, illuminating the craggy dark blue inlets of coastal Maine. "Brad's pretty cool," I said.

"I don't think it's working out," Mona confided.

I'd never been to coastal Maine. It appealed to me, the idea of idling away sometime on a craggy inlet, whittling and watching the weather patterns.

"We have great sex, but we don't want the same things out of life."

"I'm thinking of spending a few days on tour with Zapatú," I mused. "I'm thinking that would really be a good thing to do." A hollow, lonely feeling had crept up on me despite the recent resuscitation of the business. Like everyone else, I needed something to look forward to.

Mona stood directly behind me with her arms folded like a night club bouncer. Her scowl implied some displeasure with my impromptu plan.

Like a fool, I asked, "Is there something wrong?"

"No," was her answer, but her way of saying it was so unconvincing that it left me brooding over all the things that were, or might be, wrong. At any given moment, that can be a hell of a long list.

Chapter 8

For a fall afternoon, the air was unusually warm and sticky as Mona and I motored up to the Baltimore airport. Summer, the season of languid resuscitation, should have given way to the crisp demands of fall but this unseasonable heat wave was like a ghost of it left behind. At least Zapatú would not immediately feel estranged by the climate.

Killing time on our drive, I asked Mona how things were going with Brad. I maneuvered my still-undetonated Pinto into the center lane. In the event the conversation turned awkward, I could busy myself with rearview mirror imperatives.

"A dying leaf," she murmured sadly. "Beautiful but brittle. And ready to drop."

I checked out the traffic on all sides. "My condolences. I never did get the sense he was the one."

"*The One*? Why do men insist on such confining terms? Brad and I had a very enjoyable summer. Seasons change."

"You weren't hoping it would last?"

"Sure. You always hope that at the start. If you didn't have hope, you wouldn't even bother to start." A cement mixer barreling by on a downhill stretch forced a pause. When the roar had passed, Mona resumed with an altered focus. "Which gets us to your problem, Danny."

Distracted by the highway, I instinctively reacted. "What problem?"

"With women. The reason you're usually alone."

"And that reason is?" I felt like a talk show straight man, helplessly playing along.

"You're afraid to hope."

"And how exactly did you come upon this complex insight?"

She was unfazed by my sarcasm. "With men that's often the problem. They want a woman who's perfect but they don't believe they deserve such a woman so they sulk by themselves and pretend they're alienated from society."

Rearview, I scanned for another cement mixer. A good-sized tractor trailer would do. Finally, I conjectured, "Maybe I haven't met the right one."

"That's what they all believe."

"Well, just maybe in my case it's true."

"What's the difference if it is?"

Inadvertently I had slowed to fifty miles per hour. The groan and whoosh of passing autos, amplified by our open windows, imposed a convenient lull.

"Anyway," I feigned an apology, "I didn't mean to switch the conversation onto myself. We were talking about you and Brad."

Mona extended her arm nearly out the window in order to rearrange the interlocking ceramic loops of her gaudy bracelet." Each person you date teaches you more about your inner needs and desires. Brad taught me about biceps. I used to think I could do without them."

I scratched my chin with exaggerated thoughtfulness. "Isn't that interesting?"

"Yes, and remember Kevin? He showed me what I need in hair—not color, but texture."

I can never tell if she's pulling my leg. If so, her deadpan was extraordinary. Her bald pronouncements made it easy to settle into that gently prodding role of Johnny Carson (or was it Ed McMahon?). "So," I asked, "you're gradually completing your vision of the ideal man?"

"He's medium height," she replied dreamily, without hesitation. "European, possibly Asian, definitely not American unless it's first generation. He has all the money he needs. Don't ask me where it comes from. It's probably best that I don't know. He certainly isn't a workaholic—like some that I know. He knows how to relax and have a good time, although he desperately needs guidance in the finer things of life. Of course he's great in bed. That goes without saying. I probably shouldn't ask where on earth he learned all those little techniques. But after all, he is a man of the world, a student of the human condition. He's knowledgeable about politics and international situations, but he's committed to no single ideology."

"That rules out Zapatú," I interjected. It was a dumb statement, and my only excuse is that perhaps the highway fumes had made me irritable.

"That," Mona added, "and the biceps."

I had anticipated that Zapatú might be detained for questioning. After all, federal immigration officials had a job to do and part of it entailed giving the once-over to Third World political figures whose passionate denunciations of imperialism had been promulgated over network television. What I had not forseen was the massive traffic congestion caused by the apparently simultaneous conclusion of nearly every high school football game in the state of Maryland. Ten miles from the airport, and with plenty of time to spare, our breezy if tense expressway jaunt slowed to a miserable crawl, made more anguishing by the cacophonous honking of festive autos bedecked in the bright colors of homecoming pride and driven by loopy teenagers who seemed quite happy to be going nowhere fast.

Zapatú had been thoroughly briefed, in a memorandum prepared by an attorney for whose advice I'd paid a pretty price, on proper immigration procedures. He had been instructed to provide truthful answers to all questions except those pertaining to his experience with illicit drugs (in which case, advised the attorney in veiled, tortured language, he should lie through his teeth) and his relationship, if any, to any person or group who has advocated subversive activity (to which, in grand Socratic style, he should respond by requesting the precise definition of the term "subversive"). If truly cornered or confounded, he was instructed to plead difficulty with the English language and go mute until legal counsel arrived.

More than fifteen minutes late (presuming his plane had landed on time), Mona and I sprinted from the parking garage to the international terminal. We followed a series of multi-lingual directional signs to the immigration zone, made a frantic scan along the row of numbered customs-check chutes, double checked with an insolent porter to make certain the Taca flight from Tegucigalpa had touched down, felt that tingling infusion of anxiety-driven adrenaline that is almost titillating in this initial stage before it settles in and dominates, traced another series of multi-lingual signs to a bank of glassed-in offices and there we could see Zapatú. He was seated in a straightback chair pulled up to a slate-top desk. All we could see of his inquisitor was the back of his starched white shirt and the ridge of his smooth cheek.

Zapatú looked great. The intervening months had been kind to him. The sallow asceticism I'd observed at his island retreat had given way to a glistening bronze tan. I was happy to see that his hands looked properly aligned and fully recovered from that horrible fall. He still showed a misty myopia around the eyes, but it was the sort of feature which, from a distant seat in a crowded auditorium, would project as soulful sensitivity. Like a ballplayer reporting to spring training, Zapatú had taken good care of himself during the off season. In his richly woven, collarless shirt, he looked swarthy and almost dashing, like a toreador.

I knocked on the glass window. Zapatú's face lit up at seeing me. Mona, for some reason, lagged behind just out of view. The immigration official jerked around to check the commotion but before he could rise I opened the glass door and poked my affable face in. Too much was at stake to stay on the sideline.

With a barely concealed exasperation, the official asked, "Can I help you?" He was much younger than I would have expected, more like a graduate student in police studies. His shaggy haircut could never have passed military review. He sat with the kind of mannered slouch used by cocky adolescents to convey their strange concept of self-assuredness.

Moving my torso irrevocably into the doorway, I extended the determinedly eager glad hand of a congressional candidate on polling day. "Danny Frank," I enthusiastically introduced myself. "Mr. Zapatú's sponsor. I thought I might be able to help."

A hasty calculation began churning behind the young officer's calm but suspicious eyes. He could issue a command for me to leave, which, considering my aggressive bonhomie, might turn into a bit of a hassle. Or he could make his peace with my lurking presence and play it by ear. The choice probably depended on whether this was an obligaatory, boilerplate exam or a more complex and nefarious assignment. The fact is, Zapatú had no criminal record; in his native land he had never been formally charged with a crime. Legally, there ought to have been no impediment to his visitation.

"If there's any way I can help," I crooned, making myself at home by ostentatiously leaning against the doorframe, "I'll be right here. Don't hesitate to ask."

Grumpily the official turned back to Zapatú. I had guessed right. He wasn't about to start a rumble.

"And so, Mr. Zapatú, how long do you intend to stay in this country?"

A devilish glimmer eased into Zapatú's weary eyes. The scintillating performer in him had been insensitively dulled by this mundane process. Who knows how many dreary answers to routine questions he had already provided? But now he had an audience, however small. "I hope to remain," he stated with something close to jubilation, "as long as this great nation will have me."

The young officer busily jotted a note on the printed form fixed to his clipboard. Without looking up, he continued, "And how long do you expect that to be?"

"Sí, sí, always the enigma of time. How do we measure time? Is there any foolproof way to assess these things?"

With an impatient, theatrical rolling of his eyes and furrowing of his sleek brow, the official let it be known that responding to a question with a question, albeit one of philosophical depth, was a dumbass way to expedite this inquiry. "Could you give me an estimate, Mr. Zapatú, for my records? Number of weeks?"

Zapatú gave a jovial nod in my direction. "My agent, Mr. Frank, has informed me that the demand shows no signs of dying out."

"A number, please?"

"Why not five?"

The officer scribbled. "Fine."

"Make that seven," Zapatú amended. "That is the number that has held the most significance in my life. There were seven children in my family. And my father had seven sisters. Seven doting aunts? Can you imagine what effect that has on a young boy? I do not wish it on anyone."

With a vacuous stare, the official tried to demonstrate his utter lack of interest. "Do you have a return airplane ticket in your possession?"

"No."

"But you have sufficient funds to purchase one?"

"Ah, time and money, time and money. Is that all that matters?"

The pen dropped from the young man's hand and we watched it roll off the edge of his clipboard across the slate-top desk, where it came to a stop against Zapatú's serenely folded hands. Zapatú handed it back.

I couldn't contain myself any longer. "Sir," I implored, "Mr. Zapatú is extremely tired. He has been traveling for several days.

Your central office should have all this information by now. I furnished multiple copies of..."

"Quiet," he snapped. The longer this went on, the more the kid would be transformed into a belligerent authority figure. That's another feature of time, one that I hoped Zapatú wouldn't expound on. It can wear down the subtle ridges of character, leaving only the dull, intractable essence.

"...his itemized itinerary," I managed to complete my sentence.

"Shut up," he added.

Matters had taken a sour turn. Off in the immigration corral, a boisterous new shipment of international arrivals were pouring into the designated chutes. Most of them appeared to be American, sporting their vivid sunburns, festooned with trinkets. We would have been better off had it been a planeload of truly troublesome cases, like an Eastern bloc tour group chockful of potential spies, to remind our officious young inquisitor that the goal of efficient processing was not well served by needless detours into pointless trivia while actual security risks flooded our shores. Zapotú had a legitimate visa that I had obtained for him. He had picked it up at the embassy in Belize City. So what if his behavior tended to be cranky and eccentric? Those were precisely the characteristics that had pioneered the New World, even if it was now being administered by a new regime of personality traits.

The officer repressed a snarl while staring hard at Zapatú. Clearly he had the right stuff to rise in the ranks. "Our concern, quite frankly, is not the legality of your visa. We want to make certain that eventually you depart. That is all."

Zapatú stroked his chin as though contemplating a critical move in the rubber match of a chess tournament. I wanted to holler timeout before he uttered something rash. In this age of permanent data storage and instantaneous retrieval, one can't afford to be thoughtless and offhand with government employees who jot down notes.

I cleared my throat. "Then I don't see why..."

Immigration was suddenly militarized. "Out of line," barked the officer.

A *deus ex machina* in contemporary career woman disguise, Mona now moved in from out of nowhere, brushing me aside like I was a piece of furniture. Which was how I felt. The fluorescent lights accentuated the most glorious shades of red in her frizzy hair, and her sudden burst onto the scene had the galvanizing impact of an ambulance arrived.

"Don't worry," she informed everyone with a disarming ingenuousness. "Everything will be fine."

"Who are you?" This was the young officer's first glimpse of her, and he was understandably nonplussed.

She giggled coquettishly and, although I could barely believe my eyes, began sucking on the end of her thumb. I felt dizzy. What the hell was happening?

Mona sauntered closer to the slate desk, situating herself midway between the two men, her back to me. "I'm engaged to marry Mr. Zapatú," she announced with girlish cheer. "I assume that will take care of your worries."

Like a bad actor, the official rolled his eyes around the tiny room for confirmation of his suspicions. He wasn't instantly buying her line.

Mona slid closer to Zapatú and laid a delicate hand fondly on his cheek, her pinky finger grazing his silent lips.

A marital union in fact would definitely obviate immigration's petty concerns (while greatly exacerbating mine). The young official sank back in his chair, quelled by the prospect of a judicious surrender. Like all of us, he had better things to do.

Still, he had one last inquisitional flurry left in him. "Why," he sternly accused, "didn't you tell me this, Mr. Frank?"

I stammered, "Well, the fact is... I mean, in all candor, the real..."

Mona jumped in. "Mr. Frank didn't know until this very minute! I only met Mr. Zapatú a few months ago and," she paused to giggle, shyly averting her eyes, "it's all happened so very suddenly."

My shock and semi-revulsion at the mad brilliance of her performance was considerably sweetened by its devastating success.

The predator's craving had vanished from the young man's countenance; in its place was a placid government functionary quite content to have found an easy means of satisfying his professional obligations.

"Very well," he said, and pulled from the desk's center drawer an ink pad and rubber stamp. Chuckling to himself, he initialled a document, pressed the stamp to its corner, and handed it to Zapatú with the instruction to go to the farthest chute along the corral. Outside our glass window, another refugee, a black man in a Panama hat, awaited his turn at processing.

I wanted to hop into the air and click my heels. (But why advertise my astonishment that we'd pulled off one slick maneuver?) Instead I threw a patriarchal arm awkwardly around my two comrades and we headed off across the linoleum to aisle number eight, Mona, Zapatú, and me—the three musketeers. It was one of those rare and wondrous moments in time when a proud destiny felt almost within reach. And it fazed me hardly at all when they each, with needless ceremony, squirmed out of my grasp.

"Testing 1-2-3-4. Testing."

Madison, Wisconsin, gentle mid-afternoon of early October, U.S.A. The floppy-haired, rail-thin audio-visual technician tapped his forefinger against the stand-up microphone sending a low thump-thump bounding like a mortar explosion toward the far aisles of the empty auditorium. Zapatú and I, hovering at the wing, plugged our ears for protection.

The technician waved his arms like an airport runway flight controller. "Down! Way down," he hollered up to the glass-enclosed projection booth situated atop the balcony. The young man in the booth, a fat boy with horn-rimmed glasses, responded with a thumbs-up signal.

"Testing 1-2." The skinny technician tapped again on the foam-padded mike, then leaped backwards as a shrieking, screeching hacking rasp resounded from all corners. He waved his lanky arms. "Down, damn it!"

The chubster in the booth flashed a big aw-shucks-we'll-get-it-right-yet grin and signaled another jaunty thumbs up.

The technician wasn't buying it. He vaulted offstage, loping with his long stride up the side aisle to the balcony stairs. The next we saw of him he was up in the glass booth, jaw to jaw with his hapless, carefree colleague.

Extracting his fingers from his ears, Zapatú pointed to the microphone, the sole fixture on the barren wood plank stage. "Is it necessary that I use that?"

It hit me how untutored and rough, by sophisticated media standards, he was. True, he had performed some impressively shrewd maneuvers in constructing his reputation and captivating a following. Yet he was now making a drastic leap up to the major league. Suddenly my mind was swimming with doubts, and I was kicking myself for my inattention to potentially vital details. For instance, I still had no idea what he was going to say. We had corresponded over the summer, and I certainly had urged him to draft a speech combining autobiographical vignettes with personal observations about politics, the human struggle, whatever. His return letters were rambling and unspecific, far from reassuring, but I assuaged my concerns by attributing Zapatú's vagueness to a legitimate fear of surveillance. It was not the place of a capitalist gringo booking agent to discount the tenacity of the fascist oppressors.

"Yes, the microphone is necessary," I answered him. "There's going to be more than a thousand people out there tonight, not wanting to miss a word you say."

"I have addressed thousands, many thousands. My voice, it is loud enough."

Zapatú had dressed to accentuate his foreignness, with a navy blue shirt of Indian weave, billowing white drawstring pants, and a blazing orange headband to push back his hair, which had grown quite long. He truly looked exotic, yet I was queasy with apprehension. I should have remained safely back at the office, where all calamities can be buffered by a healthy bureaucratic distance.

Zapatú took a couple of steps toward center stage. "Technology is the tool of the oppressor," he declaimed to the thankfully empty auditorium. "Nature's way is the people's strength."

I followed him onstage. "Save the speech for later," I admonished. "Now, please, look at this from the audience's perspective. They've come all the way out here to see you. The microphone, assuming these dingbats can get it working properly, will allow your voice to reach them louder and more clearly. Not a syllable will be lost. They will have no choice but to listen."

"That's oppressive!"

I was trying to control my rampaging anxiety. Fortunately we were interrupted by the gawky A-V ace, who had descended from the control booth and emerged from backstage, radiating confidence in his accomplishments. He thumped the foam tip of the mike. "Testing 1-2. Can you hear me? Testing."

The amplification was now wondrous. The kid's voice soared forth rich and authoritative. If you ignored his slouchy, dufus demeanor, you'd swear that his was a voice of pure wisdom and noble purpose. He motioned to Zapatú. "How about you trying it?" His words vaulted to the ceiling and echoed back like the prounouncement of a celestial prophet.

With an encouraging nudge from me, Zapatú strutted over. Thrusting out his hand, he grabbed the silver microphone stand like a harpoon. Spreading his legs for optimal balance and mobility, he cocked his head and pushed sullenly forward into the mike. Somewhere along the way he had obviously been exposed to music videos.

I was hoping he might try out the opening of his speech. That would be a very professional thing to do, and it would calm his agent against this surge of worst-case anxiety. I imagined what it would be like later tonight, with the seats and aisles jammed and this fine old auditorium mystically darkened. Many months back Frankly Speakers had but the merest half-glimmer of a marginally feasible idea; tonight it would be a reality. So many ideas pass through one's mind yet so few ever pass outward into the world. I thrilled at the prospect of watching it unfold. I'd feel much better if I knew what he was going to say.

Zapatú tapped the mike with a firm forefinger, in imitation of the skinny technician. "Uno, dos, tres," he whispered. "Testing. All of life, mis amigos, is forever a test."

Following the sound check, Zapatú and I headed across campus to the student union, which was situated on the edge of Lake Mendota. It was a golden warm October afternoon, the kind of surreal surprise visit by timeless July known as Indian summer. Buoyant young women with muscular suntanned calves trounced up a steep hill, going the other way. A professor in a suede sportcoat pedaled by on a balloon-tire three-speed Schwinn relic, his back arched awkwardly straight as if seated at mock attention in one of his own classes. From up the hill an overthrown frisbee sailed past us, spiraling to a stop in the thick lawn. I hustled to it.

A shirtless young man stood at the crest of the hill waving for us to toss it back.

"Allow me," said Zapatú.

I gave him an instant lesson on how to grasp the frisbee with his fingers while cocking his wrist and extending the elbow. Zapatú, however, was absorbed in watching a lithe girl in floppy socks scamper across the lawn.

He snatched the frisbee from my hand, pivoted, and flung a smooth sailing perfect lead pass to the girl, who picked it off the air.

We continued down the hill to the union. "You've already mastered one of the main tests of a university education," I said. "The other is beer. Would you like one?"

Zapatú was still looking back over his shoulder for the girl who'd caught his toss. "This place is wonderful," he gushed. "The grass is so fresh, so green. And the people all look so hopeful and . . . occupied."

My first instinct was to dispute and refine his observations. But I was not accompanying him to act as an issues advisor or script consultant. My job was chaperon and facilitator. So what if I was overqualified? Someone had to do it.

The lake was alive with careering wind-surfers and white-sailed sunfish gliding in the amber light, against an awesome backdrop of oaks and maples brilliantly turned. On the pier, jutting out from the student union terrace, a dozen or more students, bare-skinned within the legal limits, languished in the unseasonably tranquil warmth. Fiberglass patio tables ringed the lakefront, populated by animated clusters of students and an occasional solitary thinker, lost in a book. The atmosphere was as relaxed and convivial as a European seaside resort.

Zapatú spied an empty table situated in the sun, close to the lake. Before dropping into the aluminum chair, he stretched out his arms as if to embrace the entire panorama—the shimmering lake, the meandering boats, the buoyant young students. "The Yankee, he is treacherous," said Zapatú, "but I have to compliment him. At least he's getting something for his money."

I agreed. This was a fine and prosperous country. Yet it troubled me slightly to hear Zapatú dwelling on it. The audience would be looking to him for an altogether different perspective. I slipped into my aluminum seat, just in time to avoid getting nipped by a speeding skateboarder. "What do you say to a beer?" I asked.

"So soon before my big lecture?"

His fastidiousness was reassuring. I was getting myself worked into anxiety for no good reason. "You're right; not a good idea," I concurred. "So are you feeling ready for tonight?

His eyes were tracking the progress of a pair of female joggers coming past the terrace, more breathless from chattering than exertion. "Can there be such a thing as ready?" he finally responded. "Preparedness, you know, carries its disadvantages. It can stifle spontaneity. It puts blinders on the muse."

My worries returned, yet I tried to remain supportive. "Certainly, of course . . . However, a certain amount of structure, an outline to follow, organized notes, that sort of thing, relieves some of the pressure, leaves you freer to improvise. Don't you think?"

The jogging young ladies disappeared up a ramp past the union. Back the opposite way sauntered a bare-chested Apollo, his heavy muscled arm enfolding a lithe black woman nearly melded to his ribcage. They were quite a pair, and even the ostensibly oblivious bookworms alone at their patio tables stole more than one furtive glance.

"Don't you think?" I tried to get Zapatú's attention. Like a high school coach, I couldn't resist feeling that he might not know exactly what is best. "Tell you what. Just as an exercise, why don't you run down the major points you'll be covering tonight? I know that you want to address the aspirations of Third World people and some of the historical roots of imperalism, but," here I obsequiously softened my voice, "how do you intend to start out?"

Zapatú tilted back in his chair. His eyes scanned like searchlights the intriguing sideshows of this pleasant carnival. "Please, Danny, be still," he cautioned. "A thought is forming."

My blood pressure subsided. I put my glasses back on. With a conciliatory lightness, I ogled a co-ed sauntering up the terrace. I could be a good ole boy, so long as I wasn't feeling besieged. "Back to the motel?" I suggested.

The autumn air was wonderful and warm, soothed over by the unmistakeable hint of coming coolness. We hiked back across the plush green lawns of the campus.

I squeezed into a flip-down seat along the right aisle, midway back. Beside me was an elderly couple dressed with academic propriety in wool tweed. The pair perched stiff and unperturbed by the twittering, preening, milling throng clamoring about for the remaining empty seats. A critical goal had been accomplished: the grand old hall was packed to the rafters.

The students were behaving like canaries in mating season,

darting along aisles, singing out to friends high in the balcony, perching ostentatiously on arm rests to capture the eye of someone, anyone. They were at that age when any gathering, even for a lecture on politics, becomes a scintillating chance to circulate, mingle, flaunt and yowl. The elderly couple, emeritus incarnate, managed to stare ahead unflinchingly. Myself, I was fantasizing that I was twenty again, looking forward to an evening where anything, even a new way of looking at the world, was possible.

Zapatú was backstage with Slade Carlstadt, the student activities lecture director. Everything was going smoothly. Our reasons for choosing to start out at Wisconsin appeared justified. The ambiance was intense yet supportive. This was not, thank God, opening night on the Great White Way.

The only one who really seemed edgy was me. I wished the students would behave with more calm and dignity. I feared that this adolescent foolishness might get misinterpreted by Zapatú as disrespect. A squat, loudmouth in a sleeveless sweatshirt a few rows in front of me wouldn't stop rolling his neck around and patting his perfectly hard tummy muscles. I wanted to shriek at him to sit down, face forward, and for godsakes leave himself alone! And that squadron of sorority sisters with shimmering coifs making a beeline for the front row seats (always the last ones to fill)—I cringed to consider that these sweet, blank, dolled-up faces will be at the forefront of Zapatú's field of vision. What if at the dramatic crescendo of his oration (presuming he has one) they pop their gum or start fooling with their wispy bangs? I looked to my elderly neighbors for commiseration, and was disturbed to note that they were absolutely motionless, eyes fixed straight-angle forward, not the slightest tremor in their taut blue lips. That popular newstand tabloid phrase, "Zombie Killers," came to mind.

The crowd burst into a raucous, derisive round of hoots and howls. Slade Carlstadt stepped to the microphone. I really wondered about an audience that could get so stupidly boisterous over nothing. And I worried about Zapatú's sensibilities.

"Testing, testing," Slade said tentatively. "One. Two."

A shout bounded from a middle row, "Three. Next is three, then comes four. You can do it, Slade."

Slade cupped his hand across his brow, forming a visor to shield the glaring spotlight. He leaned forward and peered out, searching the house for his antagonist. No one confessed.

Now Zapatú, mistaking this sequence of events for his cue, strutted onstage. Slade gawked at Zapatú with bug-eyed astonishment.

Miraculously, Slade had the presence of mind, learned unconsciously through years of exposure to the slick mannerisms of television variety show hosts, to announce instinctively, "I'm proud to welcome tonight's attraction, Zapatú!" And with a gracious sweep of his arm, he simultaneously beckoned Zapatú to the microphone and bid the crowd to respond with a proper reception.

It was an amazing and impressive recovery. My worst fear was that Slade might attempt to wave Zapatú back to the wing, precipitating an ugly tussle. I released my white knuckle grip on the armrest and relaxed the taut coil of my thigh muscles. I might have been making involuntary preparations to do something rash. Had the zombies noticed? From the corner of my vision I glanced at them, but they remained perched in motionless, death-like dignity.

Zapatú had dressed himself to accommodate every stereotype of Latin America. He wore his thin cotton drawstring pants, a collarless blouse of dark Indian weave, and a flaming red serape slanted across his torso which he certainly would soon discard—it was far too warm for the occasion—using a toreador's majestic swipe. On his feet he wore embroidered gaucho boots with heels that added a full inch to his height. All that was missing was the silver machete strapped to his hip.

Zapatú spoke. "A funny thing happened to me on my way to your charming campus today. I caught a taxi in from the airport and just as we were steering onto the highway, the cab driver turns around and says . . ."

Is he out of his mind? We had been met at the airport by Slade and his girlfriend, driving her dented Toyota with a plastic

Wisconsin badger stuck to the dashboard. We had asked about it and Slade related the whole dumb story behind the school's mascot.

"So the cab driver says to me, 'Aren't you on TV? Come on, help me out, what's the name of the show?' Now you can imagine my predicament. I'm in the back seat of this taxi. I've been in Wisconsin for all of five minutes. I've been in the United States for less than forty-eight hours. In recent months I have been in exile in a small undeveloped country in a place that has no electricity, much less commercial television. I want to be friendly and polite with this driver, but I am in no position to even pretend to answer his questions."

Zapatú bent down to pull a cup of ice water from the podium shelf. People seemed to be listening. "The driver then did a surprising thing. He pulled to the side of the road—we were on the ramp entering the highway—and he says to me that he will not proceed any further until I disclose who I am. He is convinced I am a television personality. He is a gruff-looking man, with a big round red face and patches of whisker sticking out from all the little folds where his razor missed. When we Latin Americans think of the United States, this is the belligerent, unhappy face we imagine. I think to myself, maybe this is the man from the secret police. My comrades had warned me that I would meet opposition. I am feeling the pressure. I don't know how to answer him. I cannot even think of a lie.

" 'Thursday afternoons,' he accuses me. 'On the cable channel. Around two o'clock, two-thirty. You're *Geraldo*, aren't you? You look a little different in person. I thought you'd be taller,' he says. 'That show you did last week about ladies whose lives are ruined 'cause they got big jugs—man, that was great.'

"His face was very red and he sprayed saliva when he talked. I want to say yes, I am this man Geraldo. But I smell a trap. I'm thinking maybe I will jump out the door, but he has my bag in the trunk, and I don't even know if it is legal to do that. I tell him my name is Zapatú, and I have never been on television. The taxi driver lifts his thumb and forefinger up to his eyes, and forms a little square window. Then he squints through it, staring at me like I was a zoo animal. 'I know, you're the weather guy!' he shouts. 'Not the bald guy, Willard, but the nice-looking one. Geez, you look different in person, shorter.' "

After another gulp of ice water, Zapatú continued. "Now bear in mind that this man is the first Yankee I've really met, outside of my agent, who is also a little strange and intense. I am wondering if I have walked into the valley of madness. Weather man? Geraldo? This driver is insane, but I am stuck with him. I plead with him, can't we just go on to the university? I try to appease him. 'Yes, that is me, the weather guy,' I tell him. 'The forecast is chile today, hot tamale.'

"My little joke does not have a positive effect. He is looking angry. His face is more red and his breath comes out in frightening little panting noises. 'Don't fool me,' he snarls. 'You're no goddamn weather guy. Now I know where I seen you. Aren't you the guy who used to be a woman?' "

Zapatú stepped back from the microphone to give the audience ample time to chortle and exchange knowing mirthful winks. Like a seasoned comic, he tossed in a few mimed gestures, screwing up his mouth in puzzlement, making a fey sweep of his tresses as if to test out the cabbie's newest hypothesis. Then he stepped back to the podium. The laughter quieted. He took a langorous sip of water while measuring the house. Zapatú had achieved that consummate performer's magic: we were waiting, hungry to learn what came next.

"A powerful idea came to me. If I am to be stuck with this maniac, I will tell him the truth. I will tell him why it is that I am here. Therefore the truth, ladies and gentlemen, is the only story I have to tell. I was born in a small industrial town in the foothills of the great mountains that climb into the heavy clouds and beyond . . ."

And his tale flowed forth like a babbling stream at last frothing free from a logjam. We in the audience had been collectively transformed into that cabbie, twisted around in the front seat to face

Zapatú as he now recounted the first time, as a boy of ten, that he encountered the brute injustice to which people are subjected for the crime of being born poor. The victim was a teenaged girl picking up vegetables for her family at the afternoon farmer's market. When the shopkeeper humiliated her for coming up a few centavos short, little Zapatú, or Zeze as he was then known, could do nothing but cuss and clench his fist and promise himself never to ignore that which he just learned. We are always witnessing situations, he told the cabbie (and us), that can alter our life's path if we have the courage to allow it.

He moved on to his university years, an episode of particular fascination to this audience. One day especially stood out. It was the first large political rally he attended. Passion was in the wind, and it was that afternoon when he first met the infamous raven-haired beauty, about whom there has been great speculation. That's all he said about her: there has been great speculation.

Zapatú's format appeared to combine vivid depictions of special incidents from various stages in his development with the truisms he drew from these experiences. There was an implicit recommendation that we heed the same lessons. He pounded his fist on the podium, and squinting just beneath the blinding beam of the spotlight, he drilled us with an intense stare. Much of what he said we'd heard before, but the fact that he was saying it while we patiently listened was what made it resound.

He stressed that it was important, in fact essential, to know oneself. He said that nothing of true value was achieved except through hard work and sacrifice. He urged us to resist the professional and cultural pressures to stick our heads in the sand, and to be sensitive to the great groundswell call for societal transformation. He related the famous observation by Mao Tse-Tung (I'd heard the same anecdote attributed to figures as disparate as Gandhi and Lyndon Johnson), in response to a laborer's complaint that the small seed he was toiling to plant wouldn't be large enough to bear fruit for at least ten years. "That is all the more reason to begin right now," replied Mao (and, Gandhi, and Johnson, or maybeit was Nixon). The future belongs to those who strive to make it their own, Zapatú emphasized, and we are fools to wait for an opportunity more propitious than now. He told the story of the legendary May Day rally, the vicious crackdown, the fiery confrontation, his thrilling escape and his lonely period of exile. Mold and create your own life like you would a story or a piece of sculpture, he implored. A person is great or diminished according to the integrity of their aspirations. Be all that you can be. Go for it. Not next year, not next month. Now!

"And do you know what the cab driver said?" Zapatú asked us.

Of couse we had no idea. Most of us had completely forgotten about the taxi.

"The cabbie burst into a triumphant smile and said, 'That's where I seen ya! Doing commercials!'"

First the crowd gushed with laughter, then as Zapatú stepped away from the podium and it became apparent that his speech was over, they began boisterously applauding, howling in praise, finally arising en masse for a full two minutes of high-volume standing ovation.

When the crowd calmed, Slade Carlstadt scampered onstage to announce that Zapatú would now answer questions from the floor. To my utter amazement, the elderly gentleman beside me lifted his frail tweed arm, and was called upon by Slade. "What I've been wanting to know," the old gent asked in a tremulous alto, "is whatever happened to the raven-haired beauty?"

Zapatú hesitated, and I thought I saw a tear forming at the corner of his eye. He certainly made a rather obvious motion to wipe one away. With difficulty, he cleared the welling lump from his throat. "A very sad story," he confided. "You do not want to know."

Then Zapatú looked forlornly out across the crowd for another question.

We were back at the Holiday Inn by 11:00 p.m. No reception had been planned for Zapatú. From my point of view that was just as well; it was going to be an arduous tour and there was no need to launch the first night with a boozy celebration. Zapatú, however, seemed genuinely crestfallen when I informed him backstage, as the exuberant crowd was filing out, that he'd done a wonderful job but there was nothing more to do. Like a lot of performers, he was all wired up and ready for action.

"Now what?" he had asked me enthusiastically.

"Nothing to do but go back home."

"Home?"

Home was the Holiday Inn. Our contract with the colleges stipulated Holiday Inns whenever logistically possible. There was a tranquilizing sameness to them that I knew would, over time, cushion Zapatú's feelings of dislocation. The light switch is always within arm's reach of the pillows. The bathroom is always located a predictable distance and direction from the big twin bed. The crisp cleanness and antiseptic air carry no hint of prior occupants or events. Let those troubadors of alienation flail away in fevered quest for that quintessential metaphor for our national soullessness, but you can't beat the American motel for reliability. In the frenzied world of one night stands, bland can be beautiful.

Slade and his girlfriend drove us back to the motel in the dented red Toyota. As we were bidding goodbye in the blinking green and gold glow of the neon sign, Zapatú asked Slade's girlfriend about the plastic badger on the dashboard. Since we'd already heard the dumb story, I wondered what he was doing. Then it struck me that he was stalling for time. I think he actually believed that Slade's girl might come in with him.

Yanking Zapatú playfully by the collar, I told everyone that we had a long day ahead tomorrow. Time to go, I announced.

"Why did you break it off?" Zapatú bitched as we entered the garishly lit lobby, with the green and gold semi-circular couches. "She was starting to warm up."

"She's not your type," I chided. "Besides, she looked good with Slade." He wasn't really angry.

"Tomorrow night . . . maybe I'll get lucky?"

"Tomorrows are what luck is all about."

At the dark edge of the lobby, where the fluorescent supermarket glow gave way to a hideous purple blacklight, a double frosted glass door swung open, emitting a throbbing disco soundtrack and a portly middle-aged couple toppling forward arm in arm. In their polyester leisure suits, it was hard to discern which was the male, which the female.

"I am permitted to go in there?" Zapatú asked.

I could have lied. "Sure," I said. "I'm going back to my room. Don't stay late. Be a good boy," I called after him.

We'd taken adjoining rooms, G-14 and G-16, each with a view of the parking lot. As I made my way down the corridor, I passed a young girl and her guy, with an eventful night clearly ahead, drunkenly fumbling to get their key in the door. I considered offering to help, but eventually they'd get it. All I did was wish them good luck, and moved on.

Entering my room I hit the wall switch, and both the bedpost and vestibule lamps popped on. I pounced onto the bed, and extended my weary limbs across the green velveteen cover spread. A fair-sized spider dangled from the ceiling. I reached for the phone, perched on the nightstand, read the long distance dialing instruction off the laminated pull-out card, and dialed up Mona. I don't know why. Two, three rings. I could have hung up, but I didn't.

Her voice was weak and groggy when she answered, and I realized it was an hour later there. I had awakened her.

"Zapatú did a great job," I told her. "The place was packed. We're off and running."

"That's very nice," she whispered.

"You okay?" I asked.

"Just a little down. My life is wasting away."

I had been geared for a more upbeat chat. Why exactly did I call her anyway? "Listen, you're doing just fine in your life." I was again playing the dutiful coach and counselor. "Don't be so hard on yourself."

"I'm almost thirty."

"You're twenty-eight."

"I don't even know what I'm doing."

"Who does? Really, who but the fanatics?"

"You do, Danny."

"This is knowing what I want to do?" I gestured, although she couldn't see me, at the mammoth color TV on its swivel pedestal, the pleated gold vinyl curtains, the spider dangling over my nose, the view of the parking lot. "How's the office?"

"Fine." Her monotone was pathetic.

"Busy?"

"Not really."

"Any bookings?"

"I'm not sure. I think so."

She sounded so miserably apathetic and lifeless, I wanted to help her out, but I was so far away. "Everything goes in cycles," I reassured her. "Tomorrow might be spectacular."

"Doubtful."

"Things always change."

"Yeah? How?"

I spoke without thinking. "You could come out and join us for a day or two."

"The company can't afford it."

Out in the parking lot a hot-rodder was gunning his souped-up engine. She had a point. We were far away.

"Do you really think it would be a good idea? For me to come out there?"

I could hardly say no. "We do have that date coming up in Ohio. The one you booked with that kid Lester."

"Chester." Now she was awake. "My god, that's only next week! I've got a million things to do before then. Someone's going to have to take care of my cat. I'm probably going to have to buy an outfit. I don't own a thing that would be right. Why is everything always done at the last minute?"

For a fleeting instant I actually thought I knew the reason, but I didn't disclose it.

Chapter 9

Habits of hinterland touring were being formed: a final check of our disheveled motel rooms (Zapatú was getting the hang of leaving the place trashed); pile into a breakfast booth by the window in the motel dining room (coffee and eggs served with customary blandness); tease the waitress while soliciting directions on the best route out to the interstate; grab the local paper (usually yesterday's) and peruse for whatever news of national or international significance found its way in among the crop prices and crime reports; then hit the road, Jack.

Reading the paper at breakfast today, we stumbled across a one-paragraph item mentioning a civil disturbance back in Zapatú's homeland that touched off a two-day work stoppage by the transporation union. The account, which reported that several protesters had been brutally beaten, was the sort of arcane foreign horror story one glides by all the time in the great morass of daily news.

"What's that about?" I asked him. "Any idea?"

Zapatú had rarely referred to the political turmoil that had made him famous, other than in his lectures and his compulsory replies to pointed questions afterward. I assumed it was a topic too troubling and painful for him to discuss glibly.

Predictably, he shrugged off my inquiry about the news item. "Is so far away," he sighed, reverting to a broken English. "Is another life, very far."

I really hungered to know more about Zapatú's former life and his feelings of estrangement. I didn't want to appear nosy, yet I was someone in whom he ought to confide. Was the struggle still smouldering in his homeland? Was he still expected to play a role? His recalcitrance was becoming unnerving. Agents get skittish, dependent as we are on the whims of the egocentric personalities we represent. Zapatú was an amazingly quick learner of gringo ways. He'd already mastered the fine points of ordering combination platters at roadside truckstops. He had a knack for finding the best FM stations on the dial. He'd even applied for a Visa Card and hoped to have it issued within a week. In sum, he was evincing almost too much enjoyment of the capitalist culture. His credibility as a firebrand and crusader seemed fragile.

I pulled the rented Buick onto the rolling interstate for the drive to Ames, Iowa. The fall air was still warm, and the automatic windows were cracked, letting the wind sluice through.

It was a glorious morning to be breezing along, cruising through the sweet, pungent smells of surrounding fields all a-glisten with the cool morning dew. A low pillow of fog hovered in the hollow of a harvested cornfield by a cattle pond. The morning sun streamed in golden vectors through a plateau thicket of colorful birch and maple—a dappled new day driving across midwest farmland.

I was seized by my habitual urge to verbalize my dumb appreciation of nature's grandeur. "The trees turning all different colors—it's quite beautiful, don't you think? Autumn is an amazing phenomenon."

"Is an illusion," Zapatú harumphed.

The roar of a passing tractor-trailor diesel allowed me to pretend I hadn't caught his words. I had merely succumbed to an urge; it's not like I thought it was such a terrific insight.

"Is an illusion," he insisted. "Change of seasons, change in weather—they are opiates of the people."

My observation had been made in a spirit that was a tad less ideological. I wasn't about to argue. "Fine," I said.

Zapatú persisted. "Yes, it is the illusion of big exciting environmental changes that keeps people in their place. It is a form of religion. In your country I see the way people fall silent in front of the television when the man with the toupee predicts the future weather. It is just like church. Everyone still accepts the idea that their fate descends from the stratosphere. They wait for the miracle of the future to be announced by satellite radar, whatever that is."

I glanced to the rearview mirror where a convoy of Winnebagos was pulling out of a rest stop. Zapatú had soared to a rather thoughtful level for so early in the morning, yet it was good to see him groping at ideas, even if I might disagree with them. As long as he clung to his provocative radicalism, the tour could withstand a measure of his cultural acclimatization. "Very interesting," I nodded.

"The only change that truly revolutionizes," he announced, as if I represented but the front row of a large auditorium, "is sexual love."

I assumed that he was trying to goad me. "No fooling?"

"Yes, Danny, I have given this matter great thought. Man is but another dumb animal along the chain of being. The continuation of life is all that we can hope to accomplish. Lust is our most direct communication with the gods. An erection may well represent our best guess about a better world."

I changed lanes to pass a big silver Greyhound bus. We swooped by an endless meadow and onto a viaduct crossing a sylvan creek. Even at 60 m.p.h. it was possible to glimpse the stream's murky, meandering flow beneath a veil of drooping willows on a shadowed grassy bank where an old man sat fishing off a shabby dock. We both were struck by it, this fleeting highway view of a tranquility so resplendent that our hearts fluttered. There is in this life the potential for a peace that, however evanescent, runs deep and forever. We all have glimpsed it.

For several minutes we fell silent. We were teenagers free and whistling on the breeze, riding the highway.

"Mona?" Zapatú relished elongating the syllables of her name. "She is your woman?"

"Not at all. She is simply a colleague."

"Colleague? I do not know that word."

"A co-worker. What you would call a comrade."

"Comrade means fighter for the same cause, with the same passion. You and Mona share a cause?"

"We work to make the business succeed. We work extremely hard, if you care to know the truth."

"And the success, as you say, of your business is what you struggle for? Profit is your cause?"

I had the feeling I had been over this turf with him before. I have my own set of misgivings about the capitalist system, but I didn't appreciate his snide insinuations. "Weren't you just lecturing me on the pointlessness of everything?"

"Everything except sexual love, yes. You and she seem to have many things in common. And," he stretched out his hands and wrung them lasciviously, "she has a nice shape."

"We're working smoothly. Why upset the apple cart?"

"Tell me again where the apple cart is going. And why?"

I rechecked the rearview mirror. Nothing coming up, no excuse to veer.

"You have someone else?" Zapatú said.

With several hours of driving ahead, there was not much point in protesting invasion of privacy. It's an unwritten rule of the road that if you're hurtling forward, locked in the same compact space with someone, you might as well be forthcoming. The highway is a mythic temple; shared secrets are the appropriate form of reverence.

So I confessed that I had no steady girl. I considered this to be wholly a function of circumstance. I professed to an at times demonic desire for female flesh, plus a heartfelt need for a bonded mate. I certainly had encountered numerous women who were ostensibly suitable but, like those ticky-tacky dime store games where you try to tilt the tiny metal ball into the perfectly aligned cardboard holes, even those relationships that appeared to fit were fragile, jarred loose by the slightest bump in the road.

I told Zapatú the little episode about encountering a former college fling at The Grotto one night, and how I didn't even recognize her until she so matter-of-factly pointed out that if I was hustling to get to first base I should pause to consider that I'd already been there with her. I told him how I went home with her to her apartment, giddy with expectations, but soon discovered there is a statute of limitations on the amount of carefree pleasure that can be shared between two people. It was a sorry little scene and I believed it to be symptomatic of a deeper issue in the life I was leading. I omitted a few details, but Zapatú didn't need to know everything.

"Jesus! You're so serious," Zapatú scolded.

It depressed me to think that he might be right.

"Women," Zapatú continued, "want a man who cares more about life in the broad world than he cares about her. They don't trust anything else. Ideally, yes, maybe. But as a practical matter, women are overjoyed to settle for a man who keeps himself alive by whatever means. A real man draws passion from adventures, from his work, from the world. Women know with a deep intuition that a man not immersed in the larger world is a man who someday will lose interest in them. He will become a poet with no themes, and soon he will be playing with himself."

All wise words, although I wasn't sure how applicable they were to my situation. Our rental car barreled along, many hours to go. I checked the rearview. Nothing approaching.

"Yes, this Mona just may be the woman for you," he said, bouncing forward in his seat. "You are too tense to notice. Relax. Meditate. Deep breathing. Slow down. Loosen up. Maybe visit a prostitute and try to conjure images of what it would be like with her. A dress rehearsal. Find a whore with her shape and try it out."

His words were so eloquent, his advice so ridiculous. "You are a man of many insights," I played along. "Maybe when I get back home."

"Why wait? Do it tonight."

"There's a lecture tonight."

"Then do it after the lecture. These college towns must have girls for hire. Mark my words, Danny. I think this Mona is the one."

"She is an extremely difficult, even disagreeable person."

"What do you want, a lapdog"?

"She harbors great animosity towards men."

"We are not God's most likeable creatures."

"I usually like them with darker skin."

Zapatú slumped back with exasperation. "Close your eyes and pretend."

Men at Work. The highway narrowed from six lanes to two, and became an obstacle course of blinking arrows and iridescent orange traffic cones. Billowing gray smoke, thickened with the smell of hot tar, rose steaming from an ugly metal vat that occupied the median strip.

We were bumper-to-bumper into a bottleneck. I was able to feign total preoccupation with the congested traffic. "There is a chance she might fly out to meet us in Ohio," I casually mentioned.

Zapatú grinned. "That was to be my next suggestion."

We arrived at the Holiday Inn on the edge of Ames a little after 4:00 p.m. It had been a very long drive. We were tired, and had probably spent a little too much time cooped up together. I had begun to doubt the integrity of Zapatú's vision; he had come to question the sincerity of his agent.

We were checked in at the registration desk by a stooped old woman with bluish hair swept fashionably to the side of her face. It's always the same at college town motels: doddering senior citizens dozing on the day shift; negligent adolescent employees prancing around at night.

"Reservation under the name Frankly Speakers," I announced with aplomb.

"Oh, wait." The old woman burrowed beneath the counter and emerged with a folded slip of motel stationery, which she handed over. "A message for you."

All it said was to call the office.

Across the lobby, beneath a makeshift green and gold plywood canopy, were several pay phones. A dim intuition told me not to leave Zapatú alone with the clerk. Like a parent with a restless child, firm hand on elbow, I escorted him to the courtesy sofa and sat him down right by the magazine pile. My call, I assured him, would take but a minute.

Marion answered, kindly accepting the reverse charges.

It was good to hear her voice. "How's tricks?" I asked.

"Please hold."

Phone cocked to my ear, I stood nervously jingling the change in my pocket while watching Zapatú leaf with furious disinterest through a dog-eared issue of *Field & Stream*. He appeared unsettled. Something was bothering him.

It was Kenny who finally picked up. "Hey, Danny," he gushed. "How's life out on the vast endless tumbleweed prairie?"

Kenny is the sort of myopic easterner who knows nothing about the territory west of the Catskills, unless you count California. He was avid to hear tales of wagon trains and magical tornadoes.

"I got a message to call," I brusquely stated. "What's up?"

"Oh, that must have been Mona," he chirped. "She's out at her hair appointment now. Probably she was just calling about that nonsense with Smooth Line."

"What?" I stiffened.

"Gosh, you haven't heard?"

"About what!"

"Well the last couple of days we've been getting this really strange—almost bizarre, I would say—response when we're pitching Zapatú. Everyone—not just Mona, who sometimes can get a trifle paranoid, as you might recall—got a whiff of it. Me too. Nothing concrete. It was just... just weird, different, if you know what I mean."

I could barely stand still. "Kenny," I snapped, "get to the point."

"Well there's a rumor making the rounds."

"Yes?"

"And we think Smooth Line's behind it. Keep in mind, we're only receiving the merest little intimations from the campuses we deal with. This morning we had an informal staff meeting and it was kind of exciting how we were able to piece it together. Not enough, mind you, to come right out and formally accuse them. I wouldn't say we could go to court with it, but if you ask me it sure looks like their handiwork."

"Kenny!" My shriek startled Zapatú into perking up. Now I had to deal with the frazzling burn of his attention. Why couldn't the motel stock some girlie magazines to captivate him? I softened my voice. "Please tell me, succinctly because I'm at a public phone, what's going on."

"Some of the schools think Zapatú might be a counter-revolutionary double agent selling out the hopes and aspirations of the valiant freedom fighters. That's pretty much the verbatim phrase we've been hearing."

"That's crap!"

"You're telling me. But hey..."

"There's not one shred of evidence!"

"No, of course not," Kenny reasoned. "They do it by innuendo."

"Even with innuendo you need evidence."

"Since when?"

He had a point. "Well, what's our strategy? What have you guys been saying in response?"

"We discussed that this morning, and decided not to overreact. You know, lay back and let the truth come out."

Suddenly, Zapatú hovered right beside me, drawn by the petty intrigue of seeing me squirm. I certainly didn't want him involved.

"Good work, very good work," I congratulated Kenny with phony chief-executive pep. "Sounds fine. Keep up the good work. Say 'hi' to the team. Hasta luego."

"A problem?" Zapatú asked as soon as I hung up.

"Naw. The team just gets lonesome to hear my voice."

We tromped back to the registration desk. With a perfunctory detachment, the old woman slid the registration form across the gold formica counter, and pretended to go about her business sorting a pile of plastic keys into their respective mail slots. However, she kept peeking at us. It was a slightly irksome trait, but one I could easily overlook: if motel clerks are denied the privilege to peep and be nosy, what vocational pleasures are left to them?

Zapatú was not so generous. "Señora," he snapped, flaunting his Latino accent. "Is something wrong?"

She jerked around, dangling a big green plastic key ring in her arthritic hand. She appeared greatly alarmed at being flushed out. One could imagine her having spent a busy career intimidating legions of sneaky students with her withering furtiveness.

"You have question for Zapatú?" His volume control was still set for auditorium range, and it bellowed ludicrously across the registration desk. We both were rumpled and oily from car travel. He cackled, a trifle demonically. "Do I look like someone from your gringo television?"

I tugged on his arm to get him to shut up. But it was too late. The old woman brightened, and pushed her glasses up on her nose for a better look.

"I give you a hint," Zapatú chuckled. "Thursday evenings. Hah. Prime time."

She squinted at him in order to achieve the narrowed, circumscribed, boxed perspective of the television screen while mindlessly chewing on the plastic key ring like a game show contestant pondering the correct answer.

I didn't like where this was going. The Iowa State lecture committee was meeting us for dinner at six. No stimulation was needed before then. "We'd prefer two rooms near each other," I said, getting back to business. "Do you have anything with a view of the parking lot?"

"I've had a number of celebrities here over the years," she noted with alacrity, as though we had asked. "We had an astronaut, not the one who walked on the moon but the one who stayed in the space capsule while that was happening. Then of course we had President Ford—not before he was President, mind you, but after. Every motel in the state of Iowa gets them on their way up, but how many get them afterward, or on the way down? Oh yes, just a few weeks ago we had news reporters and camera people all around on account of this fat little Indian boy who was visiting the university. They wouldn't let him sign in by himself, so I never got his signature, like I did the others."

"The Boy Guru was here?"

She was delighted for the small encouragement of my inquiry. "I can't tell you about the guru part," she chortled, dropping onto her swivel chair. "Being in this business you do learn a few things about people's personal habits. I probably shouldn't be telling you this."

"Scout's honor," I declared. "It won't leave this room."

"As I say, I can't tell you much about the guru part. The newspaper said the audience at the university was mesmerized. Stranger things have happened. All I know is that there were some very odd goings-on around here. Very odd indeed."

"Yes?"

"Well, they say he's only ten years old. But he had women in his room, mature women. And I have cause to believe he was doing a man's business with them!"

"No! That little phony. According to his promotional literature, the kid's celibate."

"Then it's a new definition of the term." she crowed.

Zapatú knew nothing of our cutthroat rivalry with the hucksters from Smooth Line. He viewed the Boy Guru simply as another traveling lecturer who, apparently, was getting some action. He was drifting into an ugly snit. "Ay! What a nation of imbeciles!" he snorted.

The old desk clerk pointed a quivering, crooked finger at him. "Now I know who you are! It's not Thursdays, it's..."

"Fool!" Zapatú bellowed. "I am nobody. You people are so empty that you get excited over nobody. Hah."

I thought he was being a little tough on the old girl. Contempt for the general public is never a viable marketing strategy.

"Stupid gringos," he persisted. "Deep in the jungles there are people who've never experienced electricity, and they've got more good sense. Anyone can make a fool of you. All you have to do is try."

I grabbed him around the waist. "Cool it, come on. Let's go for a walk."

He pulled away. "I'm no caged animal. It is you gringos who are in the zoo. Me, I am as free as any man has ever been." To prove his point, Zapatú helicoptered his arms about like a rambunctious orangutan.

The old woman had backed away from the counter and was eyeing the telephone on her desk. I could almost hear her mind groping for the exact digits of the police emergency number.

Throwing a firm arm around Zapatú, I used my most unctuous voice to reassure her that, "He'll be okay." I dug my fingers hard into his ribcage, letting him know that under severe stress I was also capable of demonic behavior. "He'll be an excellent and gracious guest. Won't you, Zapatú?"

She kept her eyes focused on the phone, but made no move. I kept my fingers stabbed in his ribs.

"Two rooms together?" I asked.

She fumbled hurriedly through her pile of cumbersome key rings, and slid two across the desk.

B-10 and B-12. With my free hand I scooped them up and steered tonight's distinguished speaker along a soothingly homogenized vanilla corridor. Shopping music tinkled down from the ceiling.

The stale air carried the scent of pine trees deep in the northern woods. A whiff of storm came off the horizon.

Iowa State was also a date booked by Mona, and the first question as we assembled for dinner at the Villa Italia, just off the highway, was what she was really like.

"She just sounds so understanding and, you know, smart," gushed Yvonne Williams, the lectures chairperson. "Once I told her something about me and my boyfriend, and wow!, she knew just the right thing to do."

There were five of us gathered at a circular table in a semi-private alcove ornamented by protruding busts of Roman heroes. Joining myself, Zapatú, and Yvonne, a freckle-faced black, was Dr. Wayne Terwilliger, chair of the Political Science Department and an authority on repressive Third World democracies, and Skip Yablonski, the director of student activities.

As Yvonne's comment fairly begged for follow-up, and since stony silences at social dinners give me indigestion, I felt justified in asking, "What advice, if you don't mind, did Mona give you?"

Yvonne scrunched up her freckled pug nose, and giggled demurely into her linen napkin. "Basically—it's sort of a long story—basically she told me to dump him. But first make him suffer."

"Excellent advice," I agreed.

The table, unlike the cluttered walls, was covered simply with a red-and-white checked cloth. These three representatives of the university community had little in common, except shared responsibility for the lectures program. Zapatú was their focus, and they were keenly aware that he had not spoken.

Each moment of his dead silence expanded many fold beyond its minor magnitude. There was a limit to how long each of us could pretend fascination with the Roman busts, the streams of crepe paper dangling from the ceiling, the map of Italy on the sugar packets. These lecture committee dinners always involve a delicate diplomacy: everyone wants the distinguished visitor to be comfortable, to enjoy the town and think fondly of its appointed ambassadors; on the other hand, the hosts subtly pressure the visitor, in order to extract some pithy disclosure or memorable intimacy, even if it's only watching him deal with some mundane mishap, like an accidental dribbling of spaghetti sauce on his tie.

Skip asked Zapatú about the motel accommodations.

"Bueno," Zapatú replied.

That did it for Skip. It had taken him many minutes to develop that question, and it was a serious blow getting shot down. He was the sort of affable fraternity boy who'd never left dear alma mater, scene of his greatest glories. Talk to him about sports, girls, weather, food, beer, or motel accommodations and old Skip would be right there for as long as you wanted. Shoot him down on any of these topics—well, you might as well be ripping his heart out.

Professor Terwilliger attempted to step into the void. That, in fact, was why he had been asked along. Or asked to come along, depending on whose account you listened to. He cleared his throat, and zeroed in on Zapatú. "I assume you read where the transportation workers in your homeland are on strike. Is this the start of a new offensive?"

Zapatú did not even bother to answer. His eyes were downcast, blank, with no expression. We were all starting to squirm, not just me. Where the hell was the waitress?

Professor Terwilliger cleared his throat again. "The syndicated columnist Barclay Dilsworth has called you a Fidel figure for the modern Latin American youth movement. Is there any accuracy in that assessment?"

Zapatú shrugged, but did it with a gracious smile. At least there was no hint of reproach. I wished I were back at the office. Or better yet, The Grotto.

The waitress finally arrived with laminated menus as large as pep rally placards. Dressed in a brief black skirt and a puffed white blouse that looked more Alpine than Italian, she stood primly before us and presented a dutiful recitation of today's specials. As she struggled to squeeze her midwest twang around each polysyllabic Italian delicacy, I pondered how to get through this meal with no further agony. It was clear that Zapatú was hereby exercising his star's prerogative to hibernate if he so pleased. It was up to me to start yapping.

Breathlessly, the waitress concluded by saying she'd be back in a few minutes to take our orders. I almost begged her to stay, maybe recite today's specials again, or tell us a story, or yodel. We sat in silence, studying our vast menus. At least there was a lot to read, even if each entree did come out tasting like tomato sauce in the end. A vibraphone version of "O Solo Mio" leaked down from the ceiling sound system. The professor looked to be gearing up to deliver another essay question.

I jumped in. "So tell me about Mahara Jo, the Boy Guru. I understand he lectured here recently."

The professor frowned. "If you call that a lecture."

"We had a real fine turnout," offered Skip. He was attempting a comeback, self-consciously fingering his wispy blond moustache. "I thought he was a nice little fella."

"Nice little fellas," sniffed the professor, "are something we have on every schoolyard in the state. We don't pay them thousands of dollars to preach homilies."

Skip ducked back behind his menu. He was now firmly out of the picture.

I wondered how the kid behaved. "Did you take him out to dinner like this?"

Professor Terwilliger eyed Yvonne coolly. "Sort of," she replied with a hesitant giggle. "His contract rider called for no activities of any sort prior to the actual lecture. He needs to meditate and prepare himself. Mentally, you know. After the lecture, I took him . . . well, we had dinner."

Zapatú straightened with interest.

"What did you think of him?" I urged.

"Like Skip said, he's very nice. Not at all what you expect of a religious, you know, guru. He has the most amazing, you know, instincts. And sensitivity," Yvonne broke into the most irrepressible smile. "He really is amazing. I felt like I'd known him for a thousand years."

Professor Terwilliger almost gagged on his buttered roll. "Why not ten thousand years? I believe that's the figure he cited in his speech."

"Did he come here, to the Villa Italia?" I asked.

Yvonne cast her eyes downward. "Well, no. This closes at ten. We only had time for carry-out pizza."

To our utter surprise, Zapatú spoke up. His voice seemed to come out of nowhere, like the night I first heard it by the campfire. "Carry out?" he inquired. "That means you leave the restaurant to eat elsewhere?"

Yvonne nodded pleasantly.

Zapatú muttered. "Where?"

She gazed down, not out of shame, but to be alone with her reminiscence. "At his motel," she sighed.

Zapatú stroked his chin in eager contemplation. Through the rest of the dinner, he was far more animated. For that I was relieved.

The lecture itself went well. The crowd was large (just as big as for the Boy Guru, we were assured) and respectful. Zapatú again employed the taxi driver format, this time inventing a few nuances. For example, he had the cabbie initially recognizing him not as Zapatú but as the co-host of the popular daytime game show, "Glitter of Gold." Zapatú's total lack of resemblance to that pudgy, effeminate motormouth with the cotton candy hairstyle elicited great laughter, as did the unfolding story of his futile effort to persuade the driver that he was, in truth, a charismatic Latin American revolutionary. I might have had some reservations about the depth of Zapatú's political zeal, but there was no doubting his insight into the tag-ends of our culture. The audience was his, and at the end they rose with appreciation to applaud him.

The first question came from a wiry young man who had remained standing in order to catch Zapatú's attention. He wore a khaki army jacket patched over with swatches of the American flag. His long hair was slicked back behind his ears and there was a caffeine skittishness in the way he clawed at his scraggly goatee. Every college philosophy department harbors the type: they linger like a gloomy conscience in the rear rows of classrooms, and, after several aimless years of incompletes, they vanish. Zapatú had no way of recognizing the symptoms.

The youth had a powerful voice for someone who appeared so ascetic and wasted. "Why," he challenged, "are you here instead of back there? Don't the poor, powerless peasants of your homeland need your leadership more than the students of Iowa State?"

Those students seated nearest the kid pushed themselves sideways and backwards, to distance themselves as much as possible.

Zapatú cupped his hand to his ear to indicate incomprehension. This was clearly a hostile question, and I guess he thought he might be able to duck behind a hastily constructed language barrier. Whereas Zapatú's command of English was almost impeccable, even with street-slang locutions, he reserved the prerogative to wax clumsy and obtuse in a pinch.

The renegade inquisitor stood his ground. "*Los pobrecitos de su pais*," he began to translate.

"*Yo comprendo*!" Zapatú's enranged voice boomed like the Almighty from the public address sytem. "I understand your question, señor. You give voice to the hidden thoughts that run through my mind every day that I spend in this most prosperous of nations. Every morning I awake in a plush motel room, alone in a bed that is big enough to comfort an entire family. I open the curtains and gaze upon a parking lot filled with clean new cars and watch the salesmen in their spotless suits climb behind the wheel to begin the day's business. And yes, in my scorn I wonder if I am so very different from these sad, inessential men, shuffling along the highways. In answer to your question: yes, I do ask myself what I am doing here while suffering and repression run rampant in my homeland and across this sorry planet."

Zapatú stepped back, believing he had dispensed with his inquisitor. I could feel his discomfort in realizing, as he peered out, that the scraggly kid continued to stand with insolence, scratching at the undergrowth of his chin. I wished that Zapatú would simply call out for another question. The kid had him unnerved.

Zapatú threw back a gulp of ice water, and reluctantly resumed. "Honesty compels me to disclose my innermost thoughts, even if they are not what you have come to expect from a man called Zapatú. In truth, my deepest thoughts are often troubling to me. For example, I believe that the remote and unmodernized parts of the world have suffered since the onset of history and, sadly, may be condemned to perpetual suffering. This is not to exempt the avaricious and deceitful ruling class, but in my heart I must admit that forces at least as oppressive as fascist rulers govern the fate of the masses. There are dry hot winds which turn the soil to a dead scab. Seasonal rains flood valleys with torrents of mud. The great thunder of nature's will drowns out even the unified voices of men."

Zapatú lifted his arms like a preacher, rolling his eyes upward. "Life, for each of us, is so brief, so faint, so fragile. Oh, I believe fervently in the righteous struggle, but I also wonder if it is not self-deception to seek more from life than a vivid survival. Like the ancients, we plod across the earth's surface, unable to peer above the next rise in the same timeworn path. It is history which teaches us that the acts of men affect the events of time. That, of course, is a history that is heavily biased towards the acts of men. History, I'm afraid, may turn out to be the opiate of the people."

The audience was hushed and numb. The lean inquisitor had

slumped down in his seat. No one clamored to ask any more questions. There was a nervous outbreak of coughing and fidgeting. Uneasiness blanketed the hall like a mist.

Amdist this pall, a young woman's voice danced up from the front. It was Yvonne, who miraculously possessed enough promoter's moxie to attempt a last ditch salvaging maneuver. "Do you have any advice," she virtually begged him, "for today's college students who are concerned about underdeveloped countries?"

Take the hint, Zapatú. Tell them they can help. Mention the Peace Corps. Or just recommend foreign travel. Give them something to hold onto beside abstract theories on the validity of recorded history!

Zapatú leaned in to speak, then stepped back. He fumbled through his pants pocket (I hadn't realized that those flimsy drawstring beach trousers even had pockets) and finally extracted a green, kidney-shaped key ring. "At the Holiday Inn. My room number is B-10. There we can talk."

It was I, not Yvonne Williams, who came to room B-10 later that evening.

"Come right in," he sang, as I knocked on his door. "It is not locked."

The room reeked of cologne. Zapatú sat on the edge of the bed, dressed like a cartoon version of a Latin lover. He wore tight black toreador pants and an embroidered silk shirt open to his navel. He actually was anticipating a midnight visit from Yvonne.

I made no effort to mask my disgust. "How'd you get those rags through customs?"

"I explained they are necessary to my act," he quipped.

"Good answer." I dropped into the armchair by the TV and switched off the set. He'd again been watching Johnny Carson. "Because it's your act that I'd like to discuss."

"You're the boss." Zapatú somehow managed in those tight pants to cross his legs lotus-style. "Only do me a favor. If that young girl shows up, please disappear."

I gave him a stern, reprimanding stare. "I was hoping we would never have this discussion."

"Last night on Johnny Carson, there was an actress who told a joke about her agent," he said affably. "It was a situation just like this."

"I doubt it. Because an actress, no matter how dumb, always knows what roll she is getting paid to play. You don't!"

"Long ago, when I was bleeding on the beach, you told me all I needed to be was my real self."

"I was wrong. You need to be what people want."

"You said that I, myself, Zapatú, was what people wanted."

"What did I know about you? Only what I read in the news. My mistake. It can be corrected."

Zapatú rearranged his pretzeled legs. "Some day I will go on Johnny Carson and tell the story of how my agent instructed me to just relax and be myself, and then he changed his mind."

"Not a very funny story. They'll never invite you back." I glanced around the room for an object to fiddle with, but that's one of the problems with motel rooms: nothing homey, hand-sized and bendable, like a paper clip. Only the Bible and a phone book. What I had to say next was not going to come easily. Once upon a time I had harbored the hope that this tour would glide along like a sanctified creature through a terrible world, enhancing all whom it touched, especially me. "I don't want to have to go through this," I said to Zapatú. "But here's how it works."

I proceeded to explain in painful detail the machinations of the lecture business, the demands of the market, the complex role of agents, the ephemeral nature of promotability. Perhaps business school professors derive some joy out of dissecting such systems into their various and interlocking component parts, attributing to each elemental function a proper name and purpose as if greater human society were indeed a machine made perfectable by intelligent application of an engineer's skill. My tendency has been to recoil from such cerebration. For every reliable methodology, I always discover new frontier territories that exist without rhyme or reason. This business was something I drifted into, with no particular plan. And although I have acquired great volumes of data and insight, I prefer—in fact, believe in—the innocent act of drifting. I was as unhappy about explicating the inner working of the lecture business as a woman would be to discuss sexual frustration with an awkward lover. Once a process is flattened out and analyzed in its segmented parts, it will never again be the same. With each endeavor a transcendent simplicity is possible; achieving it ought to be our first choice.

Reluctantly, I informed Zapatú why universities and civic groups allocate funds for such ostensibly non-income-producing functions as public lectures: to foster an image of high-minded concern for the social and political issues of the day. To the extent that this image can only be promulgated if large audiences attend the lectures, another criterion comes into play: popular appeal. Thus the marketplace searches for a blending of intellectual distinction and popularity. Frankly Speakers tried to solve this problem by representing speakers who sincerely cared about issues that, for one reason or another, had captured the public imagination. We liked to think of ourselves as agents, not simply of speakers, but of enlightenment, fairness, progress. Our success—Zapatú had no way to know how flimsy it was—depended on the lecturers performing up to quite flexible professional standards, delivering generally the message the audience has come out to hear, comporting themselves in a manner consistent with the image of the cause or issue that is being addressed, displaying passion (where called for), detachment (when appropriate), humor (at intervals), dignity (throughout).

"For that you could hire an actor," Zapatú protested.

"The point," I snapped, "is that they only pay the sort of money you're being paid to listen to the real thing."

"Even if what I say isn't altogether real?"

"Yes, dammit!"

"Danny," he whined with a child's true sadness in his voice, "why did you not tell me this before?"

I was too drained and despondent to reply. I felt empty and low, like someone who's finally consummated the sex act following too much instruction.

We were diverted by a rattling at the door, an insistent scratching sound that might have been a knock. Was Yvonne Williams at last coming to the rescue?

Zapatú leapt from the bed and threw open the door. A redfaced, rotund salesman in an ill-fitting brown checked suit collapsed stone drunk into his arms, like the death scene in a bad drama.

The salesman had been trying to get into the wrong room. I helped Zapatú pick the guy up and deposit him back in the vanilla hallway. The disturbance gave me an excuse to return to my own room.

CHAPTER 10

Zapatú and I hiked from our motel down the hill towards the Miami University campus, spread out in the distance like a museum diorama of North American college life in the late twentieth century. The buildings were red brick and pseudo-Colonial. The lawns were expansive, a great soothing swath of green. Miniature figures moved across the peaceful topography, purposeful and happy. Angst and conflict, even noise, seemed to be removed from the scene.

The streets were absurdly wide for the sparse traffic they needed to accommodate. Snug houses were set back on soft grass carpets. Garage doors were left invitingly open, revealing chaotic collections of broken three-wheelers, wood-handled tennis rackets, tool racks, lawn mowers, disassembled air conditioners, dormant autos of contemporary vintage with the driver's side door left carelessly open, probably with the keys inside. Mounds of raked leaves, wafting that unsettlingly sweet fragrance of decay, sat like Buddhas at curbside, waiting for the flame.

Our destination was the student union where, at four o'clock, the shuttle bus from the Cincinnati airport was scheduled to deliver Mona. I had offered to drive down to meet her, but she had insisted on arriving on her own to optimize the chances of "meeting someone." Solitary and struggling to make her way through unfamiliar territory was precisely the circumstance she wanted to be in should she encounter a suitable male. Self-reliant yet imperiled were the qualities she hoped to project.

Nearing the campus, we passed a large, three-story clapboard house, with several cubist additions protruding out and up at odd angles. The house was painted purple and yellow. Thunderous rock music boomed from the upper windows. On the sidewalk two bare-chested guys in sweatpants tossed wobbly spiral passes back and forth, back and forth.

"Que pasa?" Zapatú said to them.

"Howdy," they nodded.

According to the written directions provided by Chester Mudge, the student union lay at the foot of the campus, past the library ("with its stacks of books"), the humanities building ("built around an arch"), before we get to the south quad. By the fastidiousness of his directions, you'd have thought Chester was steering us through darkest Manhattan. For all I knew, that's how he viewed this sleepy little town.

As we made our way past the library, "with its stacks of books," I began to notice a profusion of the official Zapatú posters stapled to the sturdy trunks of the elms and maples and oaks which lined the diagonal walk. The posters were eye-catching in exactly the way we had hoped, with Zapatú's artfully bronzed face squinting out from a backdrop of blazing jungle. It's the difference between reading a play in manuscript and watching it performed before a live audience, witnessing these posters stapled to actual trees. And bustling toward us was an actual coed, her brunette hair pulled primly back in a bouncing pony-tail, a lumpy book bag jouncing against her cashmere sweater. We paused to observe her response to the poster.

She cruised right past one, too preoccupied with adjusting the strap of her book bag to notice. Nearing us, she looked askance, probably to avoid eye contact, then turned to the poster. It was stapled to the thick trunk of a huge oak tree aflame with dancing golden leaves. She halted. She sidled closer to read the print. The lines she was reading were ones I had written. My words were filling her pretty head: "A man who cared so deeply for his homeland that he was forced to flee, a man whose passion for economic justice ignited a fiery upheaval."

She dropped her book bag to read again. She lingered rapt before the image of those dark piercing eyes springing out from the jungle fire beyond. She could be the favored daughter of a retail furniture salesman, raised in a modest suburb of nearby Dayton. This bucolic campus might represent the farthest reach of her restless spirit.

Just as we ambled by, she turned. I glanced away, not wanting to be caught staring. Zapatú, however, saluted her with his new trick, the lascivious leer. He must have learned it from Johnny Carson.

"Que pasa?" he said.

She blushed and smiled.

I wondered if she recognized Zapatú. We kept walking, slantwise toward the big classroom building, "built around an arch." We passed a yellow wooden structure, more like a nineteenth-century New England home than an institutional facility. From the upper floor we heard the sonorous trills of a flautist practicing Bach. If the museum diorama of this campus were provided a soundtrack, it would be this, the imperfect, diligent scales of a silver flute wafting from the music building, the distant four o'clock chimes of the looming belltower, the brittle crunch beneath our feet of the newly fallen leaves.

The archway we were approaching was really more like an underpass, tunneling through a wide, thick brick building. At the mouth of the underpass stretched a huge bedsheet which advertised, in bold, spray-painted, dayglo-colored lettering, the appearance by Zapatú. "EXPERIENCE ZAPATÚ," it read.

"The little beavers are doing their job," I remarked in admiration of the banner.

"I should hope so," replied tonight's star attraction.

"They don't always," I said. We had reached the archway and I noticed that the deep concave space lent a resonant echo to my voice. It was tempting, just for the sound of it, to try to state something insightful and profound. Instead, I settled for simple reiteration. "Yes, I believe we'll get a pretty good crowd tonight."

"We?" queried Zapatú.

I knew what he was driving at. I had slipped into a collective pronoun. I might argue, and present a pretty strong case for, the indispensability of my role, from tracking him down in the tropics to fashioning the promotional campaign to keeping my mouth shut about his more vulnerable traits. But in this echoing archway the words would just fly back at me in ridiculous amplification. "Excuse me," I conceded. "*You* will get a fine crowd tonight."

"They will learn more from me than from their books!" His head was thrown back and he looked pleased with his conclusion. I don't know whom he was trying to convince.

Out across the way, in the golden light, I could see the girl with the pony-tail turning back in our direction, walking briskly. I checked my watch. "We should get over to the student union," I said to Zapatú. "Never good policy to keep Mona waiting."

He had propped himself in the cool shadows against the solid stone arch, and showed no sign of moving. He was certainly not averse to the sound of his own voice. "All this beauty, all so peaceful, all so civilized," he mused. "It is a shame that it is all built on blood. All paid for through treachery and rape."

With great ostentation I rechecked my watch. The girl in the cashmere sweater and book bag was getting closer. "Right on," I commended Zapatú. "But save it for tonight. No point in giving it away for free."

My remark was intended as a jocular chiding, but Zapatú reacted angrily. He'd sighted the girl. "I speak when the passion moves," he declared, his rich voice vaulting like a saint's through the hollow underpass. "I am no actor, I am a creature of the moment. The winds stream through my soul and speak through my lips. Only the gringo thinks he can put a clock on the wind. Hah."

The pony-tailed co-ed now hovered at the mouth of the archway, cradling her book bag like an infant child. Zapatú, immersed in his philosophical gropings, pretended to pay her no attention.

"Ah, to be stranded and alone in this place they call the United States," he continued, his somber voice filling the cool stone tunnel. "To be lost and estranged in this country where tiny men like mechanical toys march about oblivious to the vast sorrowful plight..." He came to a halt and, for the first time flashing his leer, acknowledged the young lady.

Her eyes lifted slowly, as if weighted against a pulley. It appeared to take great effort for her to emit a sound. Finally she uttered, "Are you...?" but failed to complete the question.

Helping her out, Zapatú humbly acknowledged with a deft nod that, yes, he was indeed tonight's featured attraction. He reached out his hand towards her, extending his forefinger like that image on the ceiling of the Sistine Chapel. "Will you stroll with me?" he asked.

This little scene was enacted as though I were invisible, or a stone buttress with no stake in the proceedings. As Zapatú and the cashmere lassie drifted away into the golden light, I hollered after them in the measured tones of reason, "Dinner's at six with the committee." To establish a fallback position I added, "Lecture starts at eight. Sharp."

My mundane admonition vaulted and echoed every bit as dramatically as Zapatú's grand pronouncements. Except I was the only one left listening.

I found her waiting beside two monstrous purple bags of designer luggage on the steps of the student union. "Where's Zapatú?" she accused. "Did he defect *back* already?"

My tactic, as always, was to be pleasantly superficial. "How's the trip?"

"Rotten." She surveyed this picturesque display of pastel landscape with a half-cocked scowl, from which I deduced that she had met no eligible gentlemen in the course of her journey from D.C.

"We couldn't have better weather," I observed with a salesman's smile.

"So where is he?"

The bell tower clanged out the quarter hour. A young couple skipped past, glowing with newfound affection.

"Zapatú?" I innocently replied, "He's off checking out the campus. He's become quite a student of American—excuse me—U.S. culture. I've come to admire his intellectual curiosity, even his discipline and methodology. He's quite the professional, when you get right down to it. First he gathers the flavor and feel of a locale, takes its pulse, measures the mood..."

"Is he chasing women?"

"Why do you ask that?" I actually had been happy to see her. I had forgotten her skill at interrogation.

"Because that's what they all are dying to do."

"And where did you read this?"

"I'm a woman, remember? I know."

"Incidentally, I like your hair that way." Only as an emergency measure do I pay this sort of compliment. She'd had it cut even shorter, and frosted on top. The fact that it was scrunched in a lump on one side and looked slightly laminated was something she wouldn't discover until she reached a mirror. "It makes you look younger."

"Do you think Zapatú will like it this way?"

I hadn't the foggiest. "Definitely. His taste leans in that direction."

"Really? You think so?"

I couldn't tell if she was pulling my leg. "Yeah, definitely. Just yesterday he told me he's wild for women who obsess about how their hair looks."

Mona had been dreamily gazing at the thick lawn deepening into shadow. When she turned back to face me, her eyes were pearling up with baby tears. "Why," she lashed out, "do you always have to be so damn sarcastic?"

Straining to circumvent the disconcerting sight of her looking so weepy and vulnerable, I stood my ground. "It just seems to me that your expectations about men are always so far-fetched. It's like you buy them wholesale from fragrance commercials on TV and cornball movies, not from real life."

"Tell me, Mr. Smartass, what's so wrong with that?" Her eyes may have been moist and downcast, but there was a bitter taunt in her tone. "Tell me, am I supposed to be above it all like you? Am I supposed to be such a realist that I have no dreams at all?"

"The point I'm trying to make," I rattled on like a Ph.D. candidate defending his thesis, "is that your concept of what you're looking for, especially from a guy, is founded on phony Hollywood images of muscular heroes saving damsels in distress and that's causing you problems because life just isn't that way. Geez! I'm just trying to be helpful!"

"And my point," she wailed, "is that life flies by. Who's got the time to figure out the phony images from the real? So I want a boyfriend and I'd like him to be dashing, O.K.? Otherwise there's not a chance I'm going to stay excited about him or, for that matter, Mr. Smartass, that he'll stay excited about himself. You ever been in a relationship where both of you are bored? No sir, not for me. I want life to be alive, not a slow process of flipping months on the calendar. I want a guy who needs help making the most out of life. Yes, he better be attractive to me. Yes, I hope he appreciates the best in me because that's what I want to do too. If you want to mock that, Danny, go ahead—the joke's on you!"

I gasped for air. I felt like I was suffering an asthma attack. All I could manage to sigh was, "I'm sorry," which, for inchoate reasons, I truly was.

An engorged moment of silence hovered between us like a safety cushion in the sweet autumn air. This had gone too far. Time to reinstate our professional agenda. With great difficulty I lifted her luggage. "What do you say we check in with your friend Chester? Then we'll go to the motel. Then dinner. How's that sound?"

A palpable softening infused her countenance. She licked her lips and rolled her eyes, as if playing to a hidden camera. "Right," she sang, "I nearly forgot about old Chester."

Chester Mudge's office was located in the student activities suite, tucked in the far corner of the student union's ground floor, around the bend from the video game room. To get there we had to pass the main lounge, occupied by a dozen nearly supine students staring vapidly at the giant image of a televised quiz show, a ping-pong and pool room, a lineup of neon junk food vending machines, another lounge, this one for reading (those few occupants appeared actually to be sleeping) and the closed fiberglass door of the campus newspaper. A light was on inside. We could see the silhouette of a couple making out, toe to toe.

The walls of the student activities suite were a collage of pop-star posters—a giant portrait of a famous TV sit-com bombshell, a lead guitarist looking real nasty, Gerald Ford looking painfully glum. The receptionist, a goofy young man in soiled clothing, was busy on the phone. This afforded us a further minute to gaze at Marilyn Monroe fighting a rush of air to keep her dress down (the same print Kenny has beside his desk), and a football hero thrusting out a menacing straight arm to Stop Drugs.

When it grew apparent that the receptionist wasn't even considering putting down the phone to help us, Mona asked for Chester Mudge. To the rear, the kid gestured with an indolent thumb.

His office door was open. We found Chester hunched over a newspaper outspread on his littered desk, enthusiastically picking his nose, fully utilizing his forefinger and pinky. Having no appetite for wading through other people's embarrassment, I grabbed Mona to prevent her from entering.

She squirmed away. Rapping on the door only after crossing the threshold, she crowed, "You must be Chester." And, to my alarm, she bulled forward to shake the kid's hand.

It was his right hand he'd been employing to excavate his nasal cavity, and he was clearly bedeviled as to how to receive Mona's salutation. It's one of those dilemmas no etiquette book can prepare you for.

Chester fumbled. Beads of perspiration gathered on his prematurely high forehead. His smooth, pale face turned pink and beyond. Mona grinned down at him.

"Don't worry," she reassured him, in that special way she has of offering no reassurance whatsoever. "We all do it."

I moved into the office chattering a blue streak to divert the kid's embarrassment and alleviate my own. "What a wonderful campus, what tranquility," I roared. "Has to be one of the true garden spots of western civilization. It just feels so great, so rejuvenating to be here. I'm from the midwest myself, you know. Days like this, it feels like the Garden of Eden."

When I paused to take a breath I realized I'd been sounding like that idiot sidekick on "The Tonight Show." Well, it's a job someone has to do.

In person he seemed like a sweet, somewhat nerdy kid, far different from the junior shark and would-be tycoon I had been expecting. Mona had always characterized Chester as the most jaded young person in modern America, and from what little I'd heard of his phone demeanor I would have shared that assessment. He knew how to niggle and negotiate at a level way beyond his years, and projected the type of bloated self-importance that can usually be found only in veteran corporate sociopaths. It was a surprise, therefore, to find a bland, not un-handsome but utterly modest-looking young man. His light brown hair was oily and unkempt. His sta-press short sleeve shirt was too tight for the soft rolls of his torso and the wrong color (baby blue) for his pasty complexion. He appeared so uneasy with his physical self, alternately fidgety and comatose, that sexual attraction, going or coming, was unthinkable. How he managed to metamorphose into such a cunning tiger on the phone was a mystery.

My soliloquy on the pleasures of southern Ohio had provided Chester with time to mop up and get himself together. "Have a seat," he gestured with courtly aplomb to the threadbare sofa beneath the Van Halen poster. Patches of foam rubber cushion peeked out between frayed strands of the madras fabric.

"Looks like a few generations of students have done some humping on this," observed Mona as she daintily sat herself down.

I moved to the window, not wanting to be too closely identified with my colleague. As of yet there had been no proper introductions amongst us. It was a pleasant colloquialism to bypass the formality.

Seeing me peer out the window, Chester asked, "Have you seen our publicity? We've really got the campus covered. The retards at the newspaper thought our ad wasn't supposed to run until next week, so I had to take extra measures. We've got posters all over, we even have banners. Last weekend we got it announced at half-time of the Kent State game. Supposedly the faculty are mentioning it in class. Our campus radio station is running p.a.'s. 'Course, nobody can find the dang thing on the dial."

"Looks like you have all the bases covered," said Mona, picking a foam rubber crumb off her skirt.

Chester was starting to feel his oats, and it was easier to conjure the tiger of telephone communiques. "So where's Zapatú?" he asked.

I gazed out the window at a cluster of students, yapping intently as they ambled across the verdant lawn. "Zapatú—he's off getting the feel of the place," I replied. "That's what he likes to do before a major address."

I was pretty sure this response would satisfy Chester, and I shot Mona a prohibitive frown to make certain she let the sleeping dog lie.

The same intuition that prompted Mona's concern about Zapatú now activated a professional impulse on her part to absorb Chester in other matters. Tilting her head sideways to fiddle with a dangling earring, she located a breathy, sultry range in her voice and told Chester, "It's funny how much better looking you are than I would have hoped."

Chester made a valiant effort not to burst into a huge stupid smile, but it spilled out the corners of his mouth. "Likewise, m'am," he stammered.

"Call me Mona."

I thought I sensed what was going on, and I knew I didn't want to be present for it. It had been on my mind to call the office, to make certain that in the absence of its senior executives Frankly Speakers was still operating with customary efficiency. I asked Chester where I might find a pay phone. Barely able to look up, so intense was his blushing, he directed me back past the video game room.

I told them I'd return in a few minutes, and headed towards the flashing lights and the hi-fidelity explosions. The pay phones were in an alcove off to themselves.

Marion answered, graciously accepting the reverse charges.

"How's biz?" I asked.

"Danny!" she exclaimed. "Are you still with the company?"

I knew she resented Mona's recent traveling privileges, but it's not like we were out here having a picnic. "Getting any bookings?" I asked. "Any feedback from that Women's History Month mailing?"

"Please hold." Marion disappeared to another line. At least Frankly Speakers doesn't condemn the waiting caller to listen to brainwash Muzak. I was actually grateful to have a few moments of dead air, even if they were occasionally broken by the manufactured noise of rocket launches and high speed crack-ups. Marion picked up. "No, nothing much to report. It's been pretty quiet. I wouldn't say dead, just quiet."

"Nothing coming in from Marge Holman being on the 'Today Show'?" The Supreme Court was hearing a Florida case that would repeal a woman's right to vote if she was criminally neglectful of her children. Marge had appeared on TV opposite Miss Hall, now a Smooth Line client being shrewdly marketed as a fresh voice on the role of women in society. "Isn't the network forwarding letters to us?"

"Nothing. They say the only mail's been for Miss Hall."

"How's Marge taking it?"

"She's threatening to jump agencies?"

Marion obviously was in no mood to alleviate the concerns of her absent boss. "If you have nothing more to report," I said, not concealing my irritation, "can I speak with Kenny?"

"Kenny's out today."

"How come?"

"Mental health day is what he said. He sounded pretty together when he said it."

"Let me speak with Piper."

"She hasn't returned from lunch. I'd be worried except..."

"Except what?"

"Oh, nothing. Oops. Please hold." When Marion got back on line she was laughing. "That was Piper. She called in to report she's taking a mental health afternoon."

A volley of crackling machine gun fire burst from the game room. I was feeling very edgy, very tense. I told Marion I might call back in a little while, a shameless strategy for stalling her in the office for the remaining hour of the afternoon. I hung up the phone, fished into the metal slot to retrieve my quarter, turned around and nearly bumped into Zapatú stomping down the corridor.

"Hey, amigo." I tried to sound light-hearted and loose. "Where's the young lady?"

Zapatú derisively grumbled, "Hah."

We began walking back towards the student activities suite. Without knowing the details, I felt it necessary to console him. "She seemed interested. That look she gave you in the archway—it sure made me jealous."

"Is an illusion," Zapatú scoffed.

A young man in sweat pants juked by snapping his fingers. Once he was safely beyond, I put a comradely hand on Zapatú's shoulder. "I thought you and she would be in fond embrace by now, amigo."

He cleared his throat and spat. A big gob splashed onto the green linoleum.

"What happened?" I pressed.

Zapatú had that faraway stare you see on his poster. "We strolled to her apartment. On a very pretty street, in a very pretty house. Not far."

"Yes?"

"It was just the way you said it would be, Danny. She made us tea."

"O.K. I'm following you."

"She is studying international relations."

"Excellent. And then?"

"Then nothing!" he roared. "She kept asking questions. It was like a damn press conference."

We'd arrived at student activities. Something was amiss. The goony receptionist was gone. From inside a static-riddled radio voice was transmitting the news. The light within appeared dim and orange, as if a candle were burning in an attic hiding place.

I stood outside the door and coughed loudly, that time-honored clod's way of announcing one's unwelcome arrival.

No response. I put my ear to the meager crack and listened. Zapatú hovered behind me. We heard vague quiet sounds. Could that really be the puffing of hot breath, the swishing of rubbed cloth? Fretting over what I might find, I suffered a sharp pang of regret, like indigestion, at all the wrong turns that had mired me in this trivial mayhem. I could have been . . . the pang subsided. What are life's realistic opportunities if you eliminate all the thousand-to-one crapshoot aberrations?

Giving a slight push with my toe to the door, I peered in. In the burnt orange light I could barely discern the figure of Chester leaning over his desk, and Mona standing at its corner, their gazes fixed on the desktop clock radio as if it were an oracle.

I coughed again to announce ourselves.

"Quiet!" Mona snapped. Her face was hard and distant and dead serious.

Chester, on the other hand, lit up at our arrival. "Guess what?" he enthused.

"Shhh!" Mona's admonitory hiss was as loud as a locomotive chugging into Union Station.

The radio announcer was off on a tangent, reporting that the World Series had been big business indeed for the host cities, with boomtime profits in the hotel and restaurant trade.

Chester couldn't contain himself. "CBS News," he gushed, throwing open his arms. "They want to cover us tonight."

"Great," I said, but I sensed something wasn't right.

Chester held both arms high, signaling touchdown. "They just called. From New York. I talked to them." He couldn't have been happier.

I looked to Mona for clarification.

In the waning light, her face looked ashen and haunted. "They're rioting," she intoned in a spooky whisper. "At Zapatú's alma mater. Faculty are being held hostage. Buildings are barricaded. The junta has moved in tanks."

"Eighteen reported killed," added Chester with witless glee.

Zapatú still lingered in the doorway. We all turned toward him. "Killed?" he asked with a child's crestfallen sorrow. "Killed dead?"

Chester teetered on the hind legs of his chair and threw his feet upon the desk. "There's talk of Dan Rather doing an interview by satellite."

Zapatú moved ponderously to the window. The day was dimming; the campus was less green. Fall in all its glum moods and earth colors was taking over. Zapatú propped one foot on the window sill and gazed longingly at the diminishing pastoral. Another sunrise would restore the vivid hues, but that was many hours away.

"What now?" he asked, without turning to face us.

It was my role to answer him, and I was suddenly aware of how alone and isolated Zapatú really was. What did I truly know about where he came from? How could I possibly understand the mindset of someone of his background? All I knew for certain was the ineluctable unfolding of the gringo way. Soon enough all the promoters of all the big league media would come calling, like foreign ambassadors visiting a new chief of state of an oil-producing nation. Book publishers, television packagers, Hollywood itself was likely to show interest. A guest appearance on Johnny Carson's show was virtually assured. This was the nature of the insights I had to offer. Yet I doubted that was what he was seeking.

The phone rang, Chester was on it like a hawk. "Of course," he droned officiously. "Yes, totally on top of it. Right. Don't worry, just be there on time."

Chester hung up. "My advisor," he explained to us. "The guy can't handle the pressure."

Mona stomped back to the threadbare sofa and plopped down with determination. "There's only one thing to do. We've got to get Zapatú on the first flight home. His people need him."

Chester nearly plunged backwards on his chair. Before he could launch his predictable complaint, I asserted myself as moderator. "What we need to do," I said, hating my own bland monotone, "is first think through all the options. No hasty decisions."

"Why not?" Mona growled. "Time is short. Which is something *you'll* never understand. The time has come for quick decisions, and I, for one, am glad."

"Okay, fine," I allowed. "But let's just give the matter some thought."

"What does your heart say?" Mona hurled the question at me like a dagger in a vaudevile act. I was the imperiled straight man.

My heart, if she really cared to know, is a pastiche of soaring, swooping, surging, plunging bittersweet urges that are almost insanely disconnected from the day-to-day considerations of the life I lead. Can it realistically make any difference what my heart says?

"My heart," I lied, "tells me to take a moment to consider all options, then choose the smartest."

"Mine," retorted Mona, almost levitating with the ferocious heat of her resolve, "says get Zapatú to where the action is. His number is being called. Can't you hear it, Danny? How can he go around lecturing college kids?"

She had a point. There would be a credibility problem. But worse ones than this had been successfully managed in the past. Take the Boy Guru, for example. I noticed that Chester was busily rifling through his desk drawer, probably searching for his carbon copy of our contract. Did this development constitute an Act of God reason for cancelling? Slick lawyers, like priests, can always locate evidence of divine influence.

The bell tower tolled the hour. Five o'clock. It tolls for thee.

The phone rang again and Chester pounced. "Yes, he's right here." He handed the receiver to me. "For you."

It was Marion. Frantically, she began rattling off a list of media heavyweights—*Time*, UPI, Voice of America, Geraldo—who'd been desperately trying to reach us.

I cut her off. "Give them my motel number," I instructed. "Tell them to call later tonight."

"They're certainly pushy sons of bitches," Marion complained with uncharacteristic distaste.

Even in my consternation I caught the hint. "You're doing fantastic, Marion. We couldn't function without you."

"By the way, I have to take tomorrow off," she said. Fortunately, I'd hung up before her words registered with me.

Zapatú now sat on the window sill facing us, silhouetted against the crimson-streaked sky. Weirdly, the image he presented was a close approximation to the color and layout of the official Zapatú promotional flyer. He actually appeared to be burning with passionate contemplation.

"It will be no doubt dangerous for me to return," he stated with a subdued calm.

Suddenly it hit me and I felt like a fool. There was real danger in the world. Horrible, irreparable things happened to the undeserving as well as the guilty. I paced the room, which took me right past Mona. "We could wait until tomorrow," I mused aloud. "Who knows if Cincinnati airport even has flights south tonight?"

"Delta goes to Miami," Mona chipped in.

"At night?" I challenged.

"Quite possibly. And New Orleans."

"The advantage to waiting," I asserted, "is it gives us the chance to digest all the news reports. Maybe a lot of this is disinformation. Maybe Zapatú can get a call through, somehow, and speak with someone who's right on the scene."

"Fat chance," she scoffed.

I was getting angry. After all, who's side was she on? I paced back in front of the sofa and, in a deft maneuver that would go unnoticed by Chester and Zapatú, I stomped firmly on her foot. This, I hoped, would send an unambiguous message about discipline and rank and Mona's obligation to fall in line behind the wishes of her commanding officer. She glanced up at me with a look of utter hatred, beneath which I thought I detected an indication of begrudging compliance.

On the window sill Zapatú had his knees pulled up almost in a fetal position. A grave crisis loomed and I had no sense of what he was feeling. Once in his life, several years back, he'd been embroiled in a dramatic incident and sudden fame had unexpectedly mushroomed from that. To me his true beliefs remained vague, except insofar as they constituted our mutual bread and butter. Their resonance in the darker world where sweat mixed bitterly with blood was never something I needed to know. It is an unusual gift to be renowned for accomplishements that need not be tested. The news now carried intimations of a test.

Rocking almost imperceptibly in his fetal crouch, Zapatú murmured. None of us caught what he said, if in fact that sorry guttural noise represented words.

Chester was growing alarmed. "How's that?" he insisted. "Could you speak louder?"

"My heart says I should return," came Zapatú's gloomy mumble. "But there could be danger."

This was not what I wanted to happen. Not just now. Not with me here, present, on the scene, so vulnerable and involved. Perhaps mañana, or the day after mañana. I looked over to glean an eye-contact response from Mona. She hadn't made a peep since I'd stomped on her foot.

She tossed me back a dazzling lascivious and reassuringly conspiratorial wink, suggesting she was firmly on my side. Rising to her feet, she sashayed over to the window and placed a sympathetic hand on the warm skin of Zapatú's neck. He had not been touched by a woman in at least several weeks. I held my breath while she leaned her tousled head onto his tense shoulder.

Addressing him with kindly affection, yet loud enough for all to hear, she purred, "This is getting too crazy. Let's take a walk, you and I, and get some perspective."

Chester bolted forward, but I caught his attention with a very meaningful clenched fist. Mona knows what she's doing, I informed him with a wordless icy warning. Stay out of it!

Moving her arm around his waist, Mona helped Zapatú to his feet. Like weary combat veterans limping back to camp across a rice paddy, they moved heavily toward the door. The sky outside was a swirl of purple. Very little light penetrated Chester's office. Before disappearing out the door Mona sent me a mesmerizingly wry half-smile, curled at each corner of her malleable mouth like a question mark. I interpreted this gesture as an affirmation, comrade to colleague, that her feminine wiles would be dutifully employed to deliver tonight's distinguished speaker to the podium, replete with its stand-up microphone and pitcher of ice water, by eight o'clock sharp.

CHAPTER 11

Backstage at McGuffey Auditorium, fifteen minutes until showtime, and no sign, word, or hint from Mona and Zapatú. From the dusty, unventilated custodian's broom closet which functions as a dressing room, Chester and I could hear the ordinarily gratifying sounds of a venerable old lecture hall filling up: the trampling of busy feet on antiquated wooden floors; the rising chorus of expectant voices punctuated by an occasional animated cat-call; the groaning heave and creek of humanity massing together.

A full house is exactly what you want. The less the physical separation between spectators, the more profound their response, and the better the performance. A palpable chemical reaction takes place when speaker meets audience. I'd observed it numerous times under varying conditions. Factors can be isolated; effects can be analyzed; results could be reasonably predicted. This situation would be ripe for Zapatú.

The grubby, cramped little hole where we waited was airless and unsympathetic to our predicament. The two slightly damaged straightback chairs, discards from some recently modernized classroom, offered little encouragement to sit and relax. So we leaned against opposite walls, Chester and I, like death row inmates staring at the floor and pondering the thick, unforgiving earth below. In the corner was a deep porcelain sink, once shiny and white, now grimy and grayish from years of being used to rinse dust mops and wash down custodial excrescence. The thick dull faucet dripped, not methodically, but in a maddening syncopation. Above us, on the ceiling, large flecks of olive paint protruded like pop-up cardboard cut-outs, dangling acrobatically in the slight breeze caused by our taut breath. By the sink squatted a reversible blackboard, still retaining, like an archaeological relic, the last message scribbled in yellow chalk by the last instructor to use it: "Osmosis DOES NOT apply to the flow of knowledge."

For the past forty-five minutes I had been desperately attempting to soothe, divert, reassure, and otherwise mollify Chester, who had grown increasingly snappy, nervous, sarcastic, nasty, and potentially violent. He was beginning to genuinely hate me. I was not far from adopting a similar attitude toward him.

"Tell me again," Chester spat, "where the hell you think they are."

Of course I didn't know for sure. So I told Chester pretty much what I had told him several times already; that Zapatú, along with Mona, was wandering somewhere around campus, as he tended to do before important lectures. It was a method for both gauging the regional mood and stretching his legs in anticipation of the long stationary spell at the podium.

"He usually returns with some anecdote rich in local flavor that he weaves into his introductory remarks," I told Chester. "It's an excellent device."

Chester wasn't biting. "I think he split."

I too harbored that fear. But I didn't have the strength to face it. "Last night," I told Chester, with a liar's sing-song lilt in my voice, "the same thing happened and I finally discovered him out in the crowd, sitting there anonymously, listening in on their small talk, taking their pulse. Why don't I go out there and check?"

"Don't even try it!" Chester had assumed the steely ugliness of a Mafia hit man. The goofy simplicity of his face had given way to a taut, psychopathic explosiveness. I was actually afraid to move.

There were additional aggravating factors. CBS had never shown up, but two nearby TV stations had, one from Cincinnati and one from Dayton. And at least two newspapers and one affiliated radio station had contacted Chester's advisor to reserve seats. The accumulating pressure was not relaxed by the fact that Chester had taken pains to dress himself up in a most spiffy charcoal-gray pin-stripe suit. I had a horrible hunch he might have purchased it specifically for the grand opportunity of looking his best while introducing Zapatú to the assembled throng.

Suddenly, I was painfully alert to the fragile psychological skeletal system that props up the college business: since the student chairperson receives no financial remuneration for a task that exacts considerable effort and commitment, rewards are paid in adolescent forms—resumé credits, social status, and the chance at a few gleaming moments in relative limelight. Admittedly, such rewards are ephemeral and insubstantial, but without them there is nothing—a realization that Chester Mudge was beginning to come to.

I too was reluctantly arriving at an unpleasant realization: Zapatú and Mona were not going to show up. Until now my worst apprehension was that they were off in a surrounding meadow enjoying a bucolic roll in the hay (I had warned Chester that Mona might utilize this shopworn device for detaining Zapatú) that ran overtime. Those things happen. I wasn't born yesterday. Presuming that to be the case, my mission was to stall for time. I found myself surprisingly disturbed by the idea of the two of them, panting and frisking and taking those first deliciously exhilarating baby steps towards intimacy. The thought of it repulsed me; yet this was business. If it succeeded, I could make my peace with the notion.

But they had not arrived at McGuffey Auditorium, and an even more disturbing contingency presented itself: they were gone, gone to the airport, checked through the X-ray gates, launched in the sky soaring south, speeding silent and vacuum sealed above the clouds, above hesitation, beyond reconsideration, veering toward a fate that might be perilous but never drab. Zapatú was heading home. Mona, damn her, had made a bold, precipitous leap, stranding me alone with Chester Mudge.

From our cloistered position in this bomb shelter of a dressing room, we could hear the muted cacophony of an audience percolating towards restlessness. The easy din of people settling in had given way to the scrape and clank and cough of impatience. I dearly regretted my bodily proximity to this predicament. Most business is best conducted at a safe distance. I wished I were back at the office enjoying the warm rinse of routine, my feet propped executive style atop my hopelessly cluttered desk, picking up the phone to receive a frantic call from an agitated but unfamiliar student lecture chair at Miami University (the one in Ohio, according to the note Marion would scribble), my voice cruising in its most unctuous gear, buoyed by the soothing hum of long distance satellite transmission. I would reassure the nearly hysterical student that Frankly Speakers was every bit as concerned as he at the inexplicable tardiness of tonight's distinguished speaker and as president of the company (a title that speaks volumes over the phone yet means next to nothing in person), I was absolutely committed, not just legally, which goes without saying, but as a matter of profound moral obligation, to a swift and mutually agreed upon rescheduling or substitution, if that is his preference. In fact, I would point out, postponed dates often work to the promoter's advantage, blessings in disguise, since public anticipation is usually intensified over the ensuing days and weeks. "You know how it is with girls," I might quip good-naturedly, swinging my feet to the floor and honing in on the clincher, "how you want them right away but actually grow to want them more if they make you wait a little."

Yes, the situation would have been eminently manageable if I were removed by a thousand miles or so. But now I had to deal with this wretched, twisted, time-bomb of a panic-stricken adolescent.

"Tell me again what the bitch told you," Chester snapped, spittle oozing from the snarling corner of his mouth.

Earlier I had given him a line about Mona having a crush on Zapatú; her coming to Ohio was a chance for them to get to know each other better. This was something I had said without thinking except insofar as it reflected a subconscious prescience. My intention was to rationalize their absence while humanizing the dilemma. Glibly, I had told Chester that Mona had mentioned a desire to take Zapatú on a tour of a real American haystack. I figured Chester would take it as a randy little quip, one guy to another. I was just winging it.

"It's the bitch's fault," reiterated Chester, slamming his fist into his palm. "Someone's gonna pay."

We still had five minutes to showtime. "Cool down," I advised, while struggling to mask my own rampaging consternation. "There's time. He'll show."

"He goddamn better goddamn show!"

It's hard playing the role of therapist when you're in dire need of therapy yourself. "Everything will work out," I gamely counseled. "Remember, this is Oxford, Ohio, not some horrible movie."

That was all the mollification I had in me. If Chester insisted on pushing his anger further, I was prepared to tell him to stuff it.

For a moment he kept shut, and we limply faced each other in a kind of skulking standoff. Out there in the auditorium they were really starting to rattle their chains. I certainly know the sensation of being a spectator in a restless crowd. Always there's a lag time, varying widely from sports arenas to poetry readings, but inevitably civility gives way to raucous protest. The usual industry rule of thumb is that the more money people have paid for their ticket, hence the more cherished the event, the longer they will politely endure a delay. Spectators attending free admission political lectures are known to have the patience of pit bulls.

I should never have accompanied Zapatú on tour. For that matter, I probably should have left him alone in his equatorial retreat. The business had been doing decently enough with our has-been politicians and our versatile journalists. So the Boy Guru would clean up. Big deal. Civilization has endured worse affronts. I was not a one-dimensional person. There were other ways I could make my mark. I'd always wanted to learn the guitar. There were songs, pretty tunes with catchy lyrics, in me somewhere. I could always go into training for a triathalon. It was not imperative that I outdo my scumbag rivals. Christ, I wished I were safely back at the office.

Chester was really starting to look scary. He squirmed and fidgeted like someone newly injected with the wrong dose of a bad drug. Emergency measures were called for. I seized on the only weapon in my limited arsenal—diversion.

"You know, Chester," I urgently began, "I've never told this to anyone, but I once aspired to be a pro baseball player."

"Big fucking deal," he snorted.

At least he was listening. I was encouraged to shift onto a more promising tack. "When that bottomed out—oh, somewhere around the age of ten—my next big goal in life . . ."

"Who gives a shit?" Chester's feet shuffled back and forth in an almost spastic twitch, like a bull digging in to charge. He stuck out his finger at me. "You're nothin', you know. You're worse than nothin'. You're a lying son of a bitch. You're a fraud and a cheat and believe you me you're gonna pay."

At the age of ten I concluded that what I wanted to be was Abraham Lincoln healing a nation with wise words and courage. Too bad for Chester—he'd just forfeited his chance to hear about it.

"You know, you're scum,"Chester elaborated. "There's laws against people like you. You'll get yours."

"Oh, yeah?"

"Yeah!"

I thought I saw an opening. "Hey, I'm no different than you. We're really in the same boat."

"Huh?"

"People like us—this always happens to people like you and me."

He was beginning to breathe normally. His feet were still. "Huh?"

"We're always waiting, always doting on these stars. Watching them on TV, reading about them in magazines, imagining living the lives they live."

"What's the point already?"

I had to talk fast. "There's a common bond. Agents and promoters, we're the ones looking after the hopes and wishes of the average person. It's we who look out for the public, when you get right down to it. We should be bonding together instead of always being at each other's throat. We're on the same team, you and I. It's the system that pits us against each other. The infernal system! That's the way it's always been, Chester. But I can see a better day. Just around the bend."

"Where the fuck's Zapatú?"

Damn! I thought I'd been making some headway. "Do you have any idea," I beseeched, "what this is doing to me? Can you try for just one moment to broaden your perspective and consider what *I'm* having to go through? I'm a lot older than you, I'm a whole lot closer to crunch time. Look at me, Chester! I'm not some dumb corporate robot who doesn't know any better. Christ, when I was your age I sincerely believed it was my destiny to be a meaningful participant in making a better world. Can you imagine? Can you imagine how hard it hits in the gut when you realize that life just might drift along no different than when you were born into it? Do you think it's pretty for me seeing every grand notion I've ever felt reduced to threadbare subsistence essentials like making ends meet or praying for a kindly smile from a pretty girl who, because of some weird emotional chemistry I despair of ever figuring out, I'd be lucky to like for more than half an hour? Sure, I probably strike you as an ordinary guy going about my ordinary business in this wonderful land of opportunity, but I'm telling you that way down there's a deep hurt. So don't you keep growling like I've got it so good while poor old you is stuck in the corner suffering this horrible trauma. My trauma is long term, Chester! Yours will be over before you know it. I envy you, I really do. Hey, how about it—you want to switch jobs?"

Chester lunged at me, lashing out with a determined right cross. He missed by a good margin, but the message was clear. This situation was too serious for sweet words. There was one—and only one—statement that was going to make any kind of difference.

"The show," I found myself announcing, "will go on."

Chester was too disturbed to even hear me. His previously admirable commitment to being a dutiful citizen had finally eroded; he had entered that danger zone where he was ready to cast his lot with the badasses of the world. In disgust, he spat at me. But succeeded only in soiling his spiffy yellow tie.

"I'm going out there," I told him. "I've seen Zapatú's act. I know what to do."

Chester charged over and stood two inches from my face, drool glistening on his chin. "Don't fuck with me," he snarled.

"Get out there," I commanded, "and tell them that Zapatú is in mourning for a comrade who was slain but a few hours ago. Look sad when you say it. Then tell them one of his comrades is fortunately here tonight to deliver his message. Look encouraging when you say that. We've got no choice. Get your ass out there and make the announcement. Pronto!"

He stuck his fist menacingly near my nose. His eyes were crossing with rage. "You hot shot agent, you think I'm some dumb hick. I don't fall for that crap."

Emergencies can give birth to a resolve that takes on a life of its own. I grabbed him with both hands by the throat. "You got a better idea?"

As I suspected, Chester did not.

"Can you hear me out there?" My voice boomed with preposterous force out into the darkened void of McGuffey Auditorium.

"No," came a hollered reply. A ripple of agitation, like wind across a wheatfield, wafted over the crowd. When it calmed, another lone voice (bellowed outcries come always from males) yelled, "We don't need to hear you."

I had traveled too far in this life to be derailed by a few wise guys, even if they had a valid point. "But I have a need to talk to you," I confessed into the darkness. "I really do."

They seemed to accept this remark and I could sense out there a collective leaning back to grant me a miminal interlude of indulgence. I had weathered the first wave. If I could just keep the words flowing the audience would refrain from hostilities, at least for a while.

What to say next? I had, at most, a few seconds to ponder this problem. A vulnerable performer might prove endearing; a speechless one is a different story. I quickly considered my choices. Did I have anything to say that they didn't already know? And would they sit still to hear it? Had I taken a taxicab recently, or shared a poignant exchange with a waitress that I might be able to expound on? Crucial seconds scooted by. I could feel the anxious hydrophobic panting presence of Chester Mudge in the wing. I bit down on my lower lip. I did know things of value. There had been occasions when mere acquaintances with no special reason to flatter me had stroked their chins in thoughtful admiration of my remarks. I have had insights. I have formulated complex, unplagiarized conclusions on subjects of general interest. But none of them leapt to mind. What filled my mind was an enormous, suffocating blank.

Yet I had to speak: "As you can see I'm not Zapatú. I can tell you nothing about life as an exile or of Third World revolutionary movements. I am Zapatú's agent. I am your proverbial last-minute substitute. I don't exactly know what I'm going to say, but you might find some excitement in that. I will be discovering my thoughts at the same pace you hear them. I won't make anything up; I'm too nervous to do that. I won't tell you stories that happened to someone else and pretend they happened to me. I won't embellish my own story, because for all I know one of you out there might contradict me. I won't make myself out to be a hero . . . unless I am. I won't portray myself as tragic or foolish . . . unless there is truth to those labels. Now you may be asking yourself, what the hell does that leave?"

I paused, and reached down to the podium shelf for a glass of water. The Zapatú contract rider called for several glasses of ice water, with ice, to be available within arm's reach of the podium. The crowd stayed silent. I took a long swallow, sloshing a cube languorously around my mouth, calm as a lifeguard presiding over a lazy summer lake. I replaced the glass and gripped the corners of the rostrum. I squinted out at my patient public. I was holding steady. Amazingly, it appeared that I could maintain equilibrium by holding onto the podium and speaking honestly. I don't know why it had never occurred to me before: honesty facilitates balance.

I proceeded to synopsize for them the story of Zapatú, not necessarily the one he would have told but the one I had wanted him to tell. I explained that he had been the favored son of middle class parents, a grateful and unthinking consumer of the environment in which he was raised. His college years were the usual mixture of mind-expanding stimulation and aimless, self-indulgent introspection. (I paused for the audience to ponder comparisons to their own situation.)

Zapatú, I told them, was not bred and reared to be an inspirational leader. He was brought up much like the rest of us, believing in justice, fairness, equal opportunity—those inarguable time-honored values. His path, like ours, was directed toward the mundane, nothing more. The praise he tended to receive was little more than the usual collection of vapid homilies we all have heard—nice fellow, sincere, performs to the best of his ability, there when you need him, ashes to ashes, dust to dust.

But something happened to re-route him toward that rarefied realm where one's actions echo and resound in the large world. What was it, I asked (as though I knew the answer), that transformed this ordinary youth Zapatú from one of us into a man who crosses international borders to fill large auditoriums with the power of his message?

"Once upon a time I was a college student," I continued, my bland words booming forth. "When I went to events such as this one tonight, speeches by visiting personalities, it was not to acquire information but for transformation. I was less interested in learning about the world than in learning how it could be different. I sought movement, change, excitement, transformation! Yes, what I really sought was to be a different me. To be a person ready to be born anew at the age of twenty, not to be defined by where I was raised, what my parents were, which subjects I was skilled at, or dumb in, what I looked like or would never look like. Seeing all of you out there I wonder, who has come here tonight for similar reasons? Which of you have been secretly searching, hoping for change?"

I held my breath and closed my eyes. I took a drink. I heard a few coughs, but they were prudently muffled. I heard the creak and sigh of bodyweights shifting in uncomfortable seats. Mostly I heard what I had hoped for: quiet, patient anticipation. I now had the privilege of speaking softly. I was barely worried about what to say next.

"I have been where you are," I told them, "sitting in an audience looking up. And I have said to myself what many of you are now muttering: I can do better than that clown; I've got as much to say as he does; I've got as much inside me. I have spent many, many nights sitting out there with you and thinking: if I had respect and attention I'd sure be capable of some wonderful things. If only I had the stage. If only the microphone was mine. If only it was me everyone had come out to hear. Then I'd show 'em. You bet I would!"

It's an experience every citizen should have, listening to one's own voice enlarged and propelled outward by electronic amplification. Volume is power; power bestows indiscriminate importance; importance usually gets amplified. That cycle is the dirty secret political leaders keep to themselves.

"I stand before you as a guy who is doing all right." I stretched out my arms to sardonically admire the worn sleeves of my corduroy sportcoat. "Like most of you, I glide through my days only partially tuned into the thousands of possibilities that are always available. Deep down, if we look truthfully at our lives, isn't it a fact that the person we are is just a sort of lazy guess we have made on a vast multiple choice quiz? Within each of us is the chance to be many, many different people. Haven't you had the experience of being at a party, or in your dorm with some friends, or even at your family Thanksgiving dinner, and you find yourself uttering a remark or dancing or making a gesture, a prank, mimicking someone, but doing something so insightful and clever and audacious that you can hardly believe it was you doing it?

"It's as if deep within us there's a small flame, like the pilot light on a gas stove, but we have such a dim understanding of how to turn it up. Haven't you had glimpses, a fleeting flash of some quality in yourself that's fantastic, utterly fantastic? Maybe that flash is no bigger than the tiny dot on a radar screen. But it's indisputably there. It's real. It's in you. You can deny it; you can repress it. But the spark is still there, the little flame still flickers. Sure, it's small enough to ignore—if ignoring it is what you want to do. But way down deep, hidden yet preserved in that place where dreams are, don't you keep wondering what the flame would feel like if you got up close and gave it a chance? Yes, the air would be hot. You might want to loosen your collar."

I loosened my collar and slipped off my coat. The right thing to do seemed to be to toss it into the crowd, as a rock star would do. That's just what I did! Several students actually scrambled over each other to grab it as it sailed into the third or fourth row.

My god, I had come a long way! I removed my glasses, placing them in my shirt pocket. After all, I was the object of attention; there was no one I needed to see clearly. I rolled up my sleeves. I pulled a drink of ice water and squinted out. I felt so damn sexy and mysterious, with my sleeves rolled up squinting out into a darker place.

I disclosed that my parents had wanted me to be a lawyer. Is there a C-plus student in America whose parents don't hold tight to that insipid hope? I attended college with actual designs on such a career. But it all made sense only in a world that is schematic and rational. Ours is not, my friends. Even Zapatú agrees on this. We drift and sway. You say that love can lead the way? Maybe so, but our instincts are dull, the clear river of truth that might once have coursed through our veins has become murky and polluted. There was a girl once. She had dark eyes that spoke in an ancient echo. There was a boy once with spindly legs who loved to romp the outfield grass. There was a man once and he stands before you now not knowing what to do next.

My voice sang out, informing them that I was arching to a conclusion (but concealing the fact that I didn't know what it would be). "If Zapatú were with us," I intoned, "He would ask not that you honor him, but that you honor yourselves. He would ask that you close your eyes"—like Simon Says, I stood at the podium and shut mine—"that you calm your breathing and for this moment in time quell your worries and fears."

In unison, most of the audience began to shut their eyes. I myself occasionally peeked. I was stunned to see so many people doing what I told them. It seemed that I could march them straight into battle, if I knew of a worthy one. My options appeared unlimited. My time, however, was not.

I spoke now in that voice one imagines the Lord in His consummate self-confidence employing, an amplified whisper. "Zapatú would ask you to remember that it could be any of you up on this stage, just as it has turned out tonight to be me. Remember that always: all possibilities are within you. Be ready to burst forth when your moment comes, for it surely will come. Enrich that moment by striving for the greatest good. Make the grandest gesture you can. Go forth. Now, if you need to. Perhaps tonight."

I fell silent and backed away from the microphone. People lifted to their feet with an escalating roll of applause. I opened my eyes to find some students pouring exuberantly into the aisles while others stood steadfast and contemplative at their seats. Clapping burst like thunder preceding a welcome rain.

Like someone snapping out of hypnosis, I wasn't immediately aware of what I'd done to merit this acclaim. But I knew I felt wonderful. All my senses tingled and were clear and sharp. Nothing surpasses that dazzling adrenaline rush one gets from breaking through to the perception of new possibilities. There are drugs which can mimic this sensation, but it's extraordinarily satisfying to achieve it through a real accomplishment. I stood there thinking: I'd like to do this again.

A gaggle of enthusiastic students were clamoring over the lip of the stage towards me. As an agent I'd witnessed this scene many times. Some wished to ask more detailed questions. Others just wanted to hover. All I wanted to do was stand still and savor the moment.

Like the blur before a car crash, Chester Mudge came barreling in from backstage, hell-bent to assume his rightful role as director of operations, keeper of the gate, intimate aide to the man of the hour. This was the role he'd been training for since that day many months ago when Mona first enticed him into booking the program. The fact that he was forced to enact it in relationship to me didn't appear to tarnish his zeal.

Chester pushed himself in front of the podium, rising on his tiptoes to augment his stature. Shoving his palms out flat to keep people at arm's length, he swiveled around at intervals to confidentially warn me to stand back, stay cool, don't worry. He had certainly grown since that first encounter several hours back when Mona burst in upon him picking his nose. It seemed like we were all rising to the occasion.

"Please! Back off, please," Chester barked authoritatively to the twenty or thirty surging well-wishers. In truth, they seemed very polite and only mildly curious. There certainly didn't appear to be much of a threat. When one scraggly young man sidled up, his thin shoulders drooping from the weight of a bulging canvas book bag and a stuttering inquiry formulating on his hesitant lips, Chester stopped the kid with a forceful straight arm hard to the sternum. Gasping, the kid backed away.

"Please! Stand back!" Chester insisted. "Quiet! I have an announcement."

Although there had been a mild forward surge among the people scrambling onstage, there had been little commotion or banter. Chester's demand for silence was easily accommodated.

"Stand back, please!" he shouted. "A reception for Mr. Frank will be held at the student activities suite. Anyone wishing to attend... well, just head over there."

With that, Chester threw a vigorous arm around my shoulder, clasping me protectively as we shuffled toward the wing. (Who did he think I was, Michael Jackson?) A dozen or so interested students pushed after us, flinging questions which I had trouble hearing since my head was being muffled by Chester's aggressive security maneuvers. A female voice asked me to clarify what I meant by turning up the flame? A frog-voiced male asked if it was possible to join up with Zapatú for his second semester work/study project? I was suddenly gloomy at the prospect of being trapped back at that crummy gallery of pop star posters, the activities office. I had made my statement and was damn lucky to have pulled it off; there was no encore left in this act.

While Chester grew preoccupied with beating back a phalanx of imagined assassins, a young woman managed to slip behind me. I smelled her fragrance of autumn rain even before I saw her. It was the girl with the pony-tail and cashmere sweater.

There was a calm self-assurance about her, so different from the way she had been this afternoon. She whispered, "There's an Ohio moon tonight, big and full. If you can pry yourself away?"

I was amazed at her brazenness. Maybe she had absorbed something from my presentation that I myself should know about. It had been a very big day for all of us—for her, for Chester, for Zapatú, for Mona, for me. It seemed that the least I could do was encourage the lessons we all were learning.

As surreptitiously as possible, without looking directly at her, I replied, "Please, yes, get me out of here."

CHAPTER 12

Newscasts over the ensuing days were filled with increasingly dramatic accounts of the stirring uprising in Zapatú's homeland. What had apparently begun as an ordinary labor protest over typically deplorable wages had mushroomed into a national exorcism of amorphous, pent-up outrage. Industrial workers demanded a voice in the administration of the factories. Peasant farmhands wanted land of their own, not just paltry pay and windowless shacks for their family. Intellectuals called for a monetary policy not dictated by monstrous interest obligations to U.S. banks. Brigades of women insisted on equal job opportunities and liberation from the awful tyranny of the church. Artists and writers clamored for the freedom to express themselves, no matter how crudely.

A rather predictable pattern emerged to these news broadcasts. All tended to begin with luscious, *National Geographic*-style scenes of gushing mountain cascades and quaint, gaily colored provincial plazas with barefoot women peddling ceramic objects. Then came footage of a rabble-rousing orator perched on the proverbial soap box ("actually a packing crate for bananas," noted our handsome network correspondent, gleeful at surmounting a cliché) decrying in staccato bursts some untranslated demon. Next we invariably were shown an interior shot of a vaulted conference room where a dozen stiff men, several of them bedecked in full military splendor, gathered at a long table, looking grim. There was no way to get a handle on the precise terms of the conflict—beyond assuming the perpetual one between new and old, have and have-not.

Little was clarified by the battery of "in-depth" interview programs and special bulletins. We were informed by several dour experts that these popular disruptions rarely precipitate permanant change, but "anything could happen." Former President Ford, recently returned from a five-day tour of the entire continent as head of a special fact-finding inquiry into the cause of civil unrest in impoverished regions, concurred that "these things happen" and that Americans, as leaders of the free world, had a duty to stay tuned to their TV sets.

We did just that. Safely at home in our breakfast nooks gulping coffee before prancing off to another workday, at fleeting lunch breaks in gleaming franchise restaurants, slumped in the evening with a beer on a forgiving sofa, we in America watched transfixed as the business of a nation, albeit a remote, underdeveloped one, came to a standstill. Thousands of miles away, in the dusty byways and scraggly fields and precipitous valleys an entire population was swept up in an orgy of fevered streetcorner debate coupled with a burgeoning spree of impromptu fiestas. I wished I was there.

I envied those people the consuming immediacy of their cause (whatever the hell it was). From the safe comfort of my gringo voyeur's perspective, the marching and chanting of comradely struggle appeared as an updated version of that fondest boyhood wish, to be a useful player—not necessarily the star—on a pennant contender. Most of all I envied Mona. She had escaped to a zone of existence not governed by the grinding, methodical gravity of blunt commercial imperatives. She was gone, free, weightless to float in destiny's direction. It should have been me.

The world watched and waited. But there was no horrible crackdown, no deplorable carnage. Under advice from the U.S. State Department, the Guardia Civil this time around was adopting a hands-off, wait-and-see attitude—at least until our backs were turned.

Then in *Newsweek* came the report I was searching for. Zapatú had made a gallant return to the Universidad Nacional accompanied by a "flame-haired mystery woman." We saw him in a photo standing proudly at the crest of the library steps dressed in the traditional outfit of student protest, tight blue jeans and a T-shirt advertising a thoroughly irrelevant product, this one being Point Beer. Gone were the drawstring pantaloons and brightly colored pullover blouses. A crowd of swarthy young men and intense women were gathered around him. Neither smoke nor fire could be observed. It was reported that Zapatú had once again been annointed the designated figurehead of the uprising and, given the new laissez-faire stratagem of the rulers, he was making frequent appearances on radio call-in programs, oftentimes live from the scene of the confrontation. These shows didn't exactly have the market ratings of Johnny

Carson, but all exposure was welcome.

In the background of the *Newsweek* picture I thought I could pick out the likeness of Mona. The orb of brownish-orange just to Zapatú's right was certainly a human face topped by what was approximately her hair color on last sighting. The features and general aura, to the extent discernible, were consistent with the Mona I knew, except that I personally had never witnessed her smiling radiantly with a clenched fist thrust defiantly overhead. Her taut and troubled spirit had apparently been greatly soothed at finding itself in a predicament of true strife and foreboding.

I guess I missed her. A deep and subtle comradely affection had passed between us. I recalled that car ride counseling session Zapatú had administered during our crisp morning breeze across Wisconsin. He'd made some undeniably valid points. I had become fussy and too deliberate when it came to vital personal needs, like love. My most essential instincts had grown clumsy with cobwebs. I was not a person poised to seize the moment. Maybe that was the point Mona, in her hammer-headed fashion, was trying to make. Time is short. Even when it seems to drag on to infinity, the truth is it's short.

One by one, the hunger strikers resumed eating. Dispatches arrived only sporadically. South Africa was once more erupting. Lebanon again burst into bloodshed. Typhoons ravaged Malaysia, over nine hundred dead. Soon the events which had compelled Zapatú back to his homeland were lost in the great tide of turmoil and rancor that regularly washes up in frightening volume on the shores of the nation's news desks.

Just when I had resigned myself to turning my attention back to the sorry affairs of Frankly Speakers, I received by express mail an advance copy of the highly regarded and almost universally ignored iconoclastic journal, *Global Strife*. Its lead article was titled "Home to the Hills: Zapatú Returns." The author was an American college professor, Dr. Andrew Hoffman of the University of Virginia.

At the time of the recent political turmoil, Professor Andy had fortuitously found himself on yet another field trip (don't these guys ever teach?) where he managed to parlay his unique personal connections and prior acquaintance with Zapatú into an exclusive visit to a remote hideout where the enigmatic leader and his loyal comrades had retreated in order to . . . well, it was hard to tell what they were doing.

The *Global Strife* article began with a florid description of Professor Andy's perilous ascent to the mountain village. (His ornate prose style, honed in the course of numerous academic monographs, seemed modeled on the oratorical art of filibustering.) After being inexplicably escorted through a labyrinthian series of decoy depots and circular routings (a taste of his own medicine!), the professor was deposited on a craggy footpath for the long ascent through thick mists and sweet woodfire smoke to a makeshift encampment of medieval mud huts located at the outskirts of a humble peasant village whose identity, dear reader, he was honor-bound to withhold.

Professor Andy's reportorial style made me yearn for the blunt aesthetics of wire service journalism. I was avid for hard facts—who, what, when—and resented having to slog through the unedited muck of his impressionistic blather. How did Zapatú and company fill their days? Why did they retreat? What did the villagers make of them? Could it be that people whom I actually knew firsthand entertained notions of changing the world?

Like a hyperkinetic third grader I quickly skipped down the article, flipped to the following page, desperately trying to find a section of direct, conveniently summarized information. Just the facts, I wanted to scream. But no such luck! I was rebuffed back to the start, and was forced to read every word.

After cautioning the reader yet again that he was sworn to protect the identity of the people he encountered—with the exception of Zapatú and Mona, the flame-haired mystery woman who, by some not-so-coincidental machination was also his former student (more on that anon!), Professor Andy launched into a description of his initial encounter with an older, swarthy woman who spoke in riddles like the Cheshire Cat.

"When do I get to rap with Zapatú?" Andy had inquired.

"When the peacock swims," she responded, inspiring in the good scholar a protracted rumination on the misuse of nature metaphors by political movements.

Upon being ushered to his mud hut and reflecting (at length) on the echoes he was feeling (hearing?) of the Robin Hood saga, Andy was visited by a gaunt, guitar-strumming young man.

"Do Zapatú and Mona know I'm here?"

The young man fingered his guitar. "Why do you ask?"

"Because I have come a very long way to learn their story."

"Their story? Their struggle, señor, is real. It is no story."

Having met Pepe and Rosa under similar circumstances, I felt safe in quickly skimming over Professor Andy's windy contemplation of the metaphysical portent of this remark. Rejoining the account on the next page for a communal bonfire, I learned that the moonless night was pitch black and infinite. A dozen young men and women gathered around. Dancing tongues of amber light licked the serious faces of the assembled outcasts. A lonesome howl wafted up from the valley. An omen? The young man strummed passionate chords. Then crooned. A bygone tune by Dylan from those soulful, vintage years.

Not until the following morning did Andy get to meet with Mona. On a log perch sipping cafe con leche, they watched the glistening streaks of the rising sun angle up the verdant slopes. Mona looked especially fit, he reported, in her hip-hugging army surplus slacks and Redskins T-shirt. The professor thought he detected in her placid yet stalwart countenance "a grand and instinctual wisdom that is only acquired by a radical exploration of life's deepest goals." Maybe so, but I would have welcomed a second opinion.

Mona disclosed to Andy that she had never been more fulfilled as a human being and as a woman since throwing in with *La Causa*. Released from the deadening debilitations of the modern capitalist system which, she asserted, enslaves people not through clumsy threats and blunt coercion but through a treacherous quicksand of petty worries and hopeless values, Mona now felt rejuvenated and whole, born again and bursting with fervor.

Andy, the ace cross-examiner, asked her to expound on her relationship with Zapatú. Flinging open her arms to the bounteous hills, like Julie Andrews in *The Sound of Music*, Mona replied with a girlish trill which the good professor recalled only too vividly from his own days of tutoring the rambunctious co-ed. "I'm deliriously happy," she sang. "Which sure beats being delirious."

Andy pressed Mona on the specifics of their, you know, their program for the future. She declined to go into specifics, except that it would combine some of the basic tenets of socialism with contemporary marketing techniques. "As Zapatú says," Mona elaborated, "watch what we do, not what we say."

So reporter Hoffman set out to inspect just that. But since Zapatú and his band had been located in this primitive outpost for less than two weeks, there wasn't a lot to go on beyond rhetoric and speculation.

He did manage to accompany Pepe on a visit to a local crafts cooperative, housed in the crumbling wing of an abandoned eighteenth-century convent. Before a handful of sullen women earnestly preoccupied with their projects, Pepe (the article referred to him as "Guillermo") introduced himself by performing a clever jingle of Madison Avenue succinctness that extolled the skill and passion which goes into the creation of these fine shawls and urns and little wooden donkeys with tails that wag.

The women, most of whom squatted against the dank stone walls—there were no chairs or tables—politely covered their mouths to conceal their tittering. Who was this boy in a loin cloth with the sonorous voice and the silly ideas?

Pepe explained that this co-op was founded many years before at the instigation of some U.S. Peace Corps volunteers who neglected to imbue the weavers and potters with an appropriate understanding of the mercurial global marketplace for native crafts. Money is not a force of nature, Pepe told him. Its comings and goings are not to be patiently suffered as if they are whimsical episodes of storm and drought. Life can be improved by exploiting the secret promotional formulas that the gringos in their modern glass cities prefer to keep to themselves. These objects you create with your bare hands can be worth a little or a lot, and it is within your power to determine which.

A stout woman with mud-caked knees complained, "Nothing here ever changes."

Pepe lashed out a raucous chord on his guitar. "Until now!"

The stout woman stood her ground. "All the newcomers like you tell us that."

"Si, señorita. But we are different. Soon we will map out a plan." Pepe strummed a conciliatory chord. "You will see; the power is within you."

To Andy's profound disappointment, Zapatú was never available for an interview. According to Mona, acting in her capacity as gatekeeper, Zapatú was relishing the chance to remove himself from the day-to-day imperatives that had so feverishly compelled him in recent years.

"He is meditating, working on the ultimate statement," Mona explained. "The key is to find the right words, and weave them together in the right sequence. The world will hear no more from Zapatú until he is satisfied that he has found the right words. Oh, but when he does..."

I hungered for more, but as Mona's voice trailed off, so did the article.

Soon thereafter I received a cryptic communique from Mona. It was a postcard, oblique and unsigned, no doubt to confound the police authorities. The glossy picture on the front of the card showed the sunlit circular drive and red brick entranceway to the Oxford, Ohio, Holiday Inn. She never got to spend a night in the place, but at least she made off with her rightful allotment of stationary.

"Very tense, always looking over shoulder," she wrote with a breathless slant to her script. "Amazing progress every day. Very busy, no time for hammocks. Z sends regards, considering future lecture tour. New message next time around. Love, X."

Her handwriting, which I'd never really focused on before, had a kind of vintage curlicue soda shop lilt. It was the script you would expect to find in an adolescent girl's most private diary, recording the heart-rending nuances of looking for love and searching for meaning. For all her sharp, nasty edges, that's what she was, a girl fending off the great hurt of failed hope.

She'd written a P.S. which ran across the top border of the post card. Unfortunately, the right-most part of the sentence was obliterated by an oversized gold stamp depicting a pineapple. With uncharacteristic patience, I delicately steamed off the stamp in an attempt to discover Mona's concluding remark. Unfortunately, the remaining ink was hopelessly blurred. Until further notice, I was free to fill in the blanks of that vanished postscript. In times of upheaval, it can be consoling to have such a crutch. She might have commended me on my virtues, admonished me to live up to my ideals, or hinted at a future romance once the dust of our lives settled. It's like a lottery ticket in your pocket, having an incomplete postcard from an interesting woman stashed in your desk drawer. Even if the woman is Mona.

As for the fate of the business—forget it. Frankly Speakers was down the tubes, and it didn't take a high-priced M.B.A. analyst to ascertain the problem. We just weren't hot.

Kenny, like Mona before him, was offered a job by Smooth Line. I'd like to believe that he was no more smitten than she had been by their climate-controlled computerized office environment or the scintillating prospect of lunching with former-President Ford. For Kenny the decision to jump ship was a strictly practical matter; even a fifty percent commission of nothing amounts to nothing.

Piper quit promptly on my return from Ohio. She'd been seeing a holistic fertility counselor who, after extensive research, had prescribed a rigorous program consisting of six months languishing supine beneath the sun and frothing turquoise surf of Mexico's Pacific coast, with stalwart Alec, doing nothing but drinking cerveza and having sex. I should be getting a postcard from her any time.

Marion, bless her, was kindly enough to take a job just down the hall with the Iranian exile import/export/financial consultants/ espionage specialists. She was not at liberty to tell me exactly what her job entailed, but her proximity meant that she was able to spend a few hours a week at the old office facilitating my difficult transition into insolvency.

Fall, which has a nice long run in the nation's capital, had taken an ugly turn toward winter. A cold stiff wind whistled through the cracks of my non-caulked window. Brief bursts of gray slush pelted the loose pane like a grim warning. Early in the afternoon the day's thin light was already waning.

I had my feet propped on my barren desk, clean at last! Marion was taking an extended lunch break to help me label and box up the jigsaw puzzle of our pathetic financial records. Since the Iranians were rarely in to keep tabs on her, she was not jeopardizing her new job.

"Even if they knew, they wouldn't mind," she told me. "Helping you is like charity work."

I had taken a break from the records, and was staring out the window at the gloomy alley and the dumpster being coated by slush. "I appreciate it," I thanked her.

"Don't mention it, Danny. Frankly Speakers was a public service—while it lasted."

"While it lasted." I mindlessly repeated her phrase like a mantra.

The phone chirped. We were still receiving a few stray calls, from students who'd been locked in a prolonged drug stupor, from professors who'd been on sabbatical, from prospective speakers newly released from federal prison.

The old Pavlovian response was, however, not as sharp as it used to be. It took three chirps for me to begin climbing over the scattered boxes and another two chirps to even find the phone, which was on the floor hidden beneath a Rand McNally road atlas to North America.

"Yes?" I'd already lost the habit of corporate salutation.

"Danny Frank?" The inquisitor was a male, brisk and slightly officious.

"Speaking."

"You'll never guess who this is."

I was not in a playful mood. "There's a lot of things I'll never guess."

"Jake Deaver," he stated with military crispness. "Smooth Line."

I had never met the head of Smooth Line. We had spoken over the phone on several occasions, usually when he called to apprise me that some scurrilous shyster was now under exclusive contract. Jake had a reputation for unctuousness that was legendary. "You are," he crooned, "the same Danny Frank who, by all accounts, simply captivated the audience in Oxford, Ohio?"

I did not reply. Jake Deaver is the type who responds to intervals of silence like they are the preliminary stages to an orchestrated program of torture. Responding to him was not essential to continuing the converstion.

"My sources," he prattled, "tell me you have a unique message. I said, 'Are you sure it's the same Danny Frank?' and they said, 'Yes, one and the same.'"

I punched the broadcast button on the phone console, for old time's sake. Jake Deaver was the sort of preposterously self-confident pitchman that everyone should have the opportunity to overhear at least once, just as a point of reference. I glanced over at Marion to make sure she was listening. She cocked her head in my direction, mostly, I'm afraid, out of courtesy.

Jake bulldozed ahead. "Now, Danny, I don't need to give you a lecture—ha, get it? a lecture?—anyway, I don't need to tell you about the business. You've been around. I'll put it to you straight."

Jake was actually around my age, but he'd come into the business as a teenager working for his uncle, a talent agent. He was trying an old school tactic to titillate my curiosity. I kept quiet, a kind of homage to Mona. I would do nothing on cue.

"We can get you dates."

Marion sat up. "Go on," I told him.

"Not just colleges. Some civic and religious groups."

"Doing what?"

"Doing your thing, Danny! I heard a tape. It's perfect."

There's an insidious psychological squeeze to receiving praise from someone you regard as a disreputable idiot. I felt queasy.

"And my sources also tell me that you might be available to do some dates this spring. Are my sources accurate?"

"Possibly."

"Maybe starting around the middle of March, running a month or so."

I could hold back no longer. "What the hell would I speak on?"

"Just do what you did in Ohio. Frankly—ha, get it? Sorry about the pun. If I were you I wouldn't change a word. Of course, you're the artist, Danny. The final decision is always the artist's."

I was stunned. Even unflappable Marion gazed up in utter disbelief. Either this guy was pulling my leg with an acumen and subtlety far beyond his normal range or he had truly seized upon a notion more absurd than all his others put together.

Smooth Line's track record at successfully promoting concepts I considered to be ludicrous was indeed impressive. I chose my words cautiously. "That speech was . . . well, it was kind of an emergency situation. There were factors, unique factors. I . . ."

Jake cut me off. "Let me put it to you straight. You're familiar with the Boy Guru?"

I eyed Marion to make certain I had a back-up witness. "Yes?"

"He's fucking up."

"I'm sorry to hear that, Jake. Today's youth cry out for his leadership."

"My wife's collie has more wisdom than that little dickhead. I never thought I'd say this about one of my acts. You know how we agents get attached to our acts. But this little turd is the most pampered, stuck-up, two-bit bonehead I've ever had the misfortune to work with. Also, there's reports that he might be somewhat older than his handlers led us to believe."

"Gee, Jake, his promotional literature paints such a glowing portrait of the kid."

"Ha! You got me good there, Danny. I'll put it to you straight. The Guru has a spring tour. Twelve, fifteen dates. I want you to substitute."

"You're serious?" I asked.

"Hey, this is show biz. I never know myself."

"I'm not a performer. I'm not experienced."

"Isn't that your point?"

"What I mean is, I don't exactly have credentials."

"Listen: you show up on time, you eat a nice dinner with them, you give a nice talk, you do the Q & A. Come on, you know the score."

It seemed crazy. "I get the same fee as the Guru?"

"Every penny."

The money would be great, and I knew I would be no worse than some of the acts that were out there. "And the deal is that the Boy Guru will cancel? How are you going to pull that off."

"We have ways. Don't trouble yourself about it."

A month on the circuit, summer vacation somewhere remote like the Caribbean, then back for a boffo fall tour. I could find room in my game plan for that. Indirection, however, is always the way to deal with agents. "Let me give it some thought," I replied. "How about I call you tomorrow?"

"Danny?" There was fatherly caution in Jake Deaver's oily voice.

"Yes?"

"Remember: turn up that flame." With a triumphant chortle, he clicked off.

Marion used the excuse of my momentary paralysis to pick herself up. It was time for her to be getting back to the import/export/whatever office. Upon parting, she informed me, "You're sure in one crazy business."

Outside the slush was mounting. You could feel it in your heart. Winter, the season of dark needs, was coming on.

I closed down the office, buttoned up my overcoat, and headed down to The Grotto. With a shark of an agent handling my case, who can tell where it all might lead? You stay afloat long enough with your head above water, there's always a chance you'll wash up somewhere interesting. That's right, Jake, turn up that flame! Tonight, the phony tropical drinks are on me.